Silent Sight

Jeff Neilsen

ISBN: 978-1-7322105-3-0

For my wife Chris, the soul of patience in my life.

Foreword

There are many ways of looking at the past. The wavy-glass lens of science fiction is just one of them. This is a period piece. In writing it, I attempted to be as faithful to the time and geographical settings as possible.

Jeff Neilsen

ONE

There were still a few empty seats. The Motor Vehicle License office was typically busy. The end of the month was only a few days away. The rush was on to get plates renewed, before they expired. Even thought the state gave a thirty-day grace period before penalizing a citizen, most people were uncomfortable with the idea of having expired license plates on their car.

The room was stuffy. It was beginning to become uncomfortably warm. The afternoon sun was shining through the store-front glass. The effect was that it warmed the concrete floor of the office. Added to the body heat of the people, it was overcoming the ventilation system.

Cary held his paperwork in his lap and closed his eyes. The store was busy, today. He was tired. Vander and Beste was a good place for him to be. The large department store company had great benefits. The pay was just enough to count as livable. It took nine years to get the job as a buyer. Men's Clothing was just where he wanted to be.

"Number seventy-seven!" The clerk behind the counter had the tiniest bit of rasp in her voice. Cary thought it must be an occupational hazard of clerking in government offices. In his imagination, every government office worker had a raspy voice. He fingered the plastic number card, reassuring himself that it was still there.

Cary began to weigh his job choices. With two years of college, he could stay, or move on, if he wanted. From what he knew of the pay structure, only the top executives received large salaries. He figured everybody else just stayed for the same reason he did: The work wasn't hard.

Right now, with Lennie working in the downtown store, Cary wasn't seriously thinking of going anywhere. She was what Cary imagined all men wanted. Cary had no idea of what an ideal woman was or could be. Lennie just fit. He liked her a lot. More importantly, he was sure she felt the same way about him.

"Number seventy-eight!"

With his eyes still closed, Cary momentarily let his mind go blank. As he did, an image of the people in front of him began to glow. It was like an outline or a silhouette, shining with a coronal glow. The coronal glow was salmon-colored. The outline of a woman in front of him rose from her seat and walked forward.

The appearance of the moving, glowing image startled Cary. He opened his eyes, suddenly staring, wide-eyed. Everything – no, everyone – in front of him was exactly as he had seen, in the glowing image in his closed eyes.

Cary blinked once, then again. He thought, I must be a lot more tired than I thought. The whole episode took only a second, maybe a second and a half.

"Number seventy-nine!" The woman's voice was definitely getting raspier. Cary sat and stared, still wondering what he had seen. He began to mentally check himself out, trying to remember if he had any sensations that were sign of some illness, stalking him.

"Number seventy-nine!" More rasp. Less patience, Cary thought. He felt a nudge at his elbow.

"Hey! Ain't you number seventy-nine?" The man seated next to Cary brought him back to reality.

Cary quickly rose from his chair and made for the counter. The raspy-voiced woman wore a pair of glasses that made her look twenty years older than she was. The dark frames were those pointy ones, from the 1950s. Rhinestones were embedded in the temples, evidently some consideration of fashion. The temples were fastened with a chain around the woman's neck.

Cary slid his paperwork across the counter. The woman took the number card and deftly tossed it into a bin, some ten or twelve feet away. Cary thought it was a neat shot. He wondered how many times the woman had made it. Did the office workers keep statistics on card-bin shots missed and made?

"Are you Mr. Lang, the owner of the car?" The woman kept her eyes on the papers in front of her, on the counter.

"Yes." Cary pulled his wallet out of his pocket. He had been through this process enough to know that he was going to have to show his driver's license.

"Is this your correct address?" Still not looking up. There was a very practiced pace to the way that she shuffled the papers, in and out of the pile. She checked certain boxes on the various forms with a stick pen, the kind that come in boxes of a thousand.

The small electric calculator on the counter clicked and whirred. "That'll be $17.50." At last, the clerk looked up from the papers, waiting for Cary to produce some form of payment. To her relief, Cary withdrew eighteen dollars from his wallet and handed it to the clerk.

"More than last year." Cary watched as the clerk sorted his bills into the cash drawer. She picked two quarters out of a tray and handed them to Cary.

"Always more than last year." The raspy woman had already dropped her gaze to the papers in front of her.

"Thank you." Cary picked up his papers and new tags. He began to turn away from the counter.

"Number eighty!" The words struck Cary in the back of the head. It was almost like the slap of a hand. Walking out the door of the office, Cary wondered how it was possible to speak in such a way that the words carried such practiced hostility and vitriol with them. He guessed that the repetitiveness of the job did that to people.

***

Back at the V-dub, Wheels was waiting for him, tail wagging. The golden retriever wasn't the smartest dog ever, but its affectionate nature more than made up for it. Cary had been careful to park in a shady spot and leave the windows open. He knew Wheels wouldn't jump out or let anyone in the car.

Cary got the dog as a pup. The tiny dog slid and skittered all around the sheet-goods flooring in the kitchen. The puppy spent as much of his time on his belly as on his feet. The spectacle quickly led to the name "Wheels."

Cary and Wheels "grew up" together as dog and owner. Cary went through obedience class and learned how to be a good owner. The dog learned a thing or two, as well.

With a well-behaved dog at his side, Cary seldom went anywhere alone. Cary was always careful about applying the rule of "If Wheels can't go, I won't." It was a lot easier to socialize in the summer months. Outdoor cafés and restaurants were much more understanding about pets.

Cary felt that Wheels had helped "seal the deal" with Lennie. Wheels liked her and she liked him. They began seeing each other regularly a couple of years ago. Cary felt that they had become a lot closer than they might have if Wheels wasn't part of the equation. As a doting dog owner, giving Wheels more credit than he was due, was natural.

The pair of overnight dates that they recently shared, revealed how well the three of them got along. The rhythm of dog-care activities didn't seem to interfere with any part of the evenings, or mornings.

Cary started the car and flipped on the eight-track. "Rockin' Down the Highway" was still on from when Cary left. The Doobie Brothers rode home with Cary and

Wheels. Most of the time, Wheels hung his head out the window. When Cary sang along with the music, Wheels looked in to see if the sound meant something was wrong with Cary. Cary didn't mind the dog being a critic of his singing.

The drive to his four-family flat was about a mile and a half. South St. Louis traffic was light. They only got through two songs on the tape player. Cary and Wheels got out and walked their usual route, half way up the block, cross the street, and back. No "package" to worry about this time.

They got back to the flat, just as Mrs. Roberts was finishing up her daily routine of sweeping the front steps. The entry wasn't steep, there were only three steps to keep clean. Cary thought that if she were younger, he might someday catch her scrubbing the limestone steps with kitchen cleanser. He didn't know if she was Dutch. It was an old St. Louis expression to label someone as "Scrubby Dutch."

"Hi, Mrs. Roberts." Cary carefully navigated himself and Wheels around where the landlady was working. He knew that she didn't really like dogs. He also knew that he was allowed to rent the flat from her because she thought he was cute. Mrs. Roberts had that way of looking at Cary. "Wistful" was the word that came to mind. Dead giveaway.

Another thing that worked in Cary's favor was that he was always well dressed. His job at the department store chain gave him access to greatly discounted clothing. He was even allowed to combine his employee discount with sales discounts and get clothing at ridiculously low prices. It was a job benefit that Cary took advantage of because he grew up without much in the way of nice clothes. Aside from yearly school-clothes purchases, his clothes were a combination of hand-me-down gifts from neighbor families with children, and second-hand store items.

Mrs. Roberts was one of those little, old people who managed to be tiny and frumpy at the same time. She never let anyone into her apartment, other than the maintenance people. She was pleasant enough, but no one knew her first name. Cary even asked the mailman. He said that her mail came addressed to Mrs. Roberts. Cary guessed that if she wanted to tell people her first name, she would.

Mrs. Roberts was the landlady because she owned the building. Over the couple of years that Cary rented from her, he learned that Mrs. Roberts bought the building with the proceeds from her husband's life insurance policy. She took good care of the property. Everything about the building was in working order, and freshly painted.

The only part of the four-family flat property that was not in perfect working order was the car-park area. It was originally built as a four-car garage. As cars, in general became larger, the accommodation of removing the garage doors was made. It was a solution visible in many alleyways, all over town. Garages became carports; with windows in the sides and exit doors on the yard side of the structure.

Cary thought the carport was creepy and didn't park there. The garage was built at a time when one lightbulb in a garage was thought of as a luxury. Even in broad daylight, the carport seemed dark and dingy. At night it was downright scary. Most of the time, Cary parked his Volkswagen on the street, in front of the flat. One of his upstairs neighbors, Fred Maunt, kept a car and a motorcycle in the carport. Since Cary made no use of it, he parked his motorcycle in Cary's spot.

The parking arrangements became a problem last winter when Cary wanted to use his spot in the carport. A large snowstorm was predicted, and Cary didn't want to have to shovel his VW out of a snowdrift in order to get to work. He had to get Maunt to move his motorcycle to the back of the carport. Maunt was cooperative, but Cary could tell that he was put out by having to acquiesce to the request.

Cary was very happy with his present living arrangements. The rent was well within his means. He managed to meet all of his bills and save some money every month. Mrs. Roberts' allowing Wheels to live there was the real appeal of the place. A little friction with Fred Maunt was a small price to pay for the many good parts of renting the flat.

TWO

Cary sat on his couch, reading. Wheels was on the beanbag chair. The leftover from his younger days made a great spot for the dog to curl up. Cary knew that the golden retriever spent almost all of his time there. Rough life, he thought.

The book he borrowed from the library was less exciting than he had hoped for. The writer's style didn't carry the character development very well at all. Cary read constantly. It was a habit he acquired in his youth. After his mother left, Cary was shuffled around the family. Books were a refuge for him that he sorely needed. For him, they were always there, ready to give him a form of solace nothing else could.

He landed, for a couple of years, with his uncle. He had a room in his basement. Cary's uncle was a cinder-

9

man. His job was going from house to house and collecting the coal cinders that came out of people's furnaces. Everything about and around the place he lived was coated in coal dust. The smell was something that Cary never quite got used to.

The growth of oil-fired, and natural gas furnaces made cinder collection a truly dying occupation. Every year, there were fewer remaining coal furnaces to be chased after. The solution to the problem was simple. The more you drank, the smaller the problem got.

As the need for cinder collection disappeared completely, Cary's uncle sank into totally unregenerate alcoholism. Jobless despair led him to walk out the door one day, and never come back.

The fortunate aspect of this set of circumstances was that it put Cary in the foster care system at age fifteen. Before he was even placed in a home, he found out that he could request to be emancipated from his uncle. The child welfare people were more than glad to have one less person to worry about. They even stood with him before the judge and recommended his emancipation.

The other thing that happened to Cary at this time was a name change. The judge had seen quite a number of young people wanting to make a complete break with troubled pasts. He asked Cary if he wanted to change his name.

Cary had never thought about it. He said "yes" because he disliked writing out his full name. With a whack of his gavel, the judge ordered that Cary Lang would walk out of the courtroom, leaving Cary Langenbreuner and his difficulties behind.

From there on, Cary was on his own. He managed well enough. The one-room apartment was better than the basement of his uncle's house. The judge helped him get a rental from the people who ran the converted multi-bedroom mansion, in midtown.

He worked every evening and every weekend, clerking for Vander & Beste. First, he worked in the warehouse, then on the sales floor. His knowledge of the store and commitment to work put him on a fast track to getting a buyer's position, a year after he finished high school.

The Army would have had a good place for Cary, except for an inner ear defect that affected his balance. It he tried to stand or move around in the dark, or with his eyes closed, he quickly lost his balance and toppled over.

Cary kept at it and went to the junior college as soon as he could. Starting there saved him a lot of money. He switched over to the state university for his last two years. With two interruptions for work – to get tuition money together – his college education was a five-and-a-half-year process. Cary looked at his long road to success in life as a contract, a promise he made to himself. Whatever it would take, he would become successful.

Working at Vander and Beste, with a degree in business administration, put Cary on track for a senior buyer's position. He traveled to Pittsburg, Indianapolis, Chicago, and Kansas City, becoming familiar with the store operations in each city. If everything worked out for him, Cary would be working for the parent corporation, Vanderco, within a year.

Cary let the book that he was reading rest in his lap. He thought about the strange experience at the license office. He closed his eyes and turned his head from side to side. Nothing, just darkness. He tried to recall the image, in his mind. It vaguely reminded him of something called Kirlian photography. The salmon-colored auras that he saw, surrounded the people around him in the license office. Thinking about the image, Cary realized that no objects were outlined, only people.

Cary shook his head a bit, to rid himself of the sense of confusion. He rose from the couch and went to the kitchen of the small flat, to fix a small dinner for himself. Wheels padded after him. Dinner time was for both of them. Cary occasionally dropped a bit of Kraft Macaroni and Cheese Dinner into Wheels' dog food. Wheels didn't mind a bit.

***

The next morning, Cary began to awaken. A glimmer of an image momentarily flickered before him. It was another one of the auras, like the ones in the license office. It was an outline of a person sitting upright. Behind the seated person, other, less obvious auras stood, sat or moved about. They were smaller, as if in the background. The image roused Cary from his half-awake state and faded away. He opened and closed his eyes a few times, but no residual images remained.

What did remain was the memory of an unusual sensation accompanying the image of the aura. Cary couldn't quite "put his finger on it." The whole thing was fleeting and nearly ephemeral. The original image was rock-solidly tied to what was actually happening right in front of him. Otherwise, he would have thought it was all in his imagination.

Cary needed to get his morning routine started. Wheels needed walking, after breakfast. The seasonal change was in full swing, at least Cary's portion. New goods were being brought in. He needed to make sure it was all correct. Any time he had for wondering about the strange images was lost in the demands of the day.

***

A few more days went by. Cary returned to his routine. No further thought about the auras troubled him. The end of the week meant an opportunity to have a date with Lennie He called her on Thursday and asked if she was up to a pizza and a movie. Lennie said the pizza was a good idea, but no flicks. Her roommate, Ramona, had her boyfriend over three nights in a row and she was too "strung out" to enjoy a movie.

Lennie Baerd was a head shorter than Cary. She was petite, but well-endowed. She was happy about her attractive body, but secretly bore a disappointment about never being chosen for the cheerleading squad at school. "Blondes have more fun," was an advertising slogan. Lennie knew that it meant "Blondes make the cheerleading team." Her brunette hair was part of who, and what she naturally was. That was that.

Friday morning rolled around and the last of the new season stock was arranged. The sales staff all had a grip on where the replacement stock was. Cary expected to be able to get through the entire weekend without phone calls from salespeople lost in a search for new items.

Cary headed out from work. The traffic from downtown to midtown was predictably heavy. Cary's good mood made it seem like less of a hassle. The tiny pizza restaurant, in the basement of the apartment building, was already open. An older couple ran the place. Cary wondered how many more years the two Italian immigrants would continue to operate the little pizzeria.

Lennie and Cary stumbled upon the unpretentious pizza restaurant on one of their first dates. They went to the same high school, at the same time. Lennie was two years behind Cary. They weren't perfect strangers, but the separation of two years meant that they never socialized together until after Cary graduated. They met at a party. Since they already knew something about each other, it was easy for them to strike up a relationship.

Cary rode home with the pizza making the inside of his car smell like an Italian restaurant. It was humid – surprise, it was humid in St. Louis – the moisture in the air made the whole thing almost too much. He knew that Wheels would be doubly glad to have him come through the door, reeking of pizza.

Wheels got an extra-long walk on Fridays. Weekends meant that Cary had a little more time for him. Tonight, he would get fed on time. The pizza would sit on the stove for a couple of hours. Lennie didn't leave work until after seven. Her late dinner with Cary usually meant a few bits of pizza crust for Wheels.

That evening, after dinner, Lennie sat with Cary on the couch. The stereo was tuned to some rock 'n roll, but the volume was low. Cary allowed himself the luxury of the stereo, thanks to an economic stimulus check from

President Ford. The two-hundred-dollar check was just enough to buy a good mid-range stereo. Cary actually felt slightly patriotic, spending the money the way that the President wanted him to. The habit of listening to music while he read, or studied, filled most of his evenings.

The stereo was the focal point of the living room. Cary didn't own a television. When he was very young, the television occupied almost all of his free time, as it did for his parents. Living with his dirt-poor uncle led him to reading. He couldn't stand being around his uncle, who stunk of coal dust. He kept to himself, in the basement bedroom and read.

Lennie reported that the Young Sophisticates department was busy. In her mid-twenties, she was starting to age beyond the average age of her customers. The store would be looking to move her to another department. The specter of this looming change nagged at the back of her mind. She had issues with the women who worked in the other clothing departments downtown. She was used to working downtown. There were still many more things to do and stores to shop.

The pizza dinner, with the accompanying bottle of rosé wine, helped settle the excitement of finishing another week at work. Lennie spent the night for a third time. The lovemaking was wonderful for both of them. Sleep came, and the peace of it held them in its embrace.

***

The next morning, as the dawn was just beginning, Cary began to awaken. He lay still, with his eyes closed. The aura of Lennie was there, right next to him. She lay on her side. Cary could see the rise and fall of her chest, in the regular, slow rhythm of sleep. Her aura was a very pale salmon color he had seen before.

Without opening his eyes, Cary turned away from Lennie to the other side. He could see the same outline he saw before. It was the shape of a person sitting in a chair. Cary decided that he was looking at Mrs. Roberts, sitting in her chair, watching television. He picked out enough detail in the aura that he could identify her female shape, such as it was. Then he realized that there were, at least, two walls between him and where Mrs. Roberts sat.

The realization startled him enough to cause him to open his eyes. The unusual sensation was there, the one he couldn't remember earlier. He focused his mind on the sensation and closed his eyes. The aura was still there, walls literally notwithstanding.

The image before him rose from the chair and walked to another room. The pantomime of movement made Cary realize that Mrs. Roberts was in her bathroom. She sat down again.

Too much for me, thought Cary. He opened his eyes. The reality of the world re-entered his awareness. He turned back to Lennie and put his arm around her. A faint recollection of seeing other auras, in the background again, hung in his mind. He deliberately let the strange sensation, that was not quite a tingling, in his mind, subside. He didn't want any more aural visions.

THREE

Eight-years-old was a tough age to be. At least it was for this boy. His father was a Finn and called him Poika. It was the Finnish word for boy. Few people in the neighborhood ever heard him called anything else, so the name stuck. To the other children in the neighborhood, the fact that he might have another name didn't matter. He was just Poika.

Terre Haute, Indiana in the nineteen forties, could be rough as well. It could be very rough on the poor, and their children. Poika's parents both had to work. His father was a garbage man. Poika knew that he had been in prison, but that's all he knew. He knew to not ask about it, as well.

Poika's mother cleaned houses and took in laundry. Neither of Poika's parents made much money. They earned enough to get by. Together, they earned enough to put a roof over their heads, food on the table, and buy a drink or two.

The "drink or two" was the problem. Both of Poika's parents were alcoholics. Neither had anything other than their mere presence to offer, in the way of parental care and guidance. They provided what they did for their child, and that was the end of it.

The rough streets of the housing district that sat astride the railroad tracks, constantly claimed its tribute from the local residents. The children were no exception. Poika was a bit gangly and knock-kneed, even though he was shorter than average. He took more than his fair share of teasing and torture from the local toughs. His sobriquet didn't help.

Poke-a-Poika was the game that the bigger kids liked to play. Day after day, one or more of them would take their shot at punching Poika. The older boy who liked the game the most was Lon Spahl. Not one single week went by without Poika getting waylaid by Lon.

The more troublesome aspect of the physical harassment from Lon was that Poika had a crush on Lon's sister Katie. She was the cutest thing that he could ever imagine. Poika took every chance he could, just to get a look at her. Katie Spahl was in his grade school class. All day long, he sneaked looks at her, trying his darnedest to not be obvious about it.

One afternoon, Lon was walking with his sister Katie, on their way home from school. Lon spotted Poika. He took off after him, yelling back to his sister, "Watch this!"

Lon Spahl tore into the much smaller Poika, without slowing, from a full run. The initial impact completely knocked Poika off of his feet. As Poika picked himself up, Lon belted him twice, right in the chops. Knowing that his imaginary girlfriend was watching, Poika tried to defend himself. His efforts only garnered him a worse beating, with Lon Spahl cursing him, and jeering at him the whole time.

When the "fight" was over, Poika finished walking home. He cleaned up as well as he could, but he had a swollen, split lip, and a black eye. His mother was sympathetic enough, helping to get some ice on his lip. She even managed a soothing word or two. The predations of her alcoholism kept her from any sort of loving, comforting, motherly caresses. It was mothering, but just.

Poika's father reacted differently to the whole incident. Finding his beat-up son at home, he asked what happened. Poika's explanation fell on two of the coldest, deafest ears in the universe. His father worked out his response even before he was finished.

"What kind of fight did you put up? Any?" He roughly spun the slender boy around, looking him over, throwing in critical "Tsks" and a cluck or two.

"You better 'count for yourself better, or they'll walk all over you. Hear me?" The foul-smelling man went to the kitchen, for a beer. He didn't even wait for an answer from his son.

The following week was to be no better for Poika. Lon Spahl was waiting for him after school, the next Friday. The memory of beating Poika, and of how much he liked doing it, was still fresh in his mind. This day, he brought along a couple of friends, to watch.

The little gang stopped Poika and led him into an alleyway. Once there, and sure they were out of sight, Lon began throwing punches at the smaller Poika. Poika ducked the first couple of punches, but this only made Lon mad. Having to work at pounding the little squirt wasn't what he had in mind. He went after Poika with increased ferocity.

Poika remembered his father's addled cajoling about accounting for himself and threw a couple punches of his own. This was like teasing a caged animal. Whatever restraint Lon Spahl was employing left him and he tore into the hapless Poika with genuine rage.

With the last tiny vestige of his courage, Poika threw a poorly aimed, right hand, roundhouse punch at Lon, who clumsily lurched right into it. Poika's fist struck Lon's mouth with a loud "Smack!' The larger boy staggered back and felt his lip, as it began to swell. His hand came away from his face with blood on it. It was his own blood. Poika was so involved in his terror that he didn't notice the throbbing in his right hand.

The part of Lon Spahl that had any coherent thought in it disappeared; evaporated, right there, on the spot. He leapt onto the bewildered Poika, knocked him to the ground, and began a fusillade of hammer blows that would not stop. By the time Lon's two friends had the sense to pull him off of Poika, he lay there, unconscious.

Hours later, a woman walking her dog found the boy, still unconscious, in the alleyway. She called the police, who took the boy to the hospital.

Silent Sight

Poika's parents took him home from the hospital receiving ward the same night. They were deeply embarrassed to have to tell the hospital clerk that they had no money to pay for their son's care. They had to go home with their boy. They couldn't afford for him to stay even overnight, in the hospital.

They put their son to bed without a word. They both needed to have a drink. An hour or so later, the whole incident seemed like a television story, strange, unreal, and about some other people.

The next morning was Saturday. Poika woke up about noon. Neither of his parents had the sense to look in on him. Poika saw that he was clean and had mercurochrome on some of his wounds. He wondered how it got there. Rising from the bed, the many aches and pains resulting from his beating the day before assailed him.

The memory of Lon Spahl jumping on him and pounding him, the way a hammer pounds a nail into a board, came back to him. For the rest of the weekend, Poika kept to himself, leaving his room only for meals and bathroom needs. He didn't speak to his parents at all, who hardly noticed.

The throbbing in his right hand continued. It was less intense than the day before. It reminded him of how he landed that one good haymaker, right in Lon Spahl's big, fat, mouth. The knowledge that he had nailed the big jerk, at least once, did more to ease his pains than the doses of aspirin his mother gave him. Poika rubbed away the throbbing in his hand. Eventually the rubbing turned into a sort of stroking, rewarding himself for getting in one good punch.

Something new began inside Poika that weekend. It was hate. It started as a tiny spark, engendered by the presence of pain, the memory of pain, and the fear of its returning. The new feeling was warm to Poika, who received little of any kind of feeling from interacting with his parents. Poika liked the warmth of the new feeling. It flowed through him and surrounded him.

Feeling the hate was good to Poika. He played with it in his mind like a new toy. The hate began to speak to him, telling him things that he would never hear from his parents, or from teachers. Without words at all, the hate taught him to live for himself first. No one else really mattered, just him.

In a short period of time, Poika learned to avoid the other children. They couldn't hurt him at school. He took widely circuitous paths home, a different one each day, always on the lookout for any sign of anyone who could hurt him. He began to assess everyone he saw by the same set of narrow rules: Could they hurt him, or not.

The warm feeling of hate began to be a guide for everything that Poika did. Everyday activities, done with the special flavor of hatred, became easy to do. He began to get better grades. He wouldn't let anyone in class be better than him. The hate said it would be a mistake to let anyone see him be weak in any way.

Poika began to take better care of his belongings. The hate said that being a slob was weak, and stupid. Even though he really never was a messy child, Poika took special pride in keeping everything he was responsible for neat and clean.

Poika's manners improved, along with his grades. He always knew what the proper thing to do was. Before the hate, it never seemed important. Now, he wouldn't let anyone think less of him for being unmannerly. That was weak. The hate within him wouldn't allow it.

Poika also understood how weak, and therefore unimportant, his mother and father were. The hate showed him the reality of their constant drinking, and what it did to them. He felt honestly sorry for them, even though the hate said it was stupid to feel sorry for anyone. Things began to get complicated. Treating his parents with manners meant not letting on how he felt about them.

One part of Poika didn't fall prey to his new-found hate. His crush on Katie Spahl was as fresh and wholesome, in another part of his mind, as it had ever been. Even though she was Lon Spahl's little sister – maybe in spite of the fact – Poika still loved her. It was the way an eight-year-old loves, goofy, indeterminate, and overly simple. It was still his way of having love for her.

FOUR

Lennie didn't stay for breakfast, after the usual morning lovemaking. Cary stayed in bed and watched her dress before she left. Lennie promised to spend the weekend with her parents. The Baerds were nice people. Cary met them once, at a party thrown by Lennie and her roommate.

Lennie's departure left Cary, and Wheels, of course, in the lurch. They would have to fend for themselves; struggle through the remainder of the weekend. Cary figured that they would make it, just fine. He realized that it was easier to feel this way after spending the night with Lennie.

Cary thought about Lennie's given name, Lenora, for the umpteenth time. She said that she didn't like being called by her real name. She said that she heard it more than enough, when she was little. For Cary, that was more than enough direction on the issue. Her name was Lennie, period.

Lennie grew up in a small town in southern Illinois. Her family moved to St. Louis, after Lennie finished grade school. She started at public high school the same year Cary started his junior year. They were stranger-schoolmates for two years, separated by age and class level. It wasn't until after Lennie graduated, and began working at Vander and Beste, that they met at a party and started dating.

Cary wished that the on-again, off-again, nature of their relationship would resolve itself. They had been "on" more than they had been not seeing each other for more than two years. The three nights that they spent together were increasing in frequency. It was a sign that Cary took to mean that they were becoming something more than dating singles spending more time together out of happenstance.

Cary wanted their relationship to be more. He was reluctant to bring up the subject, out of fear of driving her off. Lennie was always carrying around her copy of the soft-bound, Our Bodies, Ourselves. The book served as the introduction to understanding what the Women's Liberation Movement meant for young women. At least it worked that way for a lot of the women that Cary knew.

Cary saw so many copies of Our Bodies, Ourselves in women's apartments that he checked a copy out of the library for himself, just to understand what the fuss was all about. That was interesting. The look he got from the librarian could have frozen water into ice. Still and all, the book was a revelation to Cary. The subjects it covered were persistently mysterious to young men. He thought reading the book put him way ahead of the average guy.

***

Cary took Wheels to the park. The two of them romped and raced all around. The game of retrieving, and sometimes not-retrieving a thrown Frisbee, lasted into the afternoon. Wheels was a perfect companion dog. His heart was big, he loved Cary and would do anything for him. The problem was that among goldens, Wheels just wasn't the brightest. His eagerness to please Cary, and now Lennie, often led to truly comical situations.

Since he was free for the day, Cary laid down for a nap, after the trip to the park. Wheels curled up in "his" beanbag chair and di likewise. Cary never actually fell asleep. He was disused to napping and his brain would not let him sleep. Lying in bed, the first tiny tickle of the aural-sensing came over him. He purposely let it grow, focusing on it. This was the first time he had willfully started viewing auras.

Cary was on his side, facing away from Mrs. Roberts apartment. He saw the couple in the next building, or more appropriately, their scintillated outlines. The two people were moving about. Cary deduced, after a short time, that they were preparing a meal. The pantomime of activity was a perfect representation of what they were doing. The whole thing had a silent movie sense to it.

As the meal preparation ended, Cary detected an alteration in the color of the auras he was looking at. There was a definite green tint to the edges of the neutral salmon-pale white color. As the two shapes took their places at the

26

table and began the pantomime of eating, the green coloration occupied more and more of their auras.

Cary was unsure of what the color change meant. Was it a change brought about by metabolic activity, or something else? Did the food, entering the body, make the color change? Was it body heat? He wondered if it was like infra-red photography, that measured heat intensity.

The general confusion led Cary to open his eyes. The strange aural viewing sensation was still with him. He got up from the bed and maintained his focus on keeping the sensation in his mind. He strode to the living room where Wheels was curled up in the beanbag chair. The dog wagged his tailed at first sight of Cary. Cary closed his eyes immediately. The outline of the tail-wagging dog, still curled in the chair, appeared. The aura's color was green, solid green. Happy. Green meant happy.

Cary sat down on the couch and thought about his discovery. People's – no everyone's – auras were green when they were happy. He held his own arm up in front of himself and closed his eyes. The outline of his arm waved left and right, as he willed his arm to do so. The color of the aura was pale-salmon and slightly yellow. He thought of Lennie. Instantly his aura turned green. His delight at deliberately creating the color change caused an even deeper saturation of the green hue.

Unable to keep still, Cary jumped up from the couch and went to the bathroom mirror. He closed his eyes and viewed his own aura, again. He could make out only the outline of his own head. Turning his head to the side, he caught part of the profile as his vision turned out of the viewing angle. The more he saw, the greener the saturation of his aura became.

Now, utterly wild with enjoyment of what was happening, Cary opened his eyes and let the aura-viewing sensation begin to slip away. He returned to the living room and sat back down on the couch. He wondered at the strangeness of his new-found ability. Was it a gift, one of super human proportions, or a curse? Was it a brain tumor? There were a lot of questions.

Cary realized that he had become very excited during his short aura-viewing session. He took a few deep breaths and let himself calm down. Whatever was happening to him was extremely unique, at least as far as he knew. He had never heard of such an ability outside the ridiculous claims of carnival charlatans, and roadside palm-readers.

Cary suddenly realized that it would be nearly impossible to explain what he was experiencing to anyone. Who would believe him? The whole thing would sound ridiculous. People would think he was crazy. For just the time being, he would keep it to himself, not try and share his new talent with anyone.

***

The rest of the weekend went by without any further attempts at aura viewing. The strange sensation recurred a couple of times, but Cary mentally defused its onset by thinking of other things. It did occur to Cary that if he could voluntarily block the sensation, he probably would be able to voluntarily summon it into his mind; turn it on, so to speak.

The following weeks went by. Cary had several more dates with Lennie, but no more "sleepovers." Each week became an experiment in detecting different colors in the auras that he viewed. The more Cary employed his new ability, the more refined his sensitivity became.

Without being able to conduct experiments, like the one in his living room, Cary had to rely on a lot of guesswork to decipher the appearance of different colors in auras that he viewed. Over time, he got a strong sense that the green-for-happy thing was real.

He began see that people who were focused on what they were doing generally had a yellow, or salmon-colored aura. This color also appeared when they were sleeping. Cary became aware of the limitations of being able to detect only emotional states. It represented only a crude, highly generalized, information set. The colors told him a lot, but not everything.

Cary accidentally discovered that a person exhibits a distinctly red aura when anger is the governing emotional state. On the way home from work one day, he witnessed a fender-bender, in traffic. One of the drivers emerged from his car, in an extremely agitated state, ready to punch out the other driver. Cary quickly let the aura-viewing sensation come over him and closed his eyes. As the angry driver vehemently berated and threatened the other driver, Cary "saw" that his aura was bright red.

The same altercation also revealed that an aura intensely beset by fear is white; stark white. The arrival of a police cruiser on the scene led to predictably paler color hues in both of the auras. The angry man immediately exhibited a less red aura. The other driver's aura remained white but changed to a yellow tint as the police intervention ensued.

The experience of "background" auras led Cary to be able to focus the depth of his aural sensitivity, and discount images at other depths, within the field of his "vision." He practiced viewing auras at different distances, through several solid barriers, with no diminishment of detection. Only the size of people's auras shrank over distance.

Several trips to the library enabled Cary to find no mention of his kind of ability in any book, or encyclopedia. He even searched the books of the huge central library, downtown. As far as he could discover, he was totally unique in his new skill. What he did discover was that there were books available on a wide range of supposed, and falsely-claimed, superhuman sensory talents. All had been debunked thoroughly. In this regard, Cary's resolved to keep his ability to himself was strengthened.

Cary knew that he was becoming less uncomfortable with his new sense. He even thought of it as his "Silent Sight,' since all of the images he saw were pantomimes of reality. He gained control over how and when the ability would come over him. He was able to sleep and awaken, without having aural images to contend with.

FIVE

Cary continued his search for any hint that anyone else had ever experienced anything like his "silent sight." No luck. Weeks of poring over books in the public library proved fruitless. He even got an alumnus pass for the university library. He knew that it would mean getting more mail from the alumni association, but so be it. Try as he might, he could find no mention anywhere of a phenomenon like the one he was experiencing.

The extreme unusualness of Cary's new ability began to make him feel like some sort of sideshow freak. His observational skill with his aura-viewing began to develop ever so slightly more refined. He could now detect the emotional state of the person that he "viewed" from the outset. Previously, he had needed to wait for the impression of emotional color to become evident in the aura that he was viewing. The more refined his ability became, the more he felt that it was weird.

Despite his reaction to the weirdness of his aura-viewing ability, Cary caught himself taking brief glimpses of people's auras during the day. After getting a few strange looks from people, he realized that he had been staring in their direction – however briefly – with closed eyes. He could only wonder what they thought of him. He decided to pay attention to work and forego any opportunities for viewing auras.

Free time was turning out to be another matter. The weather was warm enough to allow him to take his lunch outside and get in a little "viewing" time. A "postage stamp" park, near the downtown store, had a few benches for passers-by. A pair of Ray-Bans gave him the chance to close his eyes and view auras at his leisure. His only problem, at this point, was not getting so drawn into the viewing that he lost track of time. A few lunch breaks passed in their entirety without Cary eating a bite of his food.

Cary began to let his usual evening time for reading slip. After taking care of himself and Wheels, every evening was beginning to involve more aural viewing rather than reading. The simple allure of the new ability grew into something of an obsession. He even began shortening the dog walks, so that he could devote more time to his new activity. Without noticing it, Cary began to sit in his silent apartment flat, viewing the goings-on around him, without the usual music from the stereo in the background. For his part, Wheels still just enjoyed Cary's company the way he always had.

One such very quiet evening, Cary focused his attention on a pair of auras in the building across the street. The couple he watched lived on the first floor of a six-family flat. The aura in the shape of a woman was a deep blue color. Cary understood this to reflect a state of unhappiness. The spectral outline of the man near her was pale salmon and white, a color combination that Cary had associated with people paying attention to what they were doing.

There seemed to be a lot of animated talking going on between the two people. The man kept reaching out to touch the woman, the woman turning away each time. Small streaks of red appeared in the man's aura. The physical animation of the couple increased. At last, the man held the woman in his arms, continuing to speak to her. The woman's blue aura decreased in its intensity after a few minutes of contact with the man. Cary couldn't get the watching-a-silent-movie thing out of his head.

As the minutes of talk between the two continued, the color of the woman's aura underwent a shift from blue, through all the intervening hues, to an aquamarine, more green than blue. Cary knew that the green meant that something happy had entered the conversation between the two people. They were now a single outline, walking, moving through their apartment without letting go of each other.

As the couple stopped, apparently in their bedroom, the man's aura shifted to an intense green. Cary detected from their movements that the couple were undressing. The man lay in the bed and waited for the woman, who took a moment or two longer to disrobe. After a moment, the two were making passionate love to one another.

33

Cary was astounded by the intensity of the colors revealed in the auras of the two lovers. The deep saturation of the green auras, portraying their experience of intense pleasure, wove its way back and forth between them. In each of the two lovers the colors left behind were different. As the green diminished in the woman, the bluer hues of her previous unhappiness limbed their way back into her halo of color. The edges of the woman's aura sustained thousands of shades of green, mixing back and forth with as many blue tints.

The man's aura was steadily green, occasionally brightening in intensity. To Cary's wonder and amazement, streaks of red flew across the man's aura as the love act reached its climax. Cary was left wondering exactly what he had seen.

When, at last, the lovemaking was over, Cary watched as the man's aura faded from an intense green to a green-stained salmon color. The woman, on the other hand displayed the same deep blue color that was present before the lovemaking. After a short time, both of their auras faded to a somber, pale yellow color: both were apparently asleep.

When Cary finally opened his eyes and let his natural vision resume, an ocean of feelings came over him. He was ashamed for having so deliberately spied on someone's love act. At the same time, he thought about what he had learned about emotion, and its role in loving. So much went on beneath the surface of people's outer selves.

Cary tried to sort out the implications of the emotional displays against the backdrop of the lovemaking act. He decided that all was probably not well with that particular pair of people. He then decided that since he had taken exactly one semester of psychology in college, he really knew nothing at all about the meaning of what he just saw.

Disappointed with himself, Cary went back to his reading. After a quick visit outdoors with Wheels, he went to bed. He tried to let the evening's events slip away but took a long time falling asleep.

***

The next day, and the ones after that, saw Cary Lang focusing on his work as intently as he could. He felt the need to let the aura viewing alone for a while. He took his meals in the store employees break room. He engaged more of his co-workers in conversation. He even broke a bit with his habit of not visiting Lennie at work. He managed to stop by every other day, just to say "Hi."

Cary made a point of resuming his regular schedule of play time with Wheels. His "best friend" was always ready for a romp, and the two were a regular fixture in the neighborhood parks. One day after another went by, and Cary began to feel less burdened by his special ability. He was not comfortable with it but having given it a rest enabled him to get an emotional perspective about himself.

Cary's return to amore natural lifestyle led to better times with Lennie. She intuitively reacted to Cary's heightened mood with a happier set of interactions. Opportunities for staying overnight at Cary's flat came more frequently. She even took to walking Wheels on her own.

Lennie complained about Ramona having her boyfriend over so much. On nights when Lennie stayed in the apartment, if the boyfriend was spending the night, there was too much noise. Lovemaking in the next room, even if it wasn't particularly frisky, was hard to ignore. Cary was sympathetic but declined to share his appreciation for the benefit that he received from Lennie's spending more and more nights with him.

During this time, the only thing that went sour was Mrs. Roberts beginning to report that Wheels was barking a lot. She said that the dog would bark loudly, every morning. Cary was surprised to hear this from Mrs. Roberts. He never thought of Wheels being much of a noisy dog, at all. The animal did very well adapting to the many strange noises that were a part of apartment living without barking. Cary didn't quite know what to do about Wheels' new problem.

SIX

The death of his father was a mixed blessing for Poika. It meant that there was one less alcoholic parent to deal with every day. His father had been killed on the job. One day, in the midst of slinging garbage cans, he was struck by a car. The driver of the car didn't stop; just kept on going. The company that he worked for kept no insurance on its employees, so there was no offset for the loss of income.

This meant that there was less money coming in to support their little family. Because of this, Poika's mother took a job, working in a diner, on the evening shift. Her working hours meant that her absence – from noon to midnight, every day – provided for being a mother to her boy only on weekends. Her job gave her the chance to meet a lot of new people, men mostly. Some of them came home with her.

For his part, Poika adapted readily to the need to take care of himself. At night, if his mother brought home a boyfriend, Poika let the hate within him rage inside his head, until his ears roared with the ocean-wave sound of his own blood rushing through his ears. An hour or so of this was usually exhausting enough that he could sleep.

Poika found it quite easy to get up every morning and get himself off to school. He was always very quiet. He never wanted to awaken anyone who might be in the bedroom where his mother slept. Stepping through the front door each morning and ever-so-quietly latching the front door, gave him a sense of accomplished relief. The idea of escaping a possible confrontation with a stranger, in his own house, gave him one of the few good feelings that came his way.

The transition to high school was no problem for him. The hate was still there. He would not let himself be weak. Even though he was only thirteen, he was smart enough to adjust to the new demands placed on him without faltering.

The high school was a mile farther away from his house than his school was. It was a longer walk, he just had to get started earlier. Because everyone else was in a morning stew, struggling with whatever they had to do to start their day, Poika could take a direct route to get to school.

Even though Poika had moved on to high school, his crush on Katie Spahl, as pointless as it might ultimately be, was still a part of him. It was the only part of him that he mentally kept separate from the hate which he let guide all of his other thinking. He saw her in the mornings. Her to the school was part of the one that he took. It was a simple matter of timing his departure to be late enough to see her, and yet not be late arriving at the high school.

The afternoons were different, but the same. They were different from the mornings, because he still had to take a circuitous route home, avoiding as many people as he could. Lon Spahl, and his group of friends, still stopped him and assaulted him, every chance they could. That was the part that was the same. Lon had even added a couple of new hounds to his pack. Now, depending on the day, there were eight or nine of them together.

Poika worked diligently at school. His grades were well above average. His friend, the hate within him, helped him stay focused every minute of the day. After school, the hate – and the fear that went right along with it – drove him to seek cleverer, winding, out-of-the-way routes to get home. Still, that gigantic prick, Lon Spahl, occasionally caught up with him.

Never alone, Lon delighted in finding new ways to torment and torture Poika. If exposure to the new learning of high school had helped Lon Spahl in any way, it was in providing him with new ideas for beating Poika. His group of cronies were always there to egg him on.

Some days, Poika went home wearing only some of the clothes he had worn to school. The others were stolen from him by Lon Spahl's hateful pack of high school shits. This led to

Poika having to wear some of his dead father's work clothes. There simply was no money to buy clothes to replace the ones lost to the predatory attacks of Lon and his crew.

Wearing a work uniform shirt, with the embroidered name patch removed, was a curious sort of a badge of honor. To Poika, it was a sign that he was irretrievably poor, and therefore worth less than other people. This kind of reaction, to dealing with the harsh realities of poverty, was rich food for the hate that fed on it. The sense of being made to look less worthy in any way than the people around him, made Poika's hate begin to blossom, like a flower in springtime.

It was during this time that Poika's hate got a chance to grow exponentially. Its new helpers, anger and rage, came along quite willingly after one particular attack from Lon Spahl and his buddy-thugs. Surprising themselves one afternoon, they accidentally came upon Poika, who was nonetheless still trying to avoid them.

The day was a Friday, and the gang's spirits were high, anticipating a weekend of wasted time. The serendipity of stumbling upon their usual prey fed the pack mentality of the teenagers. Surrounding Poika, they launched into a fusillade of taunts and insults. The odd jab, and punch was thrown in for good measure.

When Lon Spahl grabbed Poika's shirt and tried to rip it off of him, he hesitated momentarily, seeing the depth of unrestrained hate in Poika's eyes. For Poika, the loss of his father's stinking, stained, mess of a work shirt would be too much. He glared at the Spahl-goon, who had him hoist nearly off his feet completely, toes only, touching the ground.

For just that briefest of moments, the other hounds in the pack of boy-dogs weren't there. It was just Lon Spahl, with the diminutive Poika in his grasp. Both boys lost all sense that they were not alone. The look from Poika's eyes – a death-glare, seething with the deepest of hate – froze Lon Spahl into a statue.

A moment later, Lon Spahl realized that he had stopped, and released Poika from his grasp. Not wanting to look like a total dope, he threw a roundhouse punch at the smaller boy that knocked him off his feet. Laughing heartily, he led his band of followers off, each congratulating the others for successfully wounding their prey.

Laying in the dirt of the alley, Poika thought about Lon never being alone. He picked himself up out of the dirt and dusted himself off. The hate inside of Poika told him to look for just that: Lon Spahl alone. In addition to trying to avoid Lon Spahl, and his friends, Poika needed to find an opportunity to even things up. So far, the score was heavily in favor of Lon Spahl. That would have to change. It would have to be when Spahl was alone, of course.

***

A month later, the chance Poika hoped for came along. He heard that Lon Spahl's father had gotten him a job, working at the hardware store, on Saturday's. The store was not far, and served the part of town that included the cross-the-tracks neighborhood that Poika lived in. After checking a couple of times, Poika discovered that Lon worked from eight in the morning, to three in the afternoon. The route that he took home traversed several alleyways.

The plan was simple: Wait for him in one of the alleys and let him have it. The impatience of youth, along with the intensity of his hate, wouldn't let Poika wait.

The next Saturday, he waited for Lon to pass on his way home. He thought about how he was going to get Lon Spahl. Over and over, in his mind, he acted out his plan. With no watch to keep track of time, Poika was surprised when Lon Spahl walked past his hiding place. He excitedly stepped out behind him.

"Lon!" Poika called his name. He wanted Lon Spahl to see it coming, even though he wouldn't be able to do anything about it. As the great oaf began to turn, to see who called his name, Poika swung the piece of pipe he had brought.

"Thung!" The pipe recoiled off Lon Spahl's skull, vibrating with the residual impact, in Poika's hand. Poika let the pipe drop to his side. Lon Spahl dropped as well, like the proverbial ton of bricks.

Poika had surprised himself by dropping the larger boy with a single blow. He had fully expected to be running away by now. He stood over the larger boy, laying in a heap, in the dirt of the alleyway. The heap was utterly still. Poika thought that perhaps he had killed him. Then, the heap took a breath. Another breath, then another, slow but rhythmical.

Poika turned and ran. He realized, part way home, that he was still carrying the pipe in his hand. He quickly found a trash can to put it into. He made it home without being seen. Dinner with his mother that night was especially good. The food was the same as always, but it still tasted better than Poika could ever remember.

Going to bed that night, Poika reminded himself, over and over, just how good it felt to finally even the score with the gigantic prick, the no-good shit, the source of the worst pain in his life, Lon Spahl. The hate within him congratulated Poika for giving free reign to his anger, his rage, and yes, most of all, to his hate.

***

The courtroom was dark, even though the sun shone brightly through the windows. The paneling around the room was stained to a dark brown. The deep walnut tones seemed to soak into everything and everybody in the room. Seated next to his mother, Poika could barely stand to look at the judge. His mother was his only advocate here. This was what they called "Family Court."

The police came for him the day after he whacked Lon Spahl with the pipe. Apparently, Lon Spahl did see it coming. However hard he hit the son-of-a-bitch, it wasn't hard enough for him to forget anything. Lon Spahl spent several days in the hospital, recovering from the head injury. Poika spent exactly the same number of days in a cell at the state reformatory. He spent his time trying to think of ways he could have done what he did, and not get caught.

The state attorney talked a long time about how Poika should be kept in the reformatory until he was old enough to face adult criminal charges. He said boys like Poika never got any better, they just turned into hardened criminals no matter what the state, or anyone else, did for them.

Poika was embarrassed when his mother began speaking about how they had always been poor. She talked about his garbage-man father being killed by a hit-and-run driver. She talked about having to work evenings at the diner, and not having time to properly raise her boy. Poika sat quietly and wondered what the extra parenting from his alcohol-soaked mother would be like.

At the end of the day, the judge said that even though the state attorney was probably right, he was going to let Poika's mother take him home. If there were no further trouble from Poika, his record would be expunged. Poika didn't know what expunged was, but he wasn't going to the reformatory.

Poika was going to go back to school, where his enemy, Lon Spahl walked the halls wearing a headdress-bandage that looked like a turban. He was in the courtroom on the day of Poika's hearing. The state attorney thought it would be a graphic representation of the horror of not locking Poika up forever.

Poika had a list of people that he never knew, that he now hated: The police who came for him, the judge, the state attorney, the guard at the reformatory who looked at him like meat, hanging on a hook. He would be on probation until he graduated from high school. Poika hated that too.

The hate inside of Poika's mind wouldn't shut up. For the longest time, it reminded Poika that getting caught was what he did wrong. If he did a better job, no one would know who whacked Lon Spahl. The hate said it was childish to want Lon Spahl to see it coming; that was the fundamental mistake in his thinking. The hate had been so right about so many other things that Poika listened to it patiently, the way he would listen to a good teacher.

SEVEN

The complaints from Mrs. Roberts about Wheels' barking really bothered Cary. The last time he spoke with her, she said, "Every morning, after you leave, it's bark, bark, bark. Goes on for quite some time."

Cary didn't know what to make of this for a long time. Then it occurred to him that his neighbor, upstairs, might somehow be involved. Fred Maunt was the guy who parked his motorcycle in Cary's parking space and resented it when Cary said that he wanted to use it for his car. The very tall, slender man worked nights. Cary only occasionally crossed paths with him.

The truth was that Fred Maunt was the perfect sort of a man to be employed working as a night janitor at a car dealership. He was almost totally lacking in social skills, having been more or less allowed to grow up, on his own,

45

with no substantive input from either of his parents. Their philosophy of life and parentage was to supply the physical needs of their son, and that was that.

Fred Maunt did his job well enough, and actually had dreams – however pointless they may be – of someday being a car salesman. As life-guiding dreams and aspirations go, it wasn't the most inspiring thing, but it worked for him. The work at the car dealership wasn't arduous. It took him less than half of his shift to do what he had to. The rest of the time was usually spent in the showroom selling cars to imaginary customers, or just sitting in the break room, eating or reading.

Fred disliked almost everybody. He despised his employer, just for being his boss. He had to make sure that the place was ready every morning, so that the shit of a manager could open up the dealership and begin swindling the public. Fred knew about dealer rebates and sales bonuses from the factory. He heard it from eavesdropping on the managers who talked too much when they thought no one was around, late in the evening. The dealership made a fortune, but not for anyone like Fred.

From the puke who bagged groceries at the supermarket, to even the mailman, Fred had an axe to grind with virtually everybody. He was sure that the barber who cut his hair made fun of his bald pate after he left the shop. In Fred Maunt's entire life, his mental capacity, such as it was, would never rise to the level of understanding that his belief in other people's ill will was merely a reflection of his own deeply unhappy existence.

Fred Maunt was an equal-opportunity hater. He honestly disliked everyone. Mrs. Roberts was no exception.

He thought of her as another rich puke, just like the owner of the car dealership that he worked for. She owned the building she lived in, along with her tenants. She kept the place neat, tidy, and in good repair, all the time. That took money. It was the kind of money that Fred Maunt could only dream of, money he would certainly never see.

While he worked night after night, mopping floors and emptying wastebaskets, Fred seethed with resentments. With no one to talk to, and a set of social skills that would never gain him any friends, he spent his mental time dreaming up ways to get even with the people that he thought of as his tormentors. Rearranging the contents of the salesmen's desks was one way to mess with the dealership. Other than that, there really was little that he could do at work, without getting caught.

Not being able to do much about his resentment for his employer really pissed Fred Maunt off. He sought other outlets for his disaffection for society. The target that presented itself – herself – was Mrs. Roberts. As a hapless inept, Fred initially took to doing things like leaving the water faucet run all day long. He knew that the building was on one meter for all four units. Using more water would cost the old lady some of that money she obviously had so much of.

Aside from not being the brightest, Fred knew that there was only so much that he could do without ruining his own home environment. He thought long and hard. He finally came up with an idea. It was a really good idea, since it would focus attention on that well-dressed jerk downstairs, Cary Lang, and not on himself.

As a matter of course, Fred disliked Cary, especially after the motorcycle thing. The jerk wanted to use his parking space. For one day a year? Fred had to be the one who had to accommodate him. Fred's idea would even things up a bit with both Lang, and Mrs. Roberts. Ha! It wouldn't exactly be killing two birds with one stone, but it would be ruffling two birds' feathers at the same time.

***

Cary felt as though he had been burdened with keeping his new ability to himself. He considered what to do about it for a long time. He thought about what his family doctor would say and do. Cary believed the possibilities there would certainly involve sending Cary to a psychiatrist. No dice.

Cary's sphere of friends included only a couple of people from work, none of whom he thought of as close enough to share with. The obvious choice was one that he mentally danced around for a long time, before settling on the plan to tell her: Lennie. They had become closer than they had ever been. Cary hoped that the increase in their time spent together lately would put Lennie in a frame of mind to accept what he wanted to tell her.

The Friday date-night came when Cary planned to bring Lennie into his confidence. She arrived after work, with her overnight bag in hand, just as Cary hoped she would. As far as he was concerned, Lennie's roommate, and her boyfriend, came through, right on cue.

Neither Cary or Lennie were very religious but maintained the fish-on-Friday traditions of their respective families. This was so except for pizza nights – pizza conquered all. Tonight's dinner was the wonderful, fish sticks, macaroni and cheese, and string beans. A glass or two of Mateus Rosé set the mood for the Friday feast of the common folk.

After dinner, Cary and Lennie walked Wheels around the block. When they got back to the flat, they kicked their shoes off and curled up on the couch. Cary had the stereo on low. The sun was just setting. All in all, it was about as good an atmosphere as Cary could imagine for revealing his new ability to Lennie.

Cary began his revelation by telling Lennie that he needed her to be very discreet about what he was going to tell her. The first thing that he shared was the story about the episode in the motor vehicle license office. He was careful to include his own sense of utter surprise that a thing like this was even possible. He worked hard to convey his wonder at the whole thing.

Lennie listened patiently, and curiously, at first. Cary could tell she was thrown a bit of balance by the strangeness of what he was telling her. He eased it back a bit and described some of the other, incidental "viewings" he had experienced. He tried to emphasize how the whole experience of having such a new ability was still, more or less, bewildering to him.

Things weren't going as well as he had hoped. The more he tried to lessen the impact of the bizarre thing he was relating, the more Lennie seemed to withdraw from him. Cary decided to omit the entire story about watching the neighbors' lovemaking. He could tell that Lennie was more than just a little nervous. He hung up the talk for a while and just sipped at his glass of wine, hoping Lennie would ask a question or two.

Lennie sat silently, sipping her wine and not saying a word, for several minutes. She occasionally glance at Cary. There was confusion in her eyes, and fear. Cary decided to move the conversation along with a small demonstration. He took Lennie's glass from her and stood up.

"Go in the kitchen and follow my instructions. There will be two walls between us. Close the door too. I'll talk loudly, you'll still be able to hear me."

Lennie did as he asked, padding barefoot to the kitchen, closing the door behind her. Cary Closed his eyes. He could make out Lennie's aura easily. It was salmon-colored.

"Raise your arms." Lennie's aura raised its arms.

"Now, I want you to start raising your fingers one at a time. I'll count them as you go."

Lennie's aura began to do as he had instructed.

"One, two three, four, five, six." There was a moment of hesitation.

"Seven, eight, nine…" Lennie dropped her arms to her sides and just stood there.

For a moment, Cary was unsure what was happening. Lennie's aura had shifted from the salmon-yellow of concentration to a pale yellow tinged with blue. She put her hands to her face. Her shoulders started heaving up and down. She was crying.

Cary could see the blue overtaking the other tints in her aura. He opened his eyes and walked into the kitchen. Lennie was still standing there, sobbing. Cary wrapped his arms around Lennie. He knew that the last thing he wanted to do this evening was upset her so much.

"I'm sorry. I didn't know this would all be so upsetting."

Lennie looked up at him, pushing herself away slightly. "I don't understand any of this. What are you doing?"

"It's something that's been happening to me. I thought it was important enough to tell you about. You're important enough to me. You ought to know." Cary tried to wrap his arms around Lennie. She pushed herself farther away, out of his grasp entirely.

The look in Lennie's eyes had changed from confusion and fear to one of fearful determination. The crying had stopped. She wiped the tears from her eyes. She turned herself around and headed back to the front of the flat.

Passing through the door of the kitchen, "I gotta get out of here."

Cary followed her into the living room. Lennie slipped on her shoes. She grabbed her overnight bag, and made for the door, never looking back at Cary.

"Lennie, don't…" The door closed with a loud click of the latch. Cary was relieved that it had not been slammed. He knew he was grasping at the slimmest of straws, wondering what the next thing would be.

Cary couldn't help himself. He closed his eyes and watched as Lennie's aura walked down the half-flight of steps, and out the door of the building. There was still determination in the way she walked. The closure of the front door of the building coincided with a roll of thunder, heralding promised thundershowers.

Her aura was much less blue, now. The color was chiefly white – other colors, all of them occasionally flew through the aura surrounding Lennie She was his friend, his lover, his woman – he had to admit it, his everything. He had the impulse to go after her but was sure that she would only be more frightened by his pursuit.

Lennie drove away, in her beater of an old Ford Falcon, under the first few drops of rain. Watching her aura get smaller, as she went down the block, brought a new sensation to the confused mind of Cary Lang. He knew what the authors of all those books were talking about when they spoke of desolation that comes from the loss of another.

Cary spent a sleepless night, sitting on the couch in his living room. The stereo stayed on but he never heard a note of music. The rain intermittently tapped the windows. Cary paid no attention to it. Wheels knew something was wrong and rested his head in Cary's lap. Later, the dog simply laid at Cary's feet, just touching him, the whole night.

Cary's sense of loss was complete. The attempt at bringing Lennie closer had done more than merely backfire. Cary had no idea if he would ever see Lennie again. He cried from time to time that night, never really aware of it.

Saturday morning finally came. The first rays of sunlight did nothing to raise Cary's spirits. He looked down. Wheels was still there, asleep on the floor, across his feet. The dog awoke and Cary reached down to pet him. Gratefully, the dog didn't recoil from Cary's touch, as he had expected it to. Instead, Wheels let Cary pet and stroke him for a long time.

Whatever healing is bestowed upon a person, by touching a beloved pet, began at that moment. Cary decided that if he only had one, four-legged friend, that's who he would spend his weekend with.

EIGHT

Lennie woke with a small start, in her own bed, but not in her own bed. She was home in the house where she grew up. The Jefferson Barracks Bridge was tough to navigate last night. The rain made that crossing, and the rest of the trip down through Columbia and Waterloo, Illinois a real pain in the butt.

Leaving Cary's, she knew that going to the apartment was not going to work. She was planning on staying with Cary, since her roommate, Ramona, had Cliff over, yet again. Lennie shook her head at the thought that she had been thinking of asking Rita, her co-worker at the store, if she was interested in taking over Lennie's rent. She knew Rita was unhappy with her current living arrangements.

Lennie was seriously considering moving in with Cary. They had spent so much time together, already. She really liked him, he wasn't pushing her for anything at all. She wanted to know if living with Cary was a good choice, if he was the one, the guy. His frightening revelation, last night, left her only one choice: Drive home, to Red Bud.

Normally, she wouldn't have driven in those conditions. The few dips and turns of the highway were truly treacherous on weekend nights. You never knew who got an early start on drinking. You had to pay attention to the railroad crossings. They were still mostly elevated affairs, two, or three feet high, intended to slow vehicular traffic deliberately. Hitting one of those at highway speeds was certain disaster. The rain only made it all the more dangerous and frightening.

Her arrival, late in the evening, surprised her parents. Her father accepted her explanation that she just wanted to be home for a couple of days. The look in her mother's eye told her that a little bit of prying the truth out of her was going to be part of their weekend.

***

Cary had no idea what was going to happen next, with Lennie. He was sure that he had permanently ruined their relationship. He tried calling Lennie's apartment on Sunday, but Ramona said that she hadn't seen her at all, since Friday. Cary hoped that meant that she went home, to Red Bud, for the weekend. He decided that the only thing he could do was to look in on the Young Sophisticates department on Monday to see if she was there.

After ruining Friday night, as well as the rest of the weekend, Cary just wanted to get back to work. He would try to keep things together there, without letting his private life interfere. He had shipments to all the different stores to coordinate. The store management wanted emphasize men's clothing for the coming season. Cary recognized a double-edged sword when he saw it. A chance to show that he could run a big sales season was also a chance to fail.

One day ran into another. The big sales season started and the work of keeping shipments up with the varying sales levels in the different stores wore Cary out. Evenings were mostly for rest and recovery. He made sure that his best buddy, Wheels, was well taken care of.

The Monday after frightening Lennie away, he surreptitiously peeked in on her department. She was there. He couldn't help but do that one little thing to make sure that she was alright. He made sure she didn't see him, he didn't want any more problems than he already had. Cary knew that he counted on Lennie to keep his secret. If he stirred up any sort of trouble, that paper-thin remainder of their relationship would probably be lost.

As the weeks wore on, Cary began to get into the rhythm of the new responsibilities at work and finished earlier in the evenings. He spent even more time with Wheels. They'd pick a different park in the area, every day, and go for it. It was surprising to find out not only that you could wear out a Frisbee, but that you could do it fairly quickly. Wheels was getting quite a "trophy case" of worn-out dog toys to keep near him while he slept.

Long evenings in the park usually led to small or missed meals for Cary. He didn't care much about it. He knew he was depressed, but the awful beauty of depression is that it poisons itself so perfectly. Cary was unhappy along with being depressed. That was as good as pouring gasoline on a fire.

To keep from spending all of his non-reading time thinking about how much he missed Lennie, Cary began to explore the experience of aural viewing once again. He figured that he had made such a perfect mess of his life, he wanted to see what other people were doing. He had already worked out that it wasn't going to work, viewing auras while working, so he didn't try.

Evening after evening, he chose a different area, around his flat, to view. He became involved in figuring out exactly what people were doing, starting with a lot of guesswork. After a few weeks he began to get a sense of what he was looking at. Even if he came in on the midst of a person doing something, he could generally make out what mundane activity they were involved with, after only a short time.

There were exceptions to this, of course. Some of the aural outlines he viewed performed actions that Cary was unable to interpret. People who turned their backs to where Cary was located, hid their arms and hands from him with the impenetrable part of their bodies. Even taking into consideration that what he was looking at was not at all out of the ordinary, some things just didn't reveal themselves. Cary figured it would be this way with his new ability for quite a long time.

Cary began to deliberately refine his aural-viewing technique. He started viewing auras at a distance. As far as he could tell, if there were people within his line of aural sight, obstructions, besides other people meant nothing. A person passing between Cary, and another person's aura, would block the view of that aura. It was an aggravating limitation of his ability, but he felt that it somehow humanized the whole thing; made it less other-worldly.

Cary developed quite a habit of coming home from work, playing with Wheels, and feeding him, then beginning to view auras almost immediately. Cary's mealtimes went by the wayside. He always ate lunch at work, but these days dinner was passed over. Cary began to lose weight. At first, it was just a matter of his clothes fitting loosely. After a month, he needed to buy new clothes, in smaller sizes.

The aural viewing began to involve Cary more deeply. If, in the beginning, he had no idea what people were doing, he now had amassed quite a 'library' of viewing experiences to draw upon. He became more comfortable watching the goings-on in the neighborhood. Whenever a new set of movements caught Cary's aural-viewing eye, he would view the activity intently to see if he could determine the nature of the activity.

Cary also began to pay more attention to the displays of emotion played out before him. With little experience, the mixture of emotion-color and activity meant next to nothing to him. After a time, however, he began to get a real strong sense of what people's motives were by a process of trial and error.

The aural viewing experience began to give Cary a new sense of sympathy for the lack of variety in people's everyday lives. He saw the same thing, over and over again, so many times, that he began to feel sorry for the people that he watched. The idea that he was one of those people worked its way into his mind. As generally unhappy as he was without Lennie in his life, this new awareness did not help.

Cary thought that his life had taken a dark, problematical turn, since he acquired his new ability. He was sure he didn't like the way things were going. He was uncertain exactly what to do about it. Work was about as rewarding as it would ever be. His new ability was entertaining, but had become a problem, scaring Lennie away. He was sorting things out in his head every day, trying to make some life-sense of it all.

Adding to Cary's unhappiness was the fact that Mrs. Roberts continued to report to Cary that Wheels was still barking, for a long time every morning. Cary thought it was certainly, very strange that whatever made Wheels bark in the mornings, only did so on days when Cary went to work.

NINE

The second half of his senior year in high school was actually a happy time for the boy nicknamed Poika. Now seventeen years old, his long-standing probation would be coming to an end. No more monthly visits to the courthouse, no more disapproving looks from the probation agent. In fact, once he graduated from high school, there wouldn't be any Terre Haute, Indiana crap for him to put up with. Poika planned to enlist in the Army. His mother would sign for him, he knew it.

The last three and one-half years had been trouble-free years for Poika. After clobbering Lon Spahl with the length of pipe, no one tried to beat him up anymore. No one followed him home, no one tried to get revenge for whacking the great bully in the head. Likewise, in school, no one tried to make friends with Poika, he never expected anyone to do so in the first place.

Lon Spahl was alright, at least Poika thought so. He heard that Lon's grades were poorer than they were before the bump on the noggin, but Poika thought that was only natural. Lon always made sure to keep a lot of distance between himself and Poika, wherever he went.

Poika's inner life flourished. The hate he had fostered into a deadly weapon rested inside of him, quietly guiding him to continue doing well in his school work. Poika even began to bulk up a little bit, spending more and more of his free time at the gymnasium, during open-exercise hours. He grew a bit taller. He was no longer shorter than everyone else in his class.

During this last semester of school, the strangest thing happened. Of all the kids in the high school, Katie Spahl began to take an interest in Poika. Knowing that it was he who dented her brother's head didn't seem to be a problem for the petite brunette, with the deep brown eyes. She walked home with Poika, several days a week.

Poika couldn't have been happier about this particular state of affairs. Being a little older now, Poika had more concrete ideas about how he would act towards a young, perfectly beautiful girl like Katie. He had definite ideas about how she would act towards him, if he gave her the chance – that is to say if he created the right circumstances for romance to progress.

The time of the spring dance came and Katie Spahl suggested that Poika meet her at the dance. She told Poika that her parents wouldn't like it if they knew that she liked him. It would just be easier if they met at the dance.

Poika was pleased beyond words at this totally out-of-the-blue development. The night for the dance came, and

Poika managed to find a decent enough shirt to wear. His school trousers would just have to do the extra duty. Shoes? Well, shoes were expensive, he only had the one pair. He showered and brushed his teeth. He could hardly eat any dinner. Poika's clueless mother was pleased that he was finally making friends and participating in social events.

Time came for the dance, and Poika headed out. It seemed to take only moments for him to walk the distance to the high school. He waited outside, certain that Katie would appear at any time. Scores of other school kids filled past Poika, into the gym. The hour for the dance to start came and passed. The music was played loud and poorly, like any other high school dance band. Poika waited patiently.

After about a half-hour wait, Poika at last saw Katie Spahl walking towards the gym. She was radiant. There was pink ribbon in her hair, and a scarf around her neck. She was dressed in a skirt and blouse, her bobbysocks and saddles completing the ensemble. She was obviously wearing makeup, something not allowed in school. That only made her prettier.

Something was wrong though, Katie Spahl wasn't alone. One of the other seniors was with her, walking arm-in-arm with her. Poika knew the boy from several classes that they shared.

As the couple approached the door of the gym, Poika called out, "Katie!"

The pair of teenagers stopped. The boy with Katie said, "What do you want, poor-boy?"

Katie smiled at the taunt and chimed in, "Yeah, what do you want, poor-boy?"

Not knowing what the best way was to answer, Poika looked at Katie, "We were going to the dance. You – and me. Together."

Katie started laughing. "You – you and me?" She continued laughing. The boy with her started laughing too. Soon, there were six or seven high schoolers circled around Poika. They had all been let in on the joke and were laughing along with Katie and her date – her real date.

The next thing that happened totally surprised Poika. Still laughing, and nearly in tears, Katie Spahl reached out and slapped Poika in the face. "After what you did to my brother, I wouldn't let you take our dog to the dance." She had stopped laughing. She looked at him with a face darkened and distorted with contempt.

Poika pushed his way out of the circle of laughing teenagers. The side of his face, where Katie had struck him, stung and burned. Poika put his hand to his face, checking to see if it somehow had magically caught fire. He pulled his hand away, no fire, no blood. His face still hurt. He had been hit much harder by Lon. This hurt was different. There seemed no limits to it. It stung, all the way through him. Poika fell the pain of it, right down to his toes.

Stepping back, he held his clenched fists tightly, down at his sides, fearful that he would begin swinging them at anyone near enough to hit. He walked away from the entrance to the school gymnasium. The sound of laughter – laughter aimed at him, and his foolishness – followed him down the street. Too proud to let anyone see him run, Poika continued walking. He was several blocks from the school before he decided that the laughter he heard was just in his mind.

It was midnight before Poika got home. He spent the several intervening hours on his own, sitting on a barrel, down by the railroad tracks. As he sat there, he thought about how he had believed Katie Spahl would go to the dance with him, and what a dope he had been.

Without a "snap" or a "pop," something inside the boy called Poika changed. The hate within him now had access to that one last part of Poika that he had kept away from it. Before tonight, Poika held his esteem for Katie Spahl in his mental "crush box." He assessed and judged everything and everyone else against the seething hate in his heart. His "love" for Katie had been different. It stood on its own, strong and sweet, tender and brave.

Any barriers that Poika had erected in his mind, to keep his feelings for Katie Spahl separated from his hate, were now gone. They collapsed under the weight of the laughter, that still rang in Poika's ears. They collapsed beneath the overwhelming surge of pressure from the hate that now ran free inside the entirety of his mind.

Before tonight, Poika was just a malcontent, filled with hate, no direction or goals to deal with his unhappy circumstances. The hate truly spoke to him now, calming his heart, settling him down. He would go home, and become a new thing, he would become the hate itself.

***

Graduation day came, and the boy with the funny nickname wore his cap and gown, just like all the other students. He only did so for his mother's sake, she wanted to see him go through the ceremony. He listened to the speeches and collected his diploma. After dropping of his cap and gown at the gymnasium, Poika left high school, and its humiliations behind.

The following day, Poika and his mother made their last monthly visit to the courthouse. He thought that the probation agent looked leeringly at his mother. His name, Percival Clark Hamble, emblazoned the university diploma over his desk. The probation agent gave Poika's mother an official looking paper called a "Writ of Expungement." The fancy lettering was supposed to make it seem more important.

After signing the Writ, the agent said good-bye to both Poika's mother and to Poika. He still had that disapproving look on his face, for the boy. Poika knew that all Mr. Hamble would be looking at as they left, was his mother's ass. He secretly hoped that the probation agent would die sometime soon of a coronary, whatever that was.

The next day, it was finally time for Poika to get something that he wanted. He spoke to the Army recruiter for several weeks before graduation and had it all arranged. They went to the U. S. Army Recruitment Office. His mother signed the paper, despite the fact that she hoped her son would stay, and somehow contribute to her support. She was getting older now, prospects were few and far between. She had not brought a "boyfriend" home for more than a couple of years. Poika signed the paper, feeling like he had somehow just freed himself from some vast system of captivity and torture.

***

Two days later, the gaggle of new recruits waited for the bus that would take them to training camp. Some stood with their parents, there was the odd girlfriend here and there. Poika was alone. He stood and waited, barely aware that there were others around him. Among the animated well-wishers, and good-byes, with the necessary hugs and kisses, his quiet presence at the edge of the small group made him invisible, for all intents and purposes.

The bus came. It arrived in a cloud of its own foul diesel exhaust. It was painted in olive-drab green. The white star and Army insignia lettering were darkened with dirt and soot from the bus's engine, which had obviously been run far beyond its normal life expectancy. The whole thing had that wonderful post-war, U.S. Army quality of everything being in working order but at the same time, unattractively worn.

The last weeping good-byes were said; the good-bye kisses bestowed. The recruiting sergeant called off names from a list on a clipboard. The young men all filed onto the bus. The door closed, the bus started up, accelerated slowly and disappeared down the highway.

***

The training camp at Fort Leonard Wood was little better than the poor side of Terre Haute, Indiana. Poika found it to be nearly perfect. Its most appealing quality was that it wasn't Terre Haute.

The hate inside of him understood the motivations of military life on a gut level. It wasn't hate that made the Army what it was. The sheer aggression of it was close enough. It actually resonated with that part of Poika that was now in control of everything.

The moment he stepped off the bus, the yelling and abuse began. Poika soaked it all in like sunshine. He literally felt it warming the part of his soul that was in charge: the hate. All the other recruits were suffering shock and reeling with all the new demands. Poika was on vacation, playing one new game after another.

From that first moment on, everything about Army training seemed easy and pleasant. It never bothered him if the drill instructors singled him out for some special "attention." The hate kept him cool and helped him stay focused on whatever point was being made. He worked harder at being a soldier than anyone else. He was determined to be the best.

Poika quickly became a stand-out recruit. He excelled at every challenge put before him. His academic background didn't necessarily indicate readiness for officer candidate school. That was fine with the non-coms, the sergeants and corporals who ran the Army. They decided among themselves that Poika's skill made him likely to be one of them.

Poika fit right in with the regimentation and demanding schedule of Army life. The part that really worked for him, got his juices flowing, was combat training. He tore through the basics with no effort whatsoever. He found all the quick, efficient ways of killing "spoke" to him. He was soon doing expert drills with the instructors. His skill in the art of killing flowed over into his marksmanship. He earned his sharpshooter badge in the first round of trials.

All this put Poika on track for special attention from the Army. Opportunities to join several highly specialized forces within the Army soon came his way. He insisted that he was just an ordinary soldier, good at what he was doing and stayed with the regular troops. The Army, wise in its own ways, decided that a soldier as good as Poika turned out to be, would be good advertising, and assigned him to recruitment after only a year in the service.

With a corporal's rank, and a chance to stay stateside, Poika was ready to do whatever the Army asked of him, and gladly set off to his first assignment. He never really had any interest in traveling out of the country. The idea of serving his time with the Army, signing up other recruits, appealed to him. The only thing he asked from the Army was to not be sent back to Terre Haute, Indiana. Since it was a normal practice of the Army not to do things like that anyway, Poika was set.

The first recruiting assignment for Poika was Knoxville, Tennessee. He was only able to stay for a year before being reassigned. The Army wanted to keep fresh faces in its recruiting offices. One-year stints were mandatory. During this year, he was able to keep up his martial arts skills by volunteering to teach at the local YMCA. The access to the gym and equipment was more than fair compensation for showing a bunch a of little snots how to beat up on each other.

Poika's second assignment, now with the rank of sergeant, was as an instructor in hand-to-hand combat, at another training base. This time he was in Georgia. He had a natural ability as a physically aggressive, hate-filled, combatant. This gave him an edge in producing soldiers who really understood what they were doing. Poika was able to impart the drive to first incapacitate, then eliminate an opponent.

After that year, an assignment to return to recruiting was offered to Poika. He accepted the chance to go to a new town and send fresh meat into the Army grinder. The journey to Pittsburgh, Pennsylvania was easy enough, he hitched the whole way. He had never done that before but found that it was a good way to save money. At the time, picking up hitchhiking soldiers was looked on by a lot of people as almost an obligation. Wherever he was dropped off along the way he never had to wait long for another ride.

TEN

Cary did everything he could to plan for a late arrival on Tuesday morning. He even put in a little office time Sunday, to get ahead of orders. Monday, he stayed late and set up things for Tuesday's order flow, so that he could "hit the ground running." when he arrived. He didn't like coming in late, he felt his job was too important to mess with.

Before leaving work on Monday, he explained everything he had done to his supervisor, and told him he would be late the next morning because of an appointment. He left the type of appointment to the imagination of his supervisor. There was no sense weaving an excuse that was too complicated; a lie that was too convoluted.

Cary's supervisor knew Cary to be the best employee that Vander and Beste had. He thought of Cary as the one person who always showed up, and was always one hundred, ten percent ready to do the job. The young man had very consistently been just exactly that. Losing him for an hour or two during the week was the least that the stores could do for such a good employee.

Cary had been wondering about Mrs. Roberts complaints about Wheels' morning barking problem for some time. He felt that his apologies weren't going to be enough to keep him from being asked to move, no matter how much Mrs. Roberts liked Cary. Her wistful looks had long ago subsided. Whatever charm had gotten Cary his apartment, along with Wheels, had worn off.

He needed to do something about the situation. It was either that or get ahead of the whole moving thing. Having so successfully chased Lennie away was enough change for Cary to have to deal with. He didn't really want to consider moving to a new flat, or apartment.

Tuesday morning, Cary got up at the usual time, and went through his routine. He fed himself and Wheels, showered and dressed for work. He took Wheels out for his morning walk, and brought him back, leaving him at home with a pat on the head. He then drove off at the usual time.

This morning was to be different. Cary's appointment was with the person that he considered the architect of the entire problem with Wheels barking: his upstairs neighbor, Fred Maunt. He was an unusually slender, bald, middle-aged crab. He reacted so poorly, during the whole car parking episode, that Cary had him under suspicion from the outset.

Cary knew that Fred Maunt worked nights. It was just part of the normal background information of daily life that a person accumulates. The activity patterns of everyday living become evident to one's immediate neighbors in short order. If people didn't actively seek out the information, it comes to them anyway, in its own time.

Cary drove around the block and parked his VW on the street behind his apartment building. He waited until he was reasonably sure that Fred Maunt would have returned from his night job, at the car dealership. Cary crossed through the yard of the building across the alley from his. He passed Maunt's car, in the car park garage. He very quietly let himself in through the back entrance, making sure no one, especially Fred, saw or heard him.

Thankfully, Cary's surprise return caught Wheels already in the midst of his mid-morning nap. He awoke to find his master walking through the kitchen entrance to the back of the flat. A dozy wag of the tail was followed by slowly rising from his beanbag-throne and meeting Cary half way through the flat. Cary settled him back down, trying to maintain quiet.

Then, without warning, "Bung!" Wheels started growling, then barked.

Cary walked to the bedroom window of his apartment and pulled back the curtain. Outside the pane of glass in the upper sash, a tennis ball, hanging from a thick piece of twine swung back and forth. It swung outward and bounced off the window again. "Bung."

Cary could see the windows in the apartment across the gangway, they were all unoccupied and curtained. The other end of the twine was undoubtedly coming from the window above, Maunt's apartment.

To her credit, Mrs. Roberts would never allow maintenance that resulted in painting a window shut. Cary slid the upper sash downward as the tennis ball swung outward. At the end of its inward arc, it entered the space inside the window. Cary grabbed the twine, just above where it was attached to the ball. Quickly wrapping the twine around his hand, he yanked as hard as he could, once, then again.

The first forceful yank on the twine resulted in a thump, and a groan from above. The second pull brought down the entire length of twine. Cary quickly wound the twine and pulled it, and the ball, in through the window. He slid the window upwards to close it again, noiselessly. He couldn't help but think of Fred Maunt peering out of the window above, scanning the gangway below for some sign of what had happened.

After cutting the twine from the tennis ball, Cary tossed it into the basket of Wheels' toys. The golden retriever was instantly intrigued by the presence of a new toy, and filched it out of the basket, even before Cary could get to the back door to leave.

Stepping into the rear stairway of the apartment building Cary made no effort to conceal his movements. In fact, he gave the back door to his apartment a good slam, just to let Maunt hear it.

Crossing the small yard between the building and the garage, Cary glanced up just long enough to see a scowling Fred Maunt, watching him, through the rear window of his apartment. He stopped just long enough in the carport-garage to drop the coil of twine over the radio antenna on Maunt's car.

The latest release by the Eagles, Desperado, played on the eight-track, on the way in to work. After four more songs, Cary parked his car in the all-day lot. The block-and-a-half walk to work took no time at all. The feeling of accomplishment was very fulfilling. Cary was fairly sure that he had heard the last complaint about his dog.

***

Jesus on a bicycle! Stings like hell! Fred Maunt thought to himself while he poured rubbing alcohol on his hand. What did that little creep have to go and do that for?

The twine-burn in his right hand was a groove that penetrated through the skin. It hurt badly before he tried to clean it. The rubbing alcohol was all he had. It really didn't help. Oughtta call the freakin' cops on 'im!

Thinking better of that last idea, Fred Maunt wrapped his hand in gauze. The only pain reliever in his medicine chest was some aspirin that had been in there since he moved in, six years ago. He tried to open the bottle with his right hand, but it hurt too much. He switched hands but that hurt just as much. He finally held the bottle against the wall with his right hand in a fist. He twisted the cap off with his left hand. The pain in his hand and the effort of opening the old bottle left him covered in sweat. He choked down the aspirin with some water. He went and laid down on his bed.

Rotten, fancy-dressed shit, thought Fred.

The pain in his hand would ensure that he didn't sleep that day. He would go to work with a throbbing hand, and no sleep. His employer didn't give him any sick time, so he was just going to have to work through his suffering. His hand would continue to hurt for several days. The whole time, Fred Maunt would think only of Cary Lang as the sole reason for his pain.

ELEVEN

One of those supper-less workdays changed everything for Cary. The afternoon romp with Wheels went as usual. Cary spent part of the evening viewing the auras of people in the neighborhood. He recently began to assign identifiers to some of the people who regularly appeared before him. They weren't necessarily names. They helped Cary keep track of who was routinely doing what.

There was the woman he called "Apple Eater." Every day, she would come home from wherever she worked and have an apple. She was one of the first people Cary was able to associate movements with a specific activity. At first, Cary saw her cutting something up and eating it. When the woman came home one day and simply bit into the apple without cutting it up. Cary was delighted to finally associate a very specific action with the movements of an aural outline.

Cary learned to watched people in the area who largely went through the same set of activities every day. As mundane as it all was, Cary kept at it. To anyone else, watching the boring, everyday activities of working people wouldn't be worth the effort. There was a weird sort of reward in it for Cary. It gave some validation to all of the effort he was putting into it.

After a month or so of studious attention, he was comfortable with what he saw. Things made sense to him. He began to detect minor differences in the things people did. He still couldn't shake the weird feeling of watching some sort of bizarre silent movie.

Cary's level of comfort with his aural viewing made things different. It began to lose its grip on him. After another month, Cary began reading again, incorporating trips to the library into his afternoon sessions with Wheels. He made a point of eating an evening meal, hungry or not, at least three times a week. This last, he did because he had continued to lose weight and was now in danger of needing to buy even smaller clothes.

On a day that he did not necessarily plan on eating dinner, Cary was caught up in something he never expected. The evening was winding down and Cary was going to go to sleep. As he lay his head on the pillow and closed his eyes, an intense flash of aural red greeted him. It wasn't that unusual to see red in the auras of the neighbors. Life was fraught with anger-inducing events. Somebody was always mad about something. This was different. The red was very intense. There were two auras, both red.

Unable to ignore such a bright signal of someone's anger, Cary focused his "silent sight" on the source. Two human outlines – a man and a woman – were the ones responsible for the display of the bright red auras. The shapes were smaller. They had to be about a block over, to the rear of Cary's apartment building. He estimated the distance at about two hundred feet.

Cary went to the kitchen, at the rear of his flat. He zeroed in on the location of the two auras with his normal eyesight. He could just make out the edge of the building that the two shapes were in. He made a note of the architectural details. In this southside neighborhood, each building had a slightly different style, or character to it.

Standing in his kitchen, Cary closed his eyes again. He continued to view the two bright red auras. The two people were extremely agitated. They took turns speaking, their heads bobbed and wove back and forth with fierce animation.

Along with their energetic speaking, the two gestured wildly, apparently emphasizing their pronouncements. As the argument went on, the man's aura maintained an even, bright red color. The woman's aura tended to drift from red to purple, when she was not speaking and waving her hands wildly. Cary guessed that it was the blue of unhappiness creeping in.

Color shifts in the man's aura were another matter. The edges of his aura grew dark. At first, Cary thought that they were showing the same purple tint that the woman's aura had shown. A closer look – focusing his attention harder – led Cary to the awareness that he man's aura, as red as it was, showed darker and darker hues, until becoming black at the edge. The edge seemed to be growing, ever so slowly, taking over more and more of the bright red area.

Cary was unfamiliar with this particular color display. He saw that it was a profound deepening of the red hue, a deepening that indicated something more profound than anger. As he wondered about the significance of the color, the man struck the woman, with his hand. The blow was hard enough to cause the woman to totter backwards, off-balance. He woman's aura instantly faded from red to a pinkish salmon.

The aura of the man advanced on the woman. Her aura began to turn white – evincing fear – as she continued to move backward, away from the man. The woman's aura suddenly stopped. She had backed into a barrier, a wall. She held her hands in front of her, defensively.

The man's aura lashed out with one hand. The man's hand was at least a foot away from the woman. Her head recoiled violently, as if from a powerful blow. An unseen object, in the man's hand, had apparently struck the woman. The aura of the woman instantly dropped to the floor and began to fade. The white aura shone blue, then dulled and became more difficult to see. After a few moments, it was gone. The disappearance of the aural signature of the woman's emotional state meant only one thing to Cary: she was dead.

Cary was dumbstruck. He was vaguely aware of breathing at a high rate, as if he were running. He was sure that he had just witnessed an angry argument, culminating in a murder. Continuing to focus on where the woman had fallen, Cary noticed that the man's aura had changed colors several times. It faded through the spectrum from red to blue, then to green. Cary was feeling nauseated at the thought that the man's emotional state so thoroughly changed from angry to sad, to happy, all in a matter of moments.

The aura of the man stood over the spot where the woman had fallen for several minutes. Then he began to move about. His aura had shifted to a steady display of the blue of unhappiness. The movements were all unusual and unfamiliar to Cary, who could make little sense of them. He moved back and forth, from one part of the apartment to another. Sometimes the man was kneeling, other times bending over and moving around doing something with his hands. Cary watched, his attention riveted.

For a period of time, the aural outline of the man knelt in one place and did something with his hands. The place he knelt was not near where the woman's aura had fallen and faded out. This activity took place in another part of the apartment. Cary could not decipher what the activity was, although he watched carefully. The kneeling aural outline worked diligently at exactly the same spot for more than twenty minutes.

The man was done with the kneeling task. He returned to the spot where the woman fell and began to drag something. Those movements were unmistakable. The object was heavy. It took considerable effort to move. Cary began to suspect that it was the body of the woman, now no longer visible in the spectra of his special ability.

Cary's angle of view – both with his eyes and with his new ability – was from a slightly elevated position. The grade between the two locations was ten or fifteen feet. He watched as the man's aura worked at dragging, and sometimes carrying the ungainly object.

From the path that the man took – shrinking in size, as he moved farther away, and shifting first to one direction, then another – Cary guessed that he was moving the heavy object, the body, to the car park, in back of the building. The layout of the building and carpark was in the same orientation as Cary's building. It was fairly easy to follow this part of the macabre proceedings.

The head of the man darted back and forth constantly. Cary had a hunch that he was looking out for anyone who might see him. The aura of the man stopped at a place that Cary guessed roughly corresponded to the back of the car park. There, the man lifted the heavy object, in stages, into something. It wasn't hard to infer that it was the trunk of a car.

Throughout this process, the aura of the man – the killer – shifted back and forth from blue to green, then red and black. The mixture of emotions was evident. The colors shifted sometimes wildly, flashing one hue, then another. The thoughts racing through the mind of the man were obviously doing so at a terrific rate. Cary thought it was a safe bet that he was witnessing the emotional cost of panic.

The man got into the car and drove away, backing out of the car park, heading west along the alley. The loss of the sight of the man left Cary in a momentary vacuum. He slumped in a chair in the kitchen to tried and make some sense of what he had just witnessed. He was drained. He didn't realize, the whole time that he was viewing the scene, a half block away, that his pulse was racing. Now, he felt as though he just finished a long run.

The shock of it all began to come over him. Cary felt like he was being submerged beneath the waves of a tide of feelings – none of them good. Uncertainty and fear were drowning him. A life had been extinguished, right before him. What could he do? What could he say? Who would believe him?

TWELVE

Downtown Pittsburgh was a different sort of a place to try and recruit young people for the Army. Mostly it was a target for a relatively new social phenomenon: protesters.

People who found something wrong with what the army was doing in southeast Asia had begun to stand around the recruiting office with signs. The signs said all kinds of pointless stupid things about how the Army was evil. The sign-carriers were always dressed like hippies, long hair, bell-bottom jeans, sandals.

Poika made it in to the office every morning, well before the demonstrators got out of bed. Usually around the time that he was warming up his second cup of coffee, the dirty creeps would begin to show up, thinking that nine or ten o'clock in the morning was early.

The protestors did manage to intercept a few of the first interested potential recruits. Usually the confrontations were short. Comments were yelled at the young men walking toward the door of the office.

Every once in a while, the protestors would intercept a potential recruit and block their path, nattering at them about the wrongness of joining the Army. When this would happen Poika would go out on the sidewalk and escort the young man, or woman into the office. It wasn't difficult to push past the sign-toters. They were dirty, and usually smelled of hemp, but none of them were a physical match for Poika, or any of the other recruiting non-coms.

The day did come when a number of demonstrators tried to overwhelm the recruiting non-com by force of numbers. Their orders were clear: No fights or injuries. Call the police. That's what they did.

The Pittsburgh P.D. arrived in very short order and did everything the recruiters would have done. A few heads were busted, a few noses punched. The police hauled off the ring-leaders. Apparently, they had been surveilling the area in front of the recruiting office and knew who to focus on.

All this was just the day-to-day backdrop for Poika. He decided that he would continue his education. He enrolled in night courses at Duquesne University. After long sessions, talking with the school guidance counselor, Poika set his sights on pre-law, as a way of best preparing himself for the future.

All of the pre-law courses corresponded to his interests. He liked the way the police handled the situation at the recruiting office. He thought it could be a good direction for him to go in, after leaving the Army.

Being student gave Poika access to the recreational and gym facilities. He made use of the gym to keep himself in peak physical shape. The only Army facilities were more than an hour away.

The student scene also let Poika in on where the best places to get a drink were. In a very short period of time, he knew which places were friendliest to anyone with a crew cut, whether they were in a uniform, or not. He suspected that the places where the politically active students, and dopers went, were all under surveillance by the police. He didn't need any of the kind of trouble he would find in places like those.

There were plenty of friendly pretty young girls at, and around the university. Poika thought too many of them were blonde. They all couldn't have naturally colored hair. Making a few acquaintances usually revealed his general lack of socializing in his younger days. He clumsily made his way through one introductory conversation after another.

Poika was so inept at maintaining a conversation with women that he tended to just sit in the back of wherever he was drinking and watch the other customers. Aside from the idlest chit-chat with the barkeeps, he spoke to no one.

Situations like this are bound to change, for the worse, or for the better. Poika had developed the habit of stopping by one particular bar, after working hours. Sometimes this was five o'clock, sometimes it was seven. The later nights were determined by periodic "command sessions," needless instructional meetings with the officers in the recruiting staff.

The bar he settled on was called "Crazy's." After asking the bartender, Poika found out it was supposed to be "Crazies," like a bad trip on LSD, but the sign company got the order wrong and the name was changed to avoid extra expense.

This particular night, Poika arrived at seven-thirty. There was a group of students in the front of the bar, eight, or so of them, at a pair of tables they had pushed together. He walked passed them, and took up his usual perch, at the back of the bar. One petite brunette in the group briefly made eye contact with him. An even briefer smile crossed her lips.

After a couple of rounds of drinks, Poika sat, nursing his blended scotch. He left his drink for a bathroom break. When he returned, he found the petite brunette sitting on the stool next to his. He sat down, and returned to his drink, attention focused on it alone.

"So, you gonna talk to me, or what?" The brunette's eyes were a warm, inviting shade of brown. She calmly waited for a response.

"I wouldn't know what to say. You came in here with someone else, I'm sure." Poika used his chin to indicate the group at the front of the bar. He wasn't trying to be rude, he was just surprised that a young woman would seek him out for conversation.

"They're just people from school. I see them all the time." She kept her eyes on Poika's. Her gaze started to affect him, made him relax a little.

Poika was surprised to feel himself reacting in this way. He concentrated on not showing his inner turmoil. He was as unsure of himself as he had ever been. He held his polite smile and waited for the young girl to say something else.

"My name's Jennine." She continued to speak, but Poika had momentarily tuned her out. Some tiny little part of his mind was reacting to her name. Disappointment: That was the tiny little reaction.

Poika quickly caught himself and re-aimed his attention on the girl in front of him. He introduced himself and struggled to keep up a conversation. He worked hard to avoid all the pointless, conversation-ending mistakes of his past. He hoped that somehow, his pause before answering the girl's comments would be taken for thoughtfulness.

Mercifully, the conversation was cut short by the departure of the group. Jennine excused herself, promising to see Poika again, if nowhere else, then here, in the bar.

Poika sat until closing, nursing the same scotch. He wondered about his momentary disappointment at the sound of Jennine's name. Leaving the bar and heading for his small, shared apartment, he was unaware that his mind had wanted the petite brunette to be named Katie. The hate in Poika's mind hid its desire. Poika would only learn by doing, but not now.

***

The business of recruiting and a pair of school semesters went on. Poika observed that the anti-military demonstrators braved the typically poor weather conditions of Pittsburgh for most of the year. They were not, however, up to toughing it out through the winter. The first snows brought an end to the sandal-clad hair bags who harassed them almost constantly.

The winter season – really late fall, and early winter – let Poika concentrate on improving his grades. Fewer potential recruits came in, so time to study was more readily available. Poika had nowhere to go for the holidays and volunteered to cover the office during that time. Most of his days were spent reading and studying.

Evenings in Crazy's were quieter too. Fewer students on campus meant fewer bar patrons. Poika spent most of his evenings here or in the library. Sometimes it was a combination of both.

To his surprise, the girl Jennine stopped by once or twice, and spent time talking with Poika. He figured that she had become aware of his clumsy discomfiture and was somehow charmed by it. He had no more of the feeling of disappointment he experienced before.

Jennine was a local. She grew up in Pittsburgh and was one of a few graduates of local public high schools accepted by Duquesne. She was studying public policy, with a desire to get a political science degree. All this was just so much noise to Poika, who really had no expectations of any sort of a relationship with Jennine.

For her part, Jennine was honestly attracted to Poika. She thought his reticence was a boyish quality, appealing because it was quaint. It was a surprise and a shock to find out that he was a soldier. Unlike many of her friends, she didn't harbor the intense dislike of the military. She barely understood why they did. It all seemed like just a popular idea, gotten out of hand.

Poika's pre-law studies meshed with Jennine's political studies. At least she thought they did. She found the two most prominent features of his personality were honesty and thoughtfulness.

When Jennine found out that Poika was staying in town for the holidays, she invited him to her family's house for Christmas dinner. Poika declined, begging off, because it would be too much trouble to add another person to such a meal. He still thought in terms of how the poor dealt with things. He knew nothing of middle class life, other than it was different from what he grew up with.

Unable to coax Poika to her family's Christmas celebration, Jennine made a date to meet Poika for dinner, on the twenty-sixth. Her family had made a game of celebrating the Canadian holiday of boxing day, every year. That meant that some celebration would still be in order.

Poika agreed, feeling like he was going to do something new and unique. It was, at least to him. The pain and torture of the past wanted to fade away, but he would not let go of it. He clung to it, the way non-swimmer holds onto a life ring, in a stormy sea. His emotions were in a complete stew. Despite all of this he would still meet Jennine on campus. They would decide where to eat then, making it more of an impromptu event.

***

The twenty-sixth rolled around. The day before was just a bust. Poika spent two dollars, calling long distance trying to call his mother. Someone he didn't know picked up the phone and said they never heard of her. They said that they had the number for two years already.

Silent Sight

Today was a regular work day. No one was thinking much about coming to the recruitment center, save for the bums who occasionally tried to come in, out of the cold. They were alone, just like Poika, but he had no pity for them. He turned them away, sending them to the mission, across the river.

At the end of the day, Poika turned out the lights, went to the back of the office and changed into his civvies. Changing in the back, at the end of a shift, was routine for everyone. It meant having to deal with fewer troublemakers on their way out of the recruitment office. Today, it meant a shorter walk to the campus to meet with Jennine.

It was cold and the snow flurries were alternately intensifying and trailing off. The sidewalks were icy, everywhere around. Poika thought about going inside to wait, but it was a special occasion. His spirits were high. He felt much less of the cold than he otherwise would have.

As the last wan bit of daylight faded from a sky that had been pewter all day long, Jennine appeared. The image of her actually faded into view, then out again as the snow flew around her. She was wearing tight trousers and boots with heels. Her waist-length coat had a fur-trimmed hood. Her face, smiling was last to appear through the snow, slightly hidden by her hood.

Approaching Poika, she put her arms around him and hugged him. "Merry Christmas!"

It was so much more than Poika had anticipated. He struggled to reply. "Merry… Merry Christmas." Hugging Jennine back, Poika realized that he had not said those words to anyone. Not this year or last. Or the year before.

90

He wondered, briefly, at how strange it was that his life had become.

Momentarily lost in the reverie, Poika missed seeing Jennine looking over his shoulder, behind him. As he recovered his presence of mind, Jennine's face brightened, a broad smile on it.

Jennine lifted her hand and waved. "Terry!" Jennine took Poika by the arm and steered him toward the newcomer. When the three of them came together, Jennine let go of Poika's arm, stretched high on tip-toes and greeted the other young man with a kiss, on the cheek.

Turning to where Poika had stood, Jennine began, "This is Terry…"

Poika was already walking away. His hands were stuffed tightly, down in the pockets of his jacket. The trail of his footprints followed him across the entrance esplanade of the university.

Jennine raced after him. Her boots were designed for looks more than performance. She slid and skittered as she struggled to catch up with Poika, who was making a good pace across the slippery concrete.

Finally catching up, Jennine grabbed Poika's elbow and pulled to turn him back toward her. Her efforts only led to pulling herself around in front of him.

"I'm sorry. I thought you knew, that you understood. Terry and I are going to be engaged this year." She walked along with Poika, working hard to keep up, without falling on the slick sidewalk.

Poika never answered. It was just like Terre Haute. There weren't so many faces. No one was laughing at him. He felt exactly the same, as though he had been reamed out. The emptiness inside of him grew and colored everything a deep, dark black. The streetlights around him went dim. He could barely make out the edges of the sidewalk, to keep from stumbling into the street.

Poika never acknowledged Jennine, or anything she tried to say. He continued walking. Somewhere early on, Jennine quit trying to talk to him, and gave up. He walked on. The hours rolled past.

In Poika's mind the hate took more control than ever before. If the hate had gotten him this far, it could do better. He could do better. The hate could do so much more. It would be better. The hate would make it be better. Better.

***

Crazy's saw no more of the young regular who always took the back-end seat at the bar. Poika replaced his evenings in the tavern with long walks. He now had a lot to think about. He had a lot of feelings to try and sort through.

Poika moved about downtown and central Pittsburgh freely. The long walks took the place of long evenings spent drinking quite well. After just a day or two of the change, he felt like a burden was being lifted from his shoulders. Less alcohol in his diet meant better general health all around. He really got into the walking, ranging farther across town. Week by week, more neighborhoods saw the man who walked alone.

Poika was obviously well-built and walked with the authority of youth and strength. No one accosted him for any reason. The downtown police knew who he was, from numerous interactions at the recruiting office. They quickly passed the word to the other precincts about a "friendly" taking long walks in the evenings.

The combination of his familiarity and his determination to keep to himself created a unique situation. After only a short number of weeks, Poika became functionally invisible. Just another part of what passed as the daily parade of normalcy, no one noticed him at all.

THIRTEEN

Sleep largely evaded Cary Lang's best efforts on the night that his special ability revealed an apparent murder to him. The next day at work was a trial. He fought against the predations of sleeplessness all day long. His lunch tasted like dirt and sand. That was how bad he felt, emotionally and physically. The knowledge that one fed off the other didn't help one bit.

At the end of the day, Cary faced the prospect of going home to his apartment and feeling compelled to spy on his neighbor. As a brief, temporary dodge, he walked to the downtown bus station, on Broadway. The two-block walk added four blocks to the walk to his parking space, since it was in the wrong direction. The detour was part of his intentional avoidance behavior.

The newsstand there was one of two large newspaper outlets in town. Dozens of out-of-town newspapers, and hundreds of different magazines were on the racks. In the past, Cary had sometimes made special trips downtown, driving there to find newspapers from different cities. He would read them, page by page, through to the end. It was his way of mentally "travelling" to a different town.

Cary bought both of the local papers. Tucking them under his arm, he headed for his car. He knew Wheels was waiting for him, literally "holding his water." Twenty-five minutes later, Cary was home. The afternoon and early evening routine with his golden retriever began. Wheels got an extra-long workout. Didn't mind it a bit.

At home, Cary fed his friend and himself. Afterwards, he settled in with the newspapers. Determined to read every syllable in the local news sections, he was disappointed to find no mention of what he had seen the night before. He had to stop and think about it for a while.

Cary figured that without someone reporting an unusual event, no investigation would begin. Whoever the woman was, someone would have to notice her absence, or find her body.

That night, Cary spent a long time viewing the area behind his apartment. He only saw one thing that meant anything: The man in the apartment on the next street came home late. Either drunk or tired, he went to bed immediately.

Cary took the cue and went to bed. After the bad night before, his fatigue drove him into a deep, dream-filled sleep.

***

The next days were a form of torture for Cary Lang. He stopped by the local Rapid-Mart in his neighborhood, every day, to buy newspapers. Each day, disappointment crept in as he read through the local reporting, finding no mention of the crime he had witnessed.

Six days after the apparent killing, a small article appeared in the Globe-Democrat about a missing young woman. The article gave her name: Sharon Manning. The story talked about the woman not showing up for work and being unreachable at her home. There was no mention of any other person in the story. The article didn't give an address for the woman. It did mention that the woman was from Southampton, Cary's neighborhood. Bingo!

The appearance of the news article gave Cary a strange feeling of relief. Suddenly, he was no longer the only one who knew that something was wrong. The next day, he took a chance on driving past the apartment building he had viewed during the murder. It was another four-family flat, on the next street over. As he had suspected, the building number was the same as his own.

The article was short. There was a distinct lack of details. The feeling of disappointment began to creep back into his mind. The article said an investigation into the disappearance of the woman was started and gave a detective's name. The name meant nothing to Cary. He made a note of it, anyway.

After that one newspaper article, there was no more reporting on the story. After another week of buying newspapers that revealed nothing, Cary decided that reading the news at the branch library would be cheaper.

He could even get a number of recent issues at once. That meant he didn't have to make a daily trip to get a chance catch the story he was looking for.

One such trip to the library put Cary in front of a small placard sign promoting a film showing at the library branch. The film was a color, foreign language, art film. The date and time for the showing were on the coming weekend, so he decided to see the movie. He finished his news search and headed home.

Movie day came, and Cary drove over to the branch library an hour ahead of the start time. He completed his search of the news, pocketing his disappointment. He took a seat in the small side-room of the library. Only five other people were present. Cary thought that it surely must be this way for a lot of the film showings in the libraries around town.

The movie started. It was in French. The were no subtitles. It was a story of a couple's trip to the beach, an argument, and a return to their apartment. The locations were all unknown to Cary, who just kind of went with the flow. He knew a smattering of French, mostly from dating girls who took French in school. He could pick out a word, here and there, but the real content of the dialogue was lost to him.

At two or three points in the film, the other people watching laughed and giggled at something one of the characters said. By the third time this happened, Cary was thinking of simply leaving. The movie experience was turning out to be much less interesting than he anticipated.

He decided to stick it out. As the couple on the screen began to work out their differences – no doubt heading for a happy ending – Cary saw something in the film that caught his mind's eye. The man in the movie knelt next to a low cabinet, built into a wall. He worked at opening the locked cabinet for a minute, then withdrew a dusty bottle of wine, to share with the woman in the film.

As the movie wound down to its end, Cary wondered about the scene that made him react differently than the rest of the film. Lost in his thoughts, Cary was actually surprised when the "Fin" came up at the end. The room lights were turned on, the people began to file out of the small room.

Cary sat and thought for a moment longer. He rose from his seat and approached the projectionist. The young man was surprised to be approached by anyone and stopped preparing to rewind the film.

Cary asked, "Can I ask a favor? Can you run the film back for a minute or so? I saw something that I need to see again."

The young man's job as projectionist was one of the more interesting ones in the library. Still, it had its mundane repetitive quality too. He was happy to accommodate the unusual request. Once his film wrangling job was done, he would be replacing returned books, in the stacks.

"Sure!" The young man rethreaded the film and began to play the film in reverse, at a high speed. He quickly got to the scene that Cary was interested in.

"There! Play that again." The projectionist did as Cary requested. Cary watched. He did not understand why he felt so different during this particular sequence in the film. He asked the young man to run the film back again.

The film began going backward. This time, the reversal was at the normal frame rate for the movie. Cary watched in rapt attention. He knew why the scene was so important. It tripped his memory of the night of the murder. The scene showed the man in the film, kneeling, working to remove a concealed object from a low wall cabinet. Played in reverse, it put him through the same set of motions Cary had seen the man – the murderer – go through, after striking the woman.

The young projectionist stared at Cary, lost in thought, as the movie once again came to its conclusion. "Mister, you okay?"

Cary shook his head. The sudden return to reality was a surprise. "Thanks. I'm okay."

Cary turned and left the confused movie projectionist staring in wonder at the strange request. Cary left the library and went out to his car. There, he thought about interpreting the scene in the reversed movie. He mentally played it over and over in his head.

Ten minutes of this thinking left Cary wondering if he was inventing answers to questions that nobody was asking. Then, as he began to exit the library parking lot, it came to him: The man put something into the wall of the apartment.

Cary pounded the steering wheel of the Vee-dub. "Yes!"

"HONK!" There was a car behind him, also trying to exit the lot. The horn honk startled Cary. He put the

Volkswagen in gear and started the drive home. He knew he had figured out something important. What could he do about it? How could he tell what he knew? Who would even listen to him? Questions piled up on questions – so many questions.

FOURTEEN

The questions in Cary's mind wouldn't stop. All afternoon and evening, he tried to get to a point in his mind where there were clear answers. There was no such point. There were no clear answers. Until he decided to report the crime, as he understood it, to the police, his mind roiled and threw about.

Having made that determination, Cary discovered only more questions waited. It was as though the facts of the complex problem that he faced conspired against him. They took on a life of their own.

Cary decided that he needed a plan. He wrote done the key points of what he wanted to report. Then he worked out several important details to include in his report. Lastly, he figured out where and how he would make his story heard.

With all of that at least partly settled in his mind, it was only the excitement of anticipation that fought him for sleep that night. Tomorrow, he would call the police.

***

The next morning, Cary carefully assembled his notes. He put them in the pocket of his jacket and headed off to work. Things there were in a between-season lull. At lunch, he boiled all of his notes down, onto a single note card. He was able to leave a little early. He put his plan to report the crime into action.

After work, the two-block walk, over to the bus station, took only a few minutes. Cary went into the main hall of the station. The white tile on all the surfaces was a uniform grey color. The soot and dirt of a transit station was everywhere you looked. Cary wondered what particular genius was involved in choosing white as the color for a building that hundreds of thousands of people passed through every year.

On top of the dirt and grime, trash just kind of drifted around the interior of the station. There were always at least two doors open in the huge transportation hub. The wind found its way in and made fun with the discarded wrappers and printed matter. If you stopped in one place long enough, you became an obstacle and capture-point for the trash. Several people lolled or slept on seats in the huge hall, with trash gathered around their feet and ankles.

Cary navigated his way through the crowd, everyone walking this way and that. The sounds of the crowd were augmented by the bells and noises emanating from a room full of pinball machines, just off the main hall. He stopped at the row of pay telephones along one wall. Thirty telephones, all in one line. He chose a phone far from where any other caller stood.

The shallow baffles between the individual telephones provided some privacy, but not much. He had worked out in advance that if anyone else came to an adjacent phone while he was calling, he would hang up, and try another time.

Cary tried to glance around surreptitiously. He wanted to look around without being obvious about it. No one was near. He dialed the phone. After a couple of rings, the phone was answered, "Metropolitan Police."

Speaking in a raspy falsetto, Cary asked for the detective named in the original news article. "Detective Beckestone, please."

"What's it about ma'am?"

Cary was pleased that his vocal trick was working, at least so far. "I have some information about a case he's working on, the Sharon Manning case."

"Just a minute, please." The phone line went silent, after a click.

Cary pulled his note card from his pocket. He stole another quick look, left and right. Another click on the phone, and Cary heard, "Detective Beckestone. You have information about the Sharon Manning case?"

Cary concentrated on maintaining his high-pitched, raspy voice. He looked at his note card. He was determined to say only what was there. He would not converse with the police detective at all.

"Sharon Manning was murdered. By a man. In her apartment. He dragged her body to his car after hitting her with something heavy."

The detective's voice was tense. He rapid-fired his questions. "How do you know all this? Are you a witness? How do I know this information is reliable?"

Cary was rattled by the harsh, accusatory tone in the detective's voice. He broke with what he planned to say. He gave the date and time of the killing.

The rapid-fire questions continued. "Who are you? What is your name? How do you expect me to believe all this?"

Cary swallowed hard. The effort of maintaining his falsetto was beginning to hurt. He licked his lips, and took a slow deep breath, trying to remain calm. He got back to his planned speech.

"The man who killed Sharon Manning hid something in a wall of her apartment, after he killed her." Cary hung up the telephone.

He turned and slid his note card back into his jacket pocket. He glanced around one last time, to try and determine if he had drawn any attention to himself. No one appeared to be paying any attention to him at all.

Inside his jacket, his shirt was soaked with perspiration. He wiped some sweat from his face. The air moving through the bus terminal chilled the exposed parts of his neck. He made a shivering exit from the bus station.

***

At the Central Division Detective Bureau, Detective Second Grade, Benjamin, 'Benji' Beckestone hung up the phone. He turned to the secretary two desks down. "I'm gonna need to hear the recording of that last call. Rita, can you get it for me?"

"Yes, detective." Rita, rose from her desk and walked toward the recording closet, a separate room where the call recordings were made. *Of course, you need the recording, you never take a damn note.* The secretary's resentment was born of having to do more for the ever-needy Detective Beckestone than for any of the other officers.

Not taking notes was only one of the reasons Benji Beckestone was stuck at Detective Second Grade. He had the lowest "turnover rate" in the Bureau. He had been passed over twice for promotion. It wasn't that he didn't care enough, he just wasn't the smartest detective in the bureau.

The department regulations stated that being passed over for a third time would result in permanent rank. That brought with it all sorts of problems: parking meter and evidence locker problems. A person assigned a permanent rank could even end up as Cadet Advocate: nose wiper at the Academy. The command – management – staff of the functional units of the police department were always in need of career-path screw-ups to fill positions.

Detective Beckestone was single. In his mid-thirties, he had his own apartment. The promotion to detective had higher pay. He moved out of a flat, in the Soulard neighborhood he grew up in. He wasn't the best housekeeper. Doing laundry regularly was housekeeping so, there you go: he was a regular slob.

By way of contributing to his own problems Benji Beckestone drank too much, not always, but often enough for people to notice. Like every other detective on the force, he was looking to advance his career, but his lieutenant was as familiar with his drinking as he was with his performance.

Benji Beckestone had hit a wall in the labyrinthine path of his life. The most important part of him, the part that made life a success or a failure, didn't know it yet.

Rita, the secretary, returned in a few minutes with the portable tape recorder. She had gone to the recording closet, where the ceiling-high machines, with their twelve-inch tape reels, recorded every telephone call. The process involved plugging a patch-cord into the main machine and the portable. An ear piece let her listen to the operation. She would rewind the tape, listen for the right phone call, and transcribe the call by recording it on the portable.

She still had the earphone in her ear. "Here you go, Benj..., Detective." The nearly open show of disrespect wasn't unintentional. Rita was a civil service worker. Her job would be the same until hell froze over. She knew enough to do her job and not screw it up. Being able to be contemptuous of little shits like Beckestone was a job benefit.

"Thanks, Rita." Beckestone played it straight. The other detectives could get away with carrying on with the clerical staff, he couldn't. He knew he was thought of as the bottom of the list. He took the portable recorder from the secretary and reached in his desk drawer for his own earphone. Rita pulled her earphone from her ear. She snapped the ever-present piece of gum in her mouth as a last comment on having to help him, yet again.

Listening to the tape, Beckestone's first notation was 'woman?' he thought he heard some noise in the background of the recording but couldn't make it out. 'Noisy' was the second note. The rest of the notes reflected the content of the report given.

He thought it was an awful lot of information, broken down into the barest essentials. It was like the person who called in saw the whole thing but didn't want to have anything to do with the police. That part was not all that unusual. It just made sorting it all out that much more difficult. People didn't have a clue what was involved in trying to get solid proof of a crime. Some small part of his mind laughed at the pun he had just made: didn't have a clue.

Detective Beckestone listened to the recorded call over and over. He spent so much time with it that he finally attracted the attention of his boss, Lieutenant Dukasko. Realizing that he had done so, Beckestone put the tape in his desk and returned the portable to the locker. It was all too late. The Lieutenant was already out of his glass-walled office, headed his way.

***

Cary kept up with the newspapers for several days before a single word about the Sharon Manning case reappeared in the news. He was surprised by how upset he still was, even after making the nerve-wracking telephone call from the bus station. If anything, that had intensified his sense of being under pressure to do something. Being witness to such a crime was a burden. It was worse when you understood that no one was going to believe how you witnessed the crime.

The day after Cary called Detective Beckestone, the police were at the apartment building behind Cary's. The street was full of police cars. There was even a van marked Evidence Unit. So much commotion in a normally quiet neighborhood like Cary's automatically got a lot of gossip started. Cary heard all about it from Mrs. Roberts, who apparently had a great need to share everything she saw and heard.

Three days after the call to the police, a front-page story in the Globe-Democrat reported the arrest of a suspect in the disappearance of Sharon Manning. The next day, the story headlined the Newspaper: Murder in Southampton. There was even a sidebar story about locating the victim's body after interrogating the suspect that had been arrested.

The main story told of the police following a tip that led to the discovery of the murder weapon, a candlestick. It had been concealed in a recently-renovated room of her apartment. The work was done by a sometimes-boyfriend of the victim. Sharon Manning had hired, and even paid her own murderer. Confronting the suspect with the murder weapon led to a confession which included the location of the body.

The newspaper articles credited the work of Detective Benjamin Beckestone in solving the crime. His photograph, in the victim's apartment, in front of a hole in one of the walls, accompanied the front-page story. An interview pull-quote was inserted under the photograph, as a caption: "We searched the apartment for evidence. We found one candlestick on the fireplace mantel. Nobody has just one candlestick."

The quote was obviously Detective Beckestone's attempt at demonstrating how deductive reasoning was used to infer the existence of the other candlestick.

Impressive detective work, Cary thought to himself.

***

Cary read and re-read every word of the stories in the newspaper. He was glad that his report had turned the tide in the investigation. He still felt the sense of pressure. He still feared that he would be found out and made to explain how he had seen the crime. The outcome of that scenario was frighteningly unpredictable.

***

Detective Lieutenant, John Dukasko thought to himself, *Everybody has a high point in their life.* He threw the newspaper on his desk. Damn, Beckestone actually turned a case around!

FIFTEEN

Poika walked by himself. He was never alone. The long walks helped him balance the rage in his heart with the deep, seething, black hate in his mind. The incident with Jennine was now two and a half years behind him. He would be finished with school in a month. He was studying for the L-SATs. Who knew where all that could lead.

Walking all around Pittsburgh burned off the excess energy brought about by the inner turmoil that threatened to overcome him. Rage leapt to the forefront of his mind when the utterly lame episode with Jennine transpired. He mentally flagellated himself for weeks after it happened. He would have been lost, if not for the hate. The hate within him calmed the rest of his mind. The importance of keeping focused on his work was now greater than ever.

The meat grinder of Vietnam was in full swing, now. The Army had new call-up quotas to meet. Poika wondered how many of the kids he had signed up were still alive, or still whole. The high number of volunteers coming out of America's "Steel Belt" were gratefully acknowledged by the Army as an excellent supplement for draft inductions. The Army had rewarded his exceptional performance in recruiting a large number of soldiers. The Army knew they had a winning set-up, with the crew they had in Pittsburgh. They weren't going to mess it up. Poika's assignment here would last until his enlistment was up, at the end of summer.

The beneficial effects of the long evening walks weren't all that was going on. Little by little, the hate within Poika let slip a tiny bit of its strategy. It was hunting. At first, Poika didn't know what he was hunting for. He began to look at other people he saw on his walks with a different set of assessments: Threat, no threat; watcher, non-watcher.

His mind sometimes wandered as he walked around the city. He imagined himself as many different things. None would be even slightly connected with his past, his childhood. It was time for Poika, and all of his suffering to be dead and gone.

He needed to conjure up an identity that he felt more at home with. He thought of names for himself that reflected his new determination. Hunter. Stalker. Neither quite fit. Walker. That was simple and plain. He would think of himself as Walker, as he pursued his prey, from now on.

The path that he often took settled into a fairly routine tour of the university campus, and the nearby drinking establishments. Occasionally he included a bridge-crossing, just so he wouldn't be going past the same places too frequently. Varying his routine, by small increment, let him see different sets of people on any given day.

After two and a half years of walking, with some part of that consciously hunting, Walker spotted his target. The petite brunette walked out of a bar and headed for one of the residence buildings. Lagging behind, about a half block, he followed. It was late, on a Thursday. He made careful note of the time and day of the week.

After that. the evening walks centered on the route between the bar and the residence hall. He crossed the path several times in an evening, watching for the girl he had seen. About every other day, he spotted her. She was regularly meeting friends at the bar. It would require selection of the right time to make any sort of move.

For nearly two weeks he patiently scouted the area. Three likely "take" points presented themselves. If the conditions were right, he could capture her and proceed undetected. He strenuously avoided thinking in terms of "snatching" his target. The language was too imprecise, for what he wanted to do.

A beautiful Spring Friday evening came. Walker headed out. He was on his now-routine path. He guessed that the end-of-week celebration would last a little later than other nights. Friday was the best day to take a victim. The weekend, and its wide variety of available activities, provided cover for any absence. He went to his best "take" location and waited. He had parked his car near the location, in front of a dry cleaners, earlier in the day.

The doorway in which he concealed himself was deep. No street lights shone into it. He could wait in the shadows, unseen, until daybreak, if needed. The area immediately in front of the doorway was outside the reach of the streetlights as well. The dark location was one very important consideration. The total absence of anyone else was the other. It was a timing and happenstance thing that he could not influence. Conditions were going to be right, or they weren't.

He waited. The young petite brunette would head back to her dorm in some state of inebriation. That would only help. The time seemed to creep by, slowing with every tick of his wristwatch. He went through several mental routines to pass the time and calm himself.

Then, at 10:30, her saw her. Edging toward the front of the doorway, he scoured the street on both sides for sign of anyone else. Negative. The girl entered the block, on his side of the street. He looked at every window to see if anyone was there. Clear.

After what seemed like an eternity, the girl passed in front of his hiding place. He silently emerged from the doorway behind her. The memory of sneaking up on Lon Spahl from behind briefly flashed through his mind. He closed the gap between himself and his target.

With the speed of a leopard, he pounced. He quickly put his right hand over her mouth. His left forearm slithered around her neck, like a python. Just the right amount of pressure on the large arteries in her neck for three and a half seconds caused her to crumple in his grip, like a rag doll. He swept up her limp form in his arms and carried her the few steps to his car.

The girl was light enough to hold with one arm as he unlocked the trunk. Her shoulders dangled over his arm, her feet rested on the pavement. Moments later, the girl was in the trunk, her mouth taped, her hands and feet bound. The whole kidnapping had taken less than a minute and a half.

Walker got into the car and drove. The exhilaration and excitement rose within him. He fought to calm himself back down. The hate taught Poika that driving around too long with a body in the car meant an increasing likelihood of discovery. Stupid accidents happened. Unforeseen eventualities arose. Taking more time meant more could go wrong. Take the girl. Immobilize her. Take her to a safe location. Finish the kill. Leave no race.

Weeks ago, he had scouted several likely vacant lots to finish an attack. The hate in him wouldn't let any mistakes be made. Drive carefully, one or two miles per hour over the speed limit, never more than four. Drive like there's nothing wrong, relax. Don't attract attention. Breathe.

It didn't matter if anyone ever found the body. The object was to finish the kill. The kill was the sole reason for the planning, the scouting, the patient waiting. Being able to do it again, afterwards, was at least only secondary to the kill itself.

***

The vacant lot was at an unused trucking depot. The gate to the lot had only a broken chain on it. A large, empty building sat in the middle of the lot. Gravel, worn down to the bare earth in most places, extended on all four sides. No one had been to the property in years. Six miles outside of Pittsburgh, no lights shone anywhere. Perfect.

Poika parked his car at the back of the depot building and opened the trunk. He expected to see the terror-filled eyes of his victim, but she was still unconscious. As she lay there on the floor of the trunk, he reached down and shook her. The young girl's eyes fluttered open.

The dark, the realization the she was bound and gagged, and the specter of her assailant's face all greeted her at the same time. The expected look of terror in her eyes appeared immediately. Behind the tape on her mouth, she screamed. The noise streaming from her nose was pitiful.

Rivers of tears flowed from her eyes, now pleading. Poika pulled her from the trunk. Careful not to let her hit her head, he held her with one hand, unsteadily on her feet, for just a moment, looking at her. With regard to meeting the standards he had subconsciously set for a target, she was perfect: Five-foot-some-inches tall, slender, brunette. The faint echo of a thought, Just like Katie Spahl, flashed and faded in his mind.

Through the tape, "No! No! No! (Something else) No! No!"

He withdrew a knitted scarf from his pocket. He spun her around, facing away from him. He wound the scarf around her neck and paused.

"No! No!" He wound the scarf in his fist, tightly.

"No! No! N…" He twisted the scarf.

The girl thrashed wildly in his grip. She yanked herself left, then right, trying to get away from the iron-like grip, the scarf crushing her throat. She dug her heels, bound as they were, into the gravel and dirt, pushing with every ounce of her strength. Tears and mucus flowed full force from her nose. She struggled vainly to inhale, exhale.

Thirty seconds later, it was over. The limp body of the former college co-ed hung in Walker's hands. He dragged her to the edge of the forest that surrounded the truck depot lot. There, he untied her and removed the gag. He collected up the bindings, and the scarf. One last check for a pulse, one last look into her dead, dead eyes, and he left her there.

His intense concentration on making sure he did the job correctly finally diminished. Walker experienced the best feeling of his life. Hate had won. An enemy, of life-long extreme, had been vanquished. The feeling was like breathless happiness and drunk, without the dizziness, whirlies and nausea, all at once. He felt as though he could lift his arms and fly.

As he drove back to Pittsburgh, he held on to the feeling as long as he could. By the time he arrived at his apartment, the feeling was gone. Walking up the steps of the apartment building, a tiny hope rested in his mind that perhaps, someday, he would feel it again.

That night, Walker slept the sleep of the dead. No dreams came his way. None needed to. He had lived out his dark dream. It was a dream that he had not even fully admitted to himself.

Now, as he slept, the entirety of his mind and soul were united. There was a kind of peace, dark and deadly.

The internal struggle was over. Where there were two minds, operating on different levels, there was now one. His transformation was complete. The hate had become him. He had become the hate. Hate needed no dreams.

SIXTEEN

A week after the stories were splashed across the front page of the newspaper, Cary was starting to feel much less of the sensation of pressure. The intensity of his feelings went far beyond anything he experienced in his normal, everyday life. As a way of deliberately calming himself, he had avoided any aural viewing while at home. He worked diligently at keeping his mind focused on what was before him, in the visible world.

Long thought about how he was involved in the whole crime solving episode lead him to a realization: He was a victim of the crime too. Since he felt that the couldn't report the crime directly, he kept it to himself for several days. The toll of his silence was the pressure that he felt. It ruined everything. He had begun to neglect the daily activities that kept him going. Play time with Wheels was foreshortened. He skipped more and more meals. It wasn't until he was past the whole thing that his life began to return to normal.

Cary knew that not using his new talent at all would lead to its own problems. His new ability was there. He was becoming more accustomed to it all the time. There was even the progression in sensitivity he had experienced by becoming aware of the different colors dominating the auras that he saw. If he tried to ignore the new sense, it would just interrupt his life in some other, unpredictable way.

He spent part of each day away from home, finding quiet places to exercise his ability. The more he thought about making an effort to approach the thing in an organized way, the better he felt about doing it. His "return to normal" was less of a return and more of an adjustment to a completely new "normal."

With less pressure on him, Cary became more like his old self. He began to eat a little more and regained a pound or two. He was more inclined to stay later in the park and play with Wheels. His work was more like it was before witnessing the crime. There was more flow to it all. He had much more emotional energy to put into it.

One of the places Cary chose for his purposeful aura viewing was the park near the downtown store where he worked. After work, there were usually a number of children, supervised by one or more adults, playing on the playground. He would watch each day, for short periods of time. His main goal was to not appear to be doing what he was doing. Mostly, he sat with part of the newspaper in front of him as he scanned the people, eyes closed, behind his Ray-Bans.

The kids were easy to figure out. There was a lot of happy green to be seen, blue creeping in, here and there. The parents, or whoever they were, displayed much of the same. The park atmosphere was not conducive to a wide range of emotional reaction.

An interesting difference in some of the children arose. Along with all of the other emotional displays of aural intensity, some of the children showed a secondary color, while playing with the other children. Along with their green, or blue, or whatever color, dominating their aura, a separate color, a deep indigo blue made it self evident. The only difference in behavior that Cary could discern was that these children were the ones being leaders. They were either leading a group activity or telling the other children what to do. The ones choosing teams for group games always had an indigo blue aura displayed along with the display of their emotional aura.

This discernment of a second color in the children started Cary concentrating more intently on the adults he was viewing. After a day or two of looking for it, he saw multiple colors displayed in the aura of a woman, seated on a park bench, speaking in an animated manner to her bench partner. Cary strove to perceive the nuances of all the colors shone. He periodically checked himself. He tried to make sure that he was not obviously staring at someone.

Cary began to understand that while one emotion might dominate a person's mental state, everyone walked around with a set of emotional responses to their environment. Without realizing it, he had discounted a quality of human psychology that most people would consider grade-school learning. He realized that it was a result of his fascination and surprise at almost everything he viewed with his new sense.

***

Cary decided to invest in an even more organized approach to his new ability. The afternoons in the park worked out so well, that he wanted to be able to do a lot more investigation of his "silent sight." He had seen red-tipped, white canes for sale at the drug store. He spent the three dollars, telling the clerk that it was for a relative. For whatever reason, the clerk felt it necessary to remind Cary that not only was it immoral to pretend to be sightless, in many jurisdictions, it was illegal. Cary thanked the clerk for the elucidation. He carried the cane from the store like a fishing rod, tip held high, trying not to snag it on anything as he left.

The next day, Cary put the cane in his car and drove to a location near a bus route that he knew. He waited for the bus, dark glasses on. He had the correct change in one pocket, so he wouldn't have fumble for it.

The bus came and Cary went through his act, using the bus stop sign as an anchor, tapping along the sidewalk until his cane crossed the gap and struck the lip of the bus step. He mounted the bus steps carefully, but deliberately. He fumbled his hand across the top of the coin sorting machine and dropped in his fair.

"What stop?" The bus driver surprised Cary, asking which stop he would get off at. Pausing before answering, Cary had to realized that, of course, a blind person needs to hear the stop called out, so that they get off in the right place.

"Broadway." Cary had chosen to ride on the Arsenal Street route. It crossed the entire city from its western boundary to a point near the brewery, not far from the Mississippi River. He wanted to be able ride for a long time and engage in aural viewing.

Again, Cary had chosen a venue for his committed activity that revealed little in the way of intense emotions. The bus driver was the one on the bus who went through the greatest range of emotional response. As stoically as he might sit in the driver seat, the challenges and frustrations of driving in city traffic showed themselves. For the most part, there wasn't much to see among the passengers.

After taking two other busses back to where his car was parked, Cary decided that he was comfortable with his disguise. He refined his act of being blind, smoothly halting in all the places he had seen sightless people do. He substituted the touch of his hand for all the close-up things that the blind normally felt their way around. This part of the day's trial was okay. He needed to find better places to view auras of people displaying complex and intense emotional responses.

Two places that would meet his needs came to mind: Movie theaters and courtrooms. He realized that acting like a blind man would only be necessary in a courtroom. He could just find a seat at the back of a movie house and view auras freely, in the dark.

Cary set out to test his new idea the following Saturday. He chose a theater showing the actioner, "The Getaway," with Steve McQueen, and Ali MacGraw. He went a bit early, so that he could get a seat where he wanted. For the first time in a long while, Cary missed

Lennie. The last time he went to a movie in a theater, it was with her. He was so distracted by witnessing the murder that he didn't spend much time thinking about her. Now he realized how deeply he felt her absence.

The matinee was crowded. Before the house lights dimmed, only a few empty seats were left. From his vantage point in the back row, Cary had an excellent view of the crowd in front of him.

The display of emotional responses in the movie theater was impressive. Cary realized that the purpose of the movie was to take people out of their humdrum everyday existences and give them a thrill. This film certainly did that. The fast editing made sure that the action scenes were tightly strung together, only taking a long break for the comic relief.

Intense greens were all over the place. People showed the white aura of fear in all the intense action sequences. It was easy to tell who was completely involved in the film and who wasn't. At one point, Cary noticed a couple of aural outlines that were just steadily green, mostly so close together that they formed a single outline. A quick glance through his eyes revealed that it was a pair of teenagers making out. Other than those two, Cary got all that he wanted from his planned aural viewing experience.

A week later Cary took one of his many unused vacation days and sat in a courtroom. The one he chose was in the Civil Courts Building. It was much easier to get access to a courtroom here. The Criminal Courts had a screening system that included identification checks and metal detectors. Cary really wanted no part of trying to explain why he wanted to be a spectator in a criminal courtroom.

The Courtroom he chose was the venue for a trial concerning a wrongful death lawsuit. From a seat in the last row of spectator benches, Cary held his cane, tilted his head upward and listened. The arguments and interrogations went back and forth, all morning long. There was so much anger in the room that it was hard to pick one aura as the most intense. For whatever reason, even the jurors were showing auras tinted red with hostility. By the time the judge rapped his gavel to signal a break for lunch, his aura was as red as any of the others.

All in all, Cary had his fill of aura viewing just in the morning session of court. He made his way out of the courthouse. It was his plan to walk back to where he parked his car and shed his disguise. The doors of the courthouse were huge brass affairs. He pushed one aside to exit, holding it open for a woman behind him.

Cary's politeness got him in a bit of trouble. The woman following him out the door of the courthouse was a police detective. She quickly stepped around in front of Cary, and stopped him. She flipped open a badge wallet, revealing her gold badge. She held it forward, at belt level.

"I'm Detective Harding. I'd like to talk to you for a minute."

Cary had no idea what was going on. "Yes?" He knew that his inflection was too intense. He was taken off guard and didn't know what to do. The detective still held the badge wallet open, in front of her.

After a moment, it dawned on Cary that the detective was offering her badge for Cary to examine with his fingertips. He reached forward letting the woman guide the wallet beneath his hand. He fingered the surface of the badge, running his index finger over the lettering carefully.

"I noticed you in the courtroom. Are you a family member?" Detective Harding regarded him coolly. She closed the badge wallet with a snap.

Cary continued his head tilt – upward, the way blind people do – for just a moment longer. As he began to answer, his chin fell, just a bit, involuntarily.

"No, I was just there out of curiosity." He hoped he was on the right course of answering questions. He really wanted to get away, be somewhere else.

"You're very well dressed." The woman detective addressed him so matter-of-factly that it caught Cary's attention. He knew she was trying throw him off, by getting him to feel relaxed.

"Thank you." Cary now had a case of the "shut-the-hell-ups".

"I only stopped to ask you, because my uncle was blind, and he never looked as nicely dressed as you. He always said his outfits were picked by a blind man. It was just strange to me that a person with a white cane would be so well dressed. In fact, you're wearing brand coordinates. How's that?"

Internally, Cary breathed a sigh of relief. He was relieved that it was his clothing that was the thing that tripped him up. His mind stopped racing. After just a moment, he had it together.

He pulled his glasses from his face, squinting his eyes as tightly as he could. "I was born this way." He held his hand up, just an inch from his face. "I can see this far. That makes me legally blind. I can see to pick out my clothes, but not do much else. Even reading is out of the question. And lately, my limited vision has been getting worse."

Cary put his Wayfarers back on and stood there waiting for the detective's response. She either bought the story or she didn't.

"I'm sorry, Mr...."

Cary didn't answer. He knew an interrogation when he was the subject of one. He also knew that detectives talked that way almost completely out of habit.

Cary's reticence did the trick. Seeing no further point to her brief investigation, the woman detective turned on her heels and walked away without another word. Cary let out some of the breath that he had been holding, trying not to audibly sigh.

As he tapped his way along the sidewalk, Cary re-evaluated the whole blindman act. By the time he got ack to his car, the white cane was broken into six pieces and thrown in a trash can. He figured that right up to, and through lying to a detective, he had gotten enough use out of it.

***

That night after turning in for the night, Cary tossed and turned. The minor scare of the confrontation with the detective kept him wondering what could have happened. He lay there, worrying about how his new sense – his new ability – could likely get him in a lot of trouble. The telephone rang.

Cary swung his feet out of the bed. He looked at the clock at his bedside. It was ten-thirty-five. He wondered who could be calling at this late hour.

"Hello."

It's me, Lennie."

SEVENTEEN

Eleven-fifteen. Cary waited inside the door to his apartment. In the quiet of the residential neighborhood, he had heard Lennie drive up. Lennie's phone call had been short, terse. She had simply said, "I need to see you. I'm coming over."

Cary fought back a tremble of excited anticipation when he heard the door of her car slam closed. The front door, the steps. It was almost too much. He heard Lennie's footfall on the landing outside his door.

Cary silently pulled the door open. For a brief second or two, Lennie just stood there. She was dressed in a short-sleeve plaid blouse, and jeans-cut, khaki shorts. Just a pair of sandals on her feet. Her overnight bag was in her left hand.

Lennie reached out with her right hand and extended her fingers, spread apart. She used her fingertips to push Cary back, inside the doorway of the apartment. Her eyes were fixed on his. She stepped forward, closed the door. Click. She never took her eyes off of Cary's.

Cary said, "Lennie, I…"

Lennie's fingers moved from his chest up to his mouth. "Shut up." She pulled Cary into the hottest, wettest kiss he had ever experienced. Her quilted shoulder bag, the overnighter, fell to the floor. For a moment, Cary thought he might faint, just from the intensity of the excitement he felt. He actually had a slight whirling sensation. As they continued to kiss, he let his hand reach up under her blouse.

Lennie was only wearing the blouse. Dressing for her drive over to Cary's apartment had been an exercise in being dressed, but being prepared as well, for what she intended. Their separation had gone on too long, too silently. Their time apart taught her that she wanted to be with Cary more than anything. The strange, frightening things that he told her didn't matter. She wanted to be with him. She needed him.

Lennie pulled Cary's tee shirt over his head. The kissing behind the door to the apartment continued. As Lennie stroked his back, Cary opened Lennie's blouse and pulled her tightly against him. The heat of their bodies was starting to create a little happy perspiration.

Cary slid his hands down Lennie's back and discovered that the shorts were already unbuttoned at the waist. Lennie was bare beneath the canvas of the shorts. The thought that Lennie had come to his door "loaded for bear," drove Cary nuts. He slid the shorts to the floor.

Cary swept Lennie into his arms and carried her across the apartment, oblivious of Wheels' tail-wagging excitement at seeing Lennie. The golden retriever nimbly danced around Cary's feet as he carried her to the bedroom. As his master returned to his bed, Wheels curled up in his beanbag chair.

As the two lovers shed the last of their clothes, they never lost the physical contact. Together, they slid between the sheets. Cary was so entirely excited, he was afraid that he would do a bad job of making love to Lennie. This wasn't just sex. It was important. The last couple of days, reminded as he was of how much he missed her, Cary was on a mission, a quest, to show how much he loved Lennie.

For her part, Lennie was where she wanted to be and didn't care about the details. She needed to be with Cary, needed to be part of him. She wanted him to be a part of her. If the giving of oneself is the partial loss of self, it is also the partial gain of another. If their lovemaking was a blending together, let it be that. Lennie just knew she wanted this more than she had ever wanted anything else.

***

The night and the lovemaking went on. Cary and Lennie took turns stirring up the action. By about four o'clock, both were totally exhausted. Wheels was glad when all the noise and giggling finally stopped. It seemed to him that every time he fell asleep, there was more thrashing around in the bed, or someone was getting up to go to the little room.

At ten o'clock, the two young lovers rolled out of bed and took turns using the bathroom. Cary dressed quickly and took Wheels out for a brief walk. When he returned, he found Lennie, in just her blouse, sitting at the kitchen dinette, eating some jellied toast. The coffee maker was gurgling away on the edge of the tiny counter in the cramped little kitchen.

He sat down and pulled a chair up close. He watched her take a tiny little bite of her toast and reached out to brush a crumb from her lip. The touch of his hand was all that was needed to make Lennie forget her toast and stand up from the chair before Cary. She pressed her bared abdomen against his face, holding him there with her hands.

Cary wrapped his arms around Lennie and kissed her stomach. Again, without letting go of each other, the two made it to the bed, disrobed and resumed their lovemaking marathon. The coffee was neglected, along with the rest of the toast. In his corner of the kitchen, Wheels was grateful that his master had remembered how hungry he was and chowed down.

Cary and Lennie had been bitten by the gonna-do-this-till-we-can't-no-more lovebug. It was a good thing it was the weekend. Neither of them had any plans to go any where else for the foreseeable future. They only wanted to see each other, touch each other, have each other.

At about three o'clock in the afternoon, Lennie and Cary emerged from the apartment building and took Wheels for a romp in the park. They had tried to get out earlier in the day but, of course, the showering turned into something else. Only the limited supply of hot water, from the apartment's little water heater, brought reality back into the picture.

Neither Cary or Lennie had particularly much energy to chase after the dog but sharing the job got it done. Somehow, every chase of the dog ended up with Lennie and Cary, arm in arm, looking at little else but each other. Wheels had to work overtime, just to get a little attention.

At the end of the park visit, they dropped off Wheels at the apartment, with a dish of food, and headed out for some pizza. Both were absolutely starved, having eaten nothing since the day before. Lennie's couple bites of toast didn't count. After their "breakfast," a return to the kitchen revealed no trace of the toast that had been left behind. In the absence of any evidence, no accusations could be made, but there were a few askance looks at Wheels.

***

That night, the lovemaking continued. There was less urgency to it. There was a little more talk and sharing. Lennie told Cary that she looked for him every day at the store. Cary was embarrassed to tell Lennie that he had checked on her almost as frequently. He told her anyway. In the mood of the weekend, it all seemed sweet to Lennie.

The next day, Lennie broached the subject of Cary's ability to see auras of people without interference from solid objects. Cary explained a lot of what he had discovered. He told Lennie about the indigo aura always present in some children. He told her about being able to discriminate multiple colors in auras.

They went to the park again and Cary continued his story. The day was beautiful, there were a lot of people in the park and more than a few dogs. He told Lennie about the bus ride, the movie theater and the courtroom. He even told her about Detective Harding and how she scared him into ditching the white cane. That part of the story had enough comedic value to get him a few pokes in the ribs for being stupid enough to try the blindman act, in the first place.

Cary carefully watched Lennie's reaction to all of the things he told her about viewing auras. His best guess was that she was a lot more comfortable with the whole idea than when she left – when they separated. He decided to tell her about the murder of Sharon Manning and how he had accidentally witnessed the whole thing.

Cary was careful to include everything he could remember, every detail. He fearlessly related how scared and upset he was by the whole thing. With Lennie, he didn't feel like it made him any less of a man. He told her that even talking about it brought back a lot of the feelings he had during the whole episode.

Getting through the part about not knowing how to share what he had "seen" was difficult. When he started explaining about the bus station and his use of a raspy voice, he realized that he might sound like he was back in a comedic part of the story. He emphasized how nerve-wracking it was to try and report the whole thing and remain totally anonymous.

He understood that without being in his predicament, Lennie could only try to understand. To his vast relief, Lennie sympathized with his reactions to every part of the story. By the time he finished, Cary figured that there was one thing making the difference now.

He wanted for them both to be able to say it. "I love you, Lennie."

"I love you too, Cary." Lennie chimed in melodically. The sounds of the park around them seemed to disappear, fade away.

On the sidewalk, in the park, Cary took her by the shoulders, staring intently into her deep, brown eyes. "No, I mean I love you. You're the one. I want you to be mine, forever. Marry me."

Blinking at the sudden, earnest proposal. Lennie reached up and took Cary's hands down from her shoulders and held them in hers. She shook her head to the side; a tell-tale tear was trying to spoil everything. She thought for a moment that if he hadn't asked her, she might have been the one to take the lead and ask him. She knew she loved him with all her heart.

"Yes."

As they embraced, Cary closed his eyes and viewed their intertwined auras. There was so much happy green coloration that it was almost nauseating. He opened his eyes and looked around him. Where everything had seemed so dark and troubled, just a few days ago, clarity and brightness filled his estimation of the world around him.

Cary found something he was unaware that he had set aside. The was now a future to be reckoned with. It was a future that included Lennie. It was brilliant, shining with possibility.

Lennie held Cary as tightly as she could. She wanted to pull him to her, through her, bring him within her. Her love for Cary was huge and encompassing. Whatever his fortune brought, hers would be bound to. They would become one. Her belief in the beauty and grace of life was so strong that it seemed as though it could withstand anything.

They kissed one more, long kiss. It lasted until wheels couldn't deal with being ignored any longer and started pushing his way between them. The trio gathered up the belongings and headed for home. There was still enough park left to get in a few more frisbee tosses. As usual Wheels led the way with the frisbee, his trophy of hard running and catching, firmly locked in his teeth.

EIGHTEEN

Sleep lay on him like six feet of earth. He was involuntarily immobile. He awoke from sleep to find himself weighed down by the depth of his sleep. Conscious, deliberate effort allowed him to move his heavy arms and legs, first flexing, then stretching them.

After a couple minutes of this flexing and stretching, he sat up on the side of the bed. He never had an experience, waking from sleep, that was anything like this. He felt as though he had moved several tons of rock and earth. He knew that he had not.

The man, nicknamed Poika by his father, now knew his inner self as Walker. He momentarily wondered at his own need for another name with which to consider himself, as the killer that he was. The thought passed almost as quickly as it had come upon him.

He reflected on the events of the night before. The waiting, stalking. The capture, and the kill. Thought of the kill caused a rush of excitement to flash through him. He rose to his feet quickly. The weight of sleep fell from him like a cloak, slipping off of his shoulders. Adrenaline. He recognized its effects on him immediately. His combat and martial arts training taught him to use its presence advantageously.

The night's actions must have caused a flow of adrenaline through his body that persisted throughout the entire process. Hours of heightened alertness and strength took their toll on him now. It must be like battle fatigue. The causes were the same.

He looked at the clock, it was still early. He showered and dressed. Years of the same activity let automatic behaviors take over until he arrived at the recruiting office. Once there, he focused on his job. He successfully banished all thoughts of the night before from his mind.

There were three interviews that day, two of which resulted in signed enlistment papers. As the afternoon wore on, he made the choice to not go to class that evening. He would avoid the college campus and surrounding neighborhoods. He grabbed a to-go sandwich and a newspaper from a delicatessen. He went back to his apartment.

The television news had no report about a missing girl, or any murdered young woman found near an abandoned trucking lot. It was the same with the content of the newspaper. Finishing his sandwich, he thought about the implications of the lack of news.

His military training kicked in and started him down a path to realistic, clear-headed thinking. A stark realization slowly came over him: He had radically changed his behavior on the day after committing a serious crime. He had made the child-like assumption that some notice of the girl's absence, or the discovery of her body, would occur. No such earth-shattering revelations were made.

By not going to class, or taking his regular long evening walks, he had created an opportunity for discovery. He mentally beat himself up for being so stupid. The hate within him wasn't going to be enough to keep him out of prison, or the gas chamber. He had to think his way through things a lot better in the future or risk letting his hate eat him alive, from within.

No one knew that a murder had been committed, at least there was no report of it. He was fairly certain that the discovery of a young woman's body would, perforce, find its way to headline status in quick order. Even a city as large as Pittsburgh couldn't resist the thrall of the reporting of bloody mayhem.

This new understanding meant that if there ever was another stalk-and-kill, it would have to be dealt with more carefully. The relentless drive of his hate, now fully in command of his life, would have to allow for rationality to "prepare the way" for more successful outcomes. It would be impossible to keep doing what he had done today: call attention to himself, by changing his daily routine.

Tomorrow, he would resume his daily activities with no changes. Luck would have to cover for him, just this once. He would leave nothing to chance, ever again, if he could avoid it.

Having figured all this out, Walker now replayed the events of the night before in his mind. His choice of a stalking "blind," the darkened doorway, had been a good one. The sidewalk in front of the doorway was likewise a good choice for taking his target and rendering her immobile. The entire "take" zone was outside the light of the streetlights, including the place he parked his car, earlier in the evening.

The time required to take down his target was minimal. A person suddenly surprised from behind and seized with vastly more physical strength was subject to an enormous flow of their own adrenaline. In this case, it worked against the target individual, exhausting her store of readily available oxygen rapidly. Three and a half seconds was all the longer that the take-down lasted.

Walker then thought about how far he had driven, with the unconscious girl in the trunk of his car. The distance involved exposed him to discovery. It wasn't necessarily a bad part of the plan that he had executed. It could be improved upon.

His next painful realization was that, even though he had chosen a remote site for the actual kill, it was in the open. Anyone who just happened to be nearby, in the woods – for whatever stupid, pointless reason – could have witnessed the whole strangulation. This was a mistake he would never make again.

His next – he caught himself, thinking about making another kill. Walker wondered how hard it was going to be, gaining any mastery over his hate's wild drive, to do what it wanted. There had to be a way of sanely, rationally – yeah, right – sanely and rationally killing people. There had to be better ways to plan what he was doing. There had to be smarter ways of carrying out his ideas.

As the night after the murder wore on to its end, Walker came to another realization: The hate within him wasn't some strange, other-worldly experience. It was him. He was the hate. The hate was him. There weren't two minds, but one. This one mind would be smarter. It had to be. The whole 'Walker' thing was just a distraction. He would not let it interfere with what he did.

A strange peace came over him. He realized – admitted to himself that he was one with his hate. Sleep again came, less like battle-fatigue, more like a normal person's slumber. A fleeting dream or two, reminders of childhood trials and tortures, flowed through his sleeping mind. It was an indication that he was accepting his new self, the killer, as normal.

***

The next morning, sleep floated away, letting in the new day. None of yesterday's stone-like stiffness remained. Walker was glad that routine would take its place again in his life. A lot of the pressure that built up within him was eased by not only the act of killing, but by coming to those stark realizations about himself. His oneness was a new strength. He had accepted the hate within his mind as part of himself. In its own depraved way, it was heartening.

He cleaned up and shoved off. The drive to the office this morning included a regular once-a-week visit to a doughnut shop. Having a pastry to eat, and some to share with the other recruiters, made the humdrum that much more acceptable. All of the men in the office did something to ease the burden for the group.

Between regular duties, Walker got back into his books. He would have to work a little harder to cover the day that he missed but it wouldn't be impossible. His grades were good enough to attract a few job offers already. He had no idea that the demand for pre-law graduates was high. In fact, he had settled on pre-law as an area of study because it was a challenge. He had no real interest in going to law school.

There were only weeks remaining before the end of the semester and graduation. Walker re-established his routine walks, around central Pittsburg. He regained a bit of confidence with the knowledge that having missed a day of his regular walks could be attributed to simply having taken a different one of the many routes he covered.

After school ended, a long summer of finishing his enlistment would follow. The Army was already pressuring him to sign up for another tour. He knew he had been extraordinarily lucky in avoiding being sent to southeast Asia. He felt certain that, in a new tour, notice would be taken of that very fact. No way, José.

***

Weeks went by with no mention of the crime that he had committed. Then, on campus, "Have you seen this girl?" posters appeared. They hung on the bulletin boards, unnoticed, just like all the other dreck notices about frat parties, missing cats and apartment leases.

Just before the end of the semester, news stories appeared, about a body found in the countryside, at an abandoned truck depot. As Walker expected, the newspaper headlines literally screamed. The television news reports were as lurid as they could make them.

141

The body that was discovered was badly decomposed, and partially consumed by animals. The news stories could only speculate that the remains might be those of a Duquesne University student, missing for several weeks.

Graduation from college turned out to be the anticlimax of Walker's life. He avoided attending the ceremony itself. There was no one who would congratulate him at the end, save, perhaps for one of the men he worked with. He decided that having his fellow recruiters buy him a celebratory beer instead, would be just fine.

A couple of days later, the diploma arrived in an envelope that was so large that he had to go to the post office to pick it up. He thought that if he hadn't put so much work into it, he might have just left it, sitting in the post office, unclaimed. He knew that you could tell anyone you wanted that you had a degree, but they would still want a letter from the university anyway.

He looked at the diploma a total of one time, rolled it into a tube and stuck it in with his high school diploma. Neither document was likely to ever see the light of day again.

***

The summer in Pittsburgh wore on. After the initial "June rush" of enlistments, things slowed down. The flow of interested and acceptable candidates for recruitment stayed steady through July, but August was the really slow month of the year. It was a month that seemed to go on forever. The thing that helped was the steady flow of information about job opportunities for recent college – especially pre-law – graduates. It made for some interesting reading and a few telephone calls that really piqued his interest.

The war in Viet Nam was still growing. By the time Walker finished his enlistment, the Army was clamoring for him to "re-up." True to his intentions, he let his tour expire and was mustered out of the Army.

The big war meant that many government agencies needed to grow, right along with the military. Among the many agencies seeking new graduates was one in particular that caught his eye. It was a real stretch of the imagination to combine what he had done, with working for the government agency he was considering.

The very perversity of it finally made the choice for him. He decided to go for it, see if he could make another mark for himself in the world. He filled out the lengthy application and mailed it in.

NINETEEN

Cary awakened. He was entwined with Lennie. They had both fallen into a deep sleep, after yet another intense love-making session. Neither had risen to redress in any way. He realized the need to stay still for a short while. If he moved, he would likely wake Lennie. He wanted to just be there with her for a while. He wanted to enjoy the press of her body against his.

Cary loved the way Lennie smelled. He discovered, after she moved in, that the main component of her luscious scent was something called Jean Nate After Bath Splash. It didn't matter one bit that the scent came from a bottle. It was part of Lennie and he loved it. Learning the things that women did to make themselves attractive was another joyful set of discoveries for Cary.

The scent of Lennie's hair was equally intoxicating. Cary knew the shampoo was the most common thing available but, again, as something that was part of Lennie, Cary was enthralled by it. The shampoo. The thought of it caused Cary to think of all of the extra bottles and jars of lotions, creams, soaps, make-up, and fragrances that now took up so much space not only in the bathroom, but in the bedroom as well.

Cary turned his attention away from his lover for a minute and looked over all the extra belongings in the tiny bedroom. The closet had been the first to fall. It was crammed to the door frame with clothing. Cary's clothes were shuttled aside, and now occupied "his half" of the closet. Strange thing though, Cary's half was noticeably smaller than Lennie's. C'est la vie. Cary thought it would probably always be that way. As a thing that he had to adjust to, it was a minor consideration.

Even Wheels had to make some accommodations for Lennie. His beanbag chair was now pushed into a corner of the living room. Lennie brought a wing-back chair from her former apartment. Along with the couch and a coffee table, the living room was full.

Wheels exacted his payment, however. The first couple of days that Lennie stayed, he nabbed three of her hairbrushes, adding them to his basket of toys. Lennie took it in stride. She realized that having a collection of hairbrushes wasn't necessary, in the first place.

Lennie's departure from her shared apartment wasn't without its problems. Despite the fact that Ramona and Cliff had the apartment to themselves most of the time, disrupting the financial arrangement threatened to create serious animosity between the two young women. The whole situation was saved by another salesgirl at the store. She was looking for an apartment share and Lennie's exit created the place she needed.

Lennie left her former living arrangement, not spending a minute worrying about how the new roommate would adjust to the nights that Cliff stayed over. It was definitely time for someone else to have to deal with that.

After letting his mind wander for a bit, Cary carefully unwound himself from Lennie's sleeping embrace. He picked up his clothes and padded into the bathroom to dress. A minute later he was in the kitchen, starting a pot of coffee. The kitchen itself revealed the effects of joining households. The extra dishes and kitchenware were stacked everywhere. It was a bit of a trick to accomplish anything without knocking something over.

Wheels was at his feet the whole time and ready to go for his morning walk. The two quietly left via the back door. When the round-the-block walk was ended, Cary and Wheels went back to the flat. Lennie was up and already making breakfast.

Cary knew he was totally smitten by Lennie but still gave himself over to the experience with everything he had. Seeing Lennie – dressed only in panties, and one of his dress shirts; barefoot, cooking breakfast – filled his heart with such emotion that he could hardly stand it. This was his girl. She had given herself to him, as he to her. It all tended to make his head spin.

After breakfast, they decided that the following weekend, they would tell Lennie's parents about their marriage plans. It wasn't so much that they wanted ask permission. They still wanted to involve Lennie's mom and dad in the process.

***

The Friday afternoon drive to Red Bud, Illinois took about an hour. The traffic leaving town was heavy. The initial going was slow. The old, steel-truss, Jefferson Barracks bridge was under repairs. There was talk of replacing it with a new one – someday. Once they made the turn onto Illinois Route 3, the traffic thinned out. It was a sunny afternoon. The drive down was uneventful.

Arriving at the Baerd's home, Cary felt the first twinges of nervousness about meeting Lennie's folks. Until now, he hadn't given much thought to how they might react to the news. He mentally pushed the worry aside. It would all go well. There really wasn't a reason for it not to go well.

Lennie's parents greeted them and welcomed them into the house. Cary found it to be almost exactly as he had expected it to be. The furniture was worn and showed its age but there was nothing out of place or messy. In fact, everything was neatly arranged. Cary instinctively recognized the roll of German or Central European heritage in how the house was kept. It was not at all unlike houses he knew from his childhood.

The Friday evening dinner went well. There was a lot of conversation about the work at Vander & Beste. After the dishes were cleaned and put away, Cary and Lennie sat with her parents in the living room.

Cary decided to get right to it. "Lennie and I are planning to get married." He looked at Lennie for support, having just jumped straight into the discussion. Looking back at Lennie's parents, "We hoped that you'd be happy for us."

Lennie's parents sat stone-faced for a few seconds. Neither said a word. Cary was beginning to feel an awkward, uncomfortable sensation. He closed his eyes for just a second, to gauge the middle-aged couple's emotional state. Green.

As he reopened his eyes, Lennie's mother poked her husband in the ribs with her elbow. They both broke into wide smiles. Lennie's dad rose from his seat and extended his hand to Cary.

"Congratulations, son!" He gripped Cary's hand in a vise-like grip and pulled him to his feet. The rock-like hand released, the handshake became a bear hug. After a few sound claps on the back, "Welcome to the family!"

The Baerds were nobody's fools and had a solid inkling that they would be the recipients of such news on just this sort of a weekend visit. They had worked out in advance that when the moment came, they would tease the young people just a little by acting unimpressed with their plans. The intent was to throw in some shenanigans to lighten the mood and ease the tension.

The Baerds' little gag worked as intended. Cary realized he was being "handled" by a couple of old pros. He instantly started falling in love with the two old tricksters. Lennie was sitting quietly, her tongue in her cheek, loving her parents even more for the deliberate bit of goofiness.

The conversation that followed went on for hours. The Baerds were impressed that Cary felt close enough to them to share that his family name had been Langenbreuner. The revelation of how it became Lang impressed them even more deeply. The bonds of family attachment were forming.

The only other business tended to that evening was sleeping arrangements. The Baerds had not planned on Cary and Lennie sleeping together and left it at that. They were just old fashioned enough to know that they weren't expected to accommodate the young lovers. After everyone went to bed, Lennie snuck into the spare bedroom and slept with Cary. The single bed was small for them but then again, the way things were, not too small, after all.

The next morning, Cary woke early and chased his fiancée back to her own bedroom. They didn't fool anyone but managed to keep appearances in order. For their part, the Baerds kept the knowing glances and smirking to a minimum. A tiny bit of deception on everyone's part helped the weekend to pass, absent generational friction.

The best part of the weekend for everyone was watching Wheels run free in the fields near the Baerds' home. He had spectacular delight in discovering all the things that were new to a city dog. He had a better time than anyone else that weekend.

***

Cary extended his weekend, by taking Monday off. He sent Lennie off to her usual long day at the Young Sophisticates department. He was looking forward to catching up on a few things around the apartment and spending part of the day reading.

The rhythms and sounds of the normal daily routine echoed through the flat. After Lennie left, the neighbor who lived above Mrs. Roberts, Roberta Clemmons left for her job. She was a downtown office worker. Cary didn't know much about her. He knew she was in her thirties, and mostly kept to herself.

After Ms. Clemmons left, Fred Maunt came home from his night job. His pass up the stairs, to the apartment above Cary's was something Cary only heard a couple of times a year. Their paths simply did not cross with any regularity.

Cary's recent, deep involvement with Lennie had distracted him not only from his reading, but from spending time viewing auras. Other than the occasional peek at Lennie's aura, and the brief view of the Baerds, he had not done any aural viewing at all.

As he settled down to read, Wheels curled up in his beanbag chair. Cary planned on reading until noon, then walking Wheels and tending to his household chores. Footsteps, from above caught his attention. Cary closed his eyes and watched as the aural outline of a man – Maunt – crossed from his apartment to the one across the landing, Ms. Clemmons' flat. He watched as Maunt moved from room to room, stopping here and there, doing things Cary couldn't readily identify.

Cary knew that Maunt had no business in Ms. Clemmons' apartment but couldn't do anything about it. He might have to find a way of alerting Ms. Clemmons to what was going on. The aura of Fred Maunt stopped at one place in the apartment. Cary could make out that he was pulling drawers open and closing them again. At one point, Cary saw Maunt make a movement that suggested he was putting something in his pocket. After that, he left the apartment, returning to his own.

Cary continued viewing Maunt for a short period but there was no unusual activity the he could make out. He gave up viewing and picked up his reading. What he had seen bothered him and kept him from concentrating on his book. Cary decided that it was time to do chores. He would sneak in some reading time later. He went through the rest of his day off, greeted his fiancée with dinner ready, and settled in for the night.

After work on Tuesday, Mrs. Roberts met him at the door of the apartment building. She had watched and waited for Cary so she could tell him her important news: There had been a burglary. Ms. Clemmons' apartment had been broken into and jewelry was stolen.

Mrs. Roberts said that the police came and asked a lot of questions but nobody saw anything. Cary got a sinking feeling in his gut. He knew that he had seen the whole thing. Of all the things he ever expected, being a witness to crimes that other people tried to keep hidden was not one of them. He knew what to do. He knew how to do it.

The next day, Cary left work and went to the bus station. Finding a lone telephone, away from anyone else, he made the call and reported the crime he had witnessed. He asked for the detective bureau but not for anyone in particular.

This time, he used a gravely, low voice. It was easier for him to speak and he knew he wanted to provide as much detail as possible. His dislike for Fred Maunt had taken on an entirely new aspect. The man was not only unpleasant, he was a thief, as well.

Cary headed home from the bus station, picking up a newspaper from the stand he knew so well. He was sure that Maunt would get his comeuppance.

***

Two days later, the police woke Fred Maunt him from his sleep, in the middle of the day. They searched his apartment. A short while later, the police led him away in handcuffs.

At the end of the day, Cary was, once again, greeted by an excited Mrs. Roberts. She told Cary all about the "police raid" on Mr. Maunt's apartment. She woefully described the officers leading Fred Maunt away, his arms behind him, wrists cuffed with shiny steel.

After listening to the elaborate descriptions that Mrs. Roberts lavished on the exciting events, Cary went to get Wheels out for his afternoon romp. He picked up one small thing in his apartment and headed out the door.

In the small lobby of the apartment building, Cary stopped for a moment, drew a penknife from his pocket and used it to pry off Maunt's name from his mailbox. The thought that his former neighbor wouldn't be getting mail at this address, for the foreseeable future, gave Cary special satisfaction.

TWENTY

Chatter around the Detective Bureau work areas rose and fell throughout the day. A number of people talking on the telephone simultaneously tended to raise their voices, unconsciously competing with each other. Sometimes it was idle conversation between the staff that competed to be heard above all the other talk.

One such conversation fell across the ears of Benji Beckestone. He was in a common break room for the different bureaus, eating a warmed-over chimichanga. Last night's Mexican restaurant dinner was yet another uncomfortable date with a cadet from the academy.

The few women cadets that Benji had so far picked for dating all seemed to have more than he could offer in their minds. He knew from the outset that dating police recruits was potentially dangerous to his career but nothing else had worked out for him. He would have to try something else to find someone to – what, he didn't know. He was that far from it.

The conversation was between two burglary detectives. "Yeah, anonymous phone call. Guy gave a whole lotta details. It was like he was sittin' there, watchin' the whole thing." The burglary detective was filling in another with the tale of a minor apartment burglary. The "leg work" in solving the crime was done by whoever called in the information.

Not being a believer in coincidences, Beckestone listened carefully and got enough information. It sounded exactly like his experience with the person who called in the tip on the Manning case. He made a mental note of the two detectives, especially the one telling the story.

That conversation gave him what he needed to go to his lieutenant, later that day. "I've listened to both recordings, Lieutenant. They sound different but the words are similar, like both calls were made by people who were educated. They might even be the same person, disguising his voice."

Lieutenant Dukasko looked at his junior member of the bureau. "You expect me to give you time to investigate who's making these phone calls?" He chewed his cigar a bit. "Why?"

"Whoever the caller – or callers – are, they know an awful lot of things about the crimes they are reporting. Too much. It's almost like they were watching the crime take place and deciding to call us some time later."

"So, what?" Lieutenant John Dukasko felt that he was too busy to be entertaining the ideas of the young detective. He looked down at the mountain of paperwork he still had to wade through that day.

Beckestone said, "The similarity is that both calls came in some time after the crime took place. Neither of the calls were made right after the crime. Both calls had way too much detail for someone who hadn't seen the crime committed. I'd like to get a court order to go through the telephone company's records to see where the calls came from."

"And then what?" Dukasko was about to throw Beckestone out of his office.

"I'll go where the leads take me. It's probably going to be a lot of schlepping around town, chasing dead ends. But who knows? I can only promise that I'll keep my daily reports on time. If this is going nowhere, you can pull me off."

Dukasko knew that his current position was as high as he was likely to go in the department. He was setting any records with crime solving. The statistics were no worse than when he took over. They were no better either. It chaffed him that a young detective, who hadn't been the most productive member of the bureau, was now asking to assign himself to an investigation of – what? He sat in his chair, regarding the detective in front of him for a moment.

The kid did just bust the Manning case. Maybe he was on to something, maybe he wasn't.

"I'll tell ya what, Detective Beckestone: Three days. Get what you can get in three days, or you're back on an assignment of mine." Benji Beckestone knew that he didn't need to answer. He turned on his heels and headed out the door.

Lieutenant John Dukasko looked at the separate photographs of his two ex-wives that he kept on his desk. They were there as reminders. They reminded him of where his pay went and why he was always broke. They also reminded him that life's a bitch who don't make no promises. He reached into the bottom drawer of his desk, pulled out a bottle of Old Crow and poured himself a paper-cupful.

Kinda early to start this. Dukasko thought to himself. *Was yesterday too.*

Hustling back to his desk, Beckestone thought to himself. Three days, what generosity. He stopped in the office only long enough to grab his coat. He was headed for the order office to have a clerk fill in the information he needed to get a court order for the phone records.

***

The following afternoon, Detective Beckestone stood in front of the bank of payphones that lined one wall of the main salon of the bus station. He had been up all night, reading reams of records from the phone company. Finally, the numbers came up, both of them here. He looked up and down the line of phones.

A brief search led to the two telephones used to make the calls. Finding the phones was beginning to look like a dead end. He went to a row of seats in the main hall and sat. He watched the people who came and went at the phone bank. Some of the people making calls spoke for long periods, most were short.

Beckestone intuited that long calls made from this location might be unusual. There were probably a lot of expensive long-distance calls made here. Telephone calls would be kept short. A person who made a long telephone call would stand out. Both of the calls made to the police, reporting the crimes, were comparatively lengthy. The first call was more than three and a half minutes long, the second just at three minutes.

This was a thin finding, for all of the work put into it. The next step was the schlepping part. Detective Beckestone began interviewing the counter personnel. After getting little more than blank stares from the bus line ticket handlers, he moved on to the concessionaires. The pizza-by-the-slice counter was attended by an Armenian who apparently only spoke pizza. Beckestone's questions fell on ears on a head that could only answer, "Cheese? Meat? Pepperoni?"

He got nowhere with the clean-up crew that moved around the bus station constantly. It seemed as though they did no actual cleaning. The station was in a perpetual state of squalor that suggested more likely occupancy by bears than humans. Along with not cleaning, the janitorial staff saw nothing. The "I didn't see nuthin" responses to Beckestone's question were so strident and similar to each other, that Beckestone suspected the formation of a minor religious sect.

There was nothing but negative results, so far, from his investigation. Beckestone was tired and frustrated. At one point he strode over to one wall of the bus station and prepared to start banging his head against it. He stopped short of doing so. He realized that if he let any part of his head touch the wall of the bus station, his head would be coated with the brownish-greyish-sooty stuff that covered every surface.

Ready to give up, admit defeat and head back to Dukasko, with hat in hand, Beckestone made for the exit of the station. Outside the station he saw someone who was always there: the news vendor. Walking away from the station, the thought struck Benji Beckestone like a thrown stone, to the back of the head. He's always there.

Beckestone spun around and headed back to the station and the newsstand. The newsboy, Riggy Bodd, was always there. He was a fixture of the entire downtown area, not just the bus station. Everybody knew Riggy.

Equipped as he was with the gifts of limited intelligence, a friendly manner and a speech impediment, he made out like a bandit. Ostensibly paid ninety cents an hour, Riggy Bodd never filed income taxes. It was a good thing because his demeanor got him generous tips, all the time. He made more than thirty thousand dollars a year. He gave a lot of his money to the church he attended and lived in a small, one-room apartment.

Standing on a street corner every day of the year took its toll on Riggy's clothes. He looked as though his coat had never been cleaned. The reason for this was simple: It had never been cleaned. For whatever reason, Riggy didn't pursue a rigorous hygiene regimen. He looked and smelled the part. Frequent passers-by at the newsstand knew the trick of staying upwind of Riggy, just in case he started talking to you.

Detective Benjamin Beckestone only knew Riggy Bodd by reputation. He soon found out why it was that everyone else tossed coins to Riggy and kept on walking by. He hoped that the interview with the newsmonger would be short.

"Sure, I seen lotsa people by the telephones, all the time." Riggy's nasal, breathy speech was laced with the pungent odor of whatever it was he had eaten most recently.

"No, Riggy. I need to know about people that make long calls, calls that last a long time." Beckestone was convinced that even this was going to turn out to be a dead end.

Riggy Bodd subtly took a big breath and got into a ramble. "Oh, yeah. There's that one guy. He's always nice. Buys outta town papers. Says it's a cheap way to travel. That's weird, ain't it? He works over at the department store, Vander & Beste, you know, just a couplah blocks over. He drives one o' them German cars." Riggy, out of air now, drew another breath.

Beckestone was stunned that the seedy, dirty paper vendor was turning out to be a fountain of information. Riggy held up four stained fingers. The ends of his fingernails were black. It was the kind of dirt-black that you knew never changed, even in the unlikely event of a bath. Riggy was a street person, despite living indoors.

"See?" His breath threatened to make Beckestone turn away in disgust. It was that bad.

Riggy Bodd waved his four digits in front of Beckestone's face. "It's a vee, an' a dub-yah. Just like on his car. My dad used to call 'em sauerkraut grinders. I ask him, 'When you gonna get rid o' that sauerkraut grinder?'" Riggy laughed at his own joke.

Beckestone thanked Riggy and gave him a couple of bucks, for a tip. Walking away, he realized that other than the conversation, he had tipped him for nothing. He didn't even buy a paper. Riggy Bodd made out again.

Detective Beckestone had a lead, a slim one but a real one. He looked at his watch. It was three-thirty. There was still time to get over to the department store before the offices closed for the evening. With his intensely constrained timetable, waiting until tomorrow was not an option. If someone at Vander & Beste's personnel office went home a little late, it would just have to be that way.

***

That evening, Detective Beckestone wrote an interim investigation report. It detailed his activity for the day and cited the name that his investigation had led to: Cary Lang.

The next day of his self-directed search for the person reporting crimes in highly unusual detail would continue with an interview with Mr. Lang. Benji Beckestone could only guess at what it might all eventually lead to.

TWENTY-ONE

While Walker was a student, the landlord was generous about collecting the rent. He really liked having a member of the armed forces in one of his apartments. He said it helped keep the place quieter than normal. The Army paychecks came once a month, ten days after the rent was due. The landlord always let it slide.

He was no longer a student. He was compelled to move. The landlord said he received government grant money for renting to students. He would lose the grant if anyone other than students or members of his family lived in the building.

The month of looking for another small apartment and moving really cut into his mustering out money. The Army only had an extra month's pay for him at separation. Without having gone overseas, or to Viet Nam, he had none of the "points" that got so much extra money for soldiers mustering out of the Army.

He knew to use the university library for reading want-ads in the newspaper. Every day, he would go in at opening and get a copy from the counter. He always had a notebook to write information about job listings in.

Weeks after the start of a new semester, he saw an ad for a manager position that interested him. He went to the address in the ad and applied. Apparently, there was no stampede of people for the position. The store manager took a quick look at the application and told Walker to come in that evening. The job turned out to be night produce manager for a twenty-four-hour grocery. The job consisted of managing the produce, not other workers.

The store was a big supermarket-size operation, but an independent, not part of a chain. It's late night hours were a way of competing with the chain stores that closed up every evening. It served the inner city, the downtown area and part of the area around the university. The location of the store would allow Walker to walk to work, if he thought the weather would be tolerable.

Going in to work at eleven, Walker had the responsibility of setting up the next day's displays. It was all very self-explanatory. The first night orientation took all of thirty minutes. In addition to restocking shelves, the job called for setting up new displays as they came in, for the produce department and the rest of the store.

Hopper's Grocery only had four people on the night shift. The other three people were a store manager, a cashier, and a clean-up man. The first night of work was a new experience for Walker. He went about his work, occasionally seeing people in various states of dress come into the store, buy an item or two, and leave. He had never seen people grocery shopping in their pajamas before.

Most nights at the grocery store, Poika helped out with the clean-up work. If his set-ups were done, he used his extra time to make sure that the store was as ready for the next day's business. The atmosphere among the night staff was very relaxed and flexible. If the cashier needed an extra break, Poika would cover it until she came back. The first couple of months went by very quickly.

He took advantage of his walks to work. It was an opportunity to scout and to hunt. He looked for places that were frequented by the college crowd. He included those locations in his set of regular routes taken to work. Every night when he arrived at work he would make mental notes of the key observations he made. He considered paper notes but realized how revealing they could be and kept his notations in his head.

Walker also searched out likely intercept points along with escape routes. As time went by, he became very judgmental about his performance in his first kill. He figured that dumb luck let him get away with his first crime. The "take" point was his best effort. The lights were all far away from where he grabbed the girl and incapacitated her. The partly inhabited inner-city street was also good.

Beyond that, Walker realized that he hadn't planned adequately for his first victim. He now knew that he would need to have plastic sheeting in his trunk, in case the target was injured and bleeding. He also reconsidered his choice of strangulation weapon. He had used his own wool scarf to wring the life out of his victim. He knew such fabrics were easily matched. In the future, he would only use synthetic cloth, purchased from a mass distributor.

The combination of steady work and the chance to expand his avocational horizons gave Walker a sense of completeness. It was all he wanted out of life thus far. Walking home from work in the mornings gave him a new perspective on things he saw at night. He knew that the weather would change. Pittsburgh would live up to its reputation. The weather would get crappy. He would be forced to drive his car.

Two and a half months into the job, things changed. The grocery store was robbed one evening before Poika went to work. Driving into the parking lot, he saw all the flashing red lights of the police cars. He decided to drive because the forecast was for rain, possibly snow before morning. The entrance to the store was blocked by a police officer who lifted a yellow plastic barrier tape to let other police personnel in and out.

The night manager was already there, waiting in front of the store. The cashier was there as well. She was crying into the night manager's shirt. The manager explained that three people had been killed in the store, during the robbery. Two of the victims were customers. The other was one of the hold-up men. The obviously upset night manager could give no other details about what had happened. The fate of the other robber was known only to the police.

Poika stood there, waiting to enter the store. He watched as the police detectives went about their business. They seemed bent on photographing every inch of not just the crime scene, but the whole store. One of them stooped low and picked up some debris near a drying pool of blood. He was wearing rubber gloves.

Poika had never seen anything like that before. He realized that he was fascinated with the investigative goings-on. His view of the proceedings was through a narrow path between the display items in the front of the store and the managers kiosk, at the end of the line of cashiers' stations. Only part of what was happening was visible at any one time. The peek-a-boo nature of what he was able to see only heightened his interest.

About two-thirty in the morning, the night shift crew was let into the store. Without being told, the three workers set about cleaning up the mess left by the robbers. The manager went to his kiosk and disappeared. What his night's work would entail was a daunting mystery to anyone who thought of it.

Walker took over cleaning up the largest of the blood pools. He filled and emptied his bucket eight times before the area was clean. The blood-spattered merchandise all went into a bag so that the staff could take what they wanted. None of the rest of it would leave the store, other than in the trash. Wiping down the shelves took two more buckets of soapy water.

The mopping and cleaning took so much of his night that he rushed through the set-up work. Having only four and a half hours to complete a full shift of work was difficult. He was confident that the areas he was responsible for were clean. He left it to the day shift to finish set-ups. He hoped they were as interested in making the store operations seem normal. If they suffered a bit of pique at not having everything in perfect order, so be it.

By six in the morning, he was able to knock out about ninety percent of the set-up for the morning shift. The night manager came around and had everyone join him for a few minutes in the break room. He invited everyone to sit down. He thanked them each individually for the hard work cleaning up the store for the new day's business. He said that if the store could afford it, they would all get bonuses for "hanging in there."

Walker went home that morning wondering about the violent death that had stalked into the midst of the calm, quiet, ordinary business of the grocery store. He thought about how intriguing the work of the detectives was. Several parts of him were astir with – he didn't know what. The hate inside of him cried out to know more about the killing. The curious part of his mind wanted to know more about how the detectives did their work.

***

The night was his best friend. The cold darkness of November actually felt good. The moon was down. He didn't know if it was set already, or unrisen. It didn't matter. The vapor of his own breath, disappearing inches in front of him, somehow reassured him. The girl would be walking by any minute, now.

Walker had seen the girl the night after the killings at the grocery store. If hate could be happy, his was overjoyed. It had seethed and burned within him the day after the botched robbery. His sleep was hard in coming, despite his being overly tired from all the extra work.

The girl was a university co-ed. Not quite as petite as the first target, she would still be able to put up only feeble resistance to a blitz-attack, from behind. It became obvious, in short order, that she took the same route from wherever she spent her evening hours, to her apartment.

The "take" location was near her apartment building. The location was more than a mile from where he lived; more than three miles from where he worked. The street was typically empty at the time when the girl usually passed. Late in the evening, lights in the windows, up and down the street, were beginning to go out.

For this occasion, the parking place he was forced to use was a little farther away from where he would incapacitate the target. The extra bit of exposure, to potential observation, was a risk that he had considered at great length. Without giving in to his need for another kill, he weighed the risk. Being ruthlessly honest with himself, he decided that some risk would accompany every one of his "operations."

He continually scanned the sidewalks on both sides, in both directions. His view was wide enough to encompass the windows nearby. Right on time, the young woman approached. He waited in a dark doorway. The clip-clop of her hard-soled shoes told exactly where she was.

Controlling his breathing as she passed, Poika launched himself at her back. Left arm quickly wrapping around her neck, right hand over her mouth, he brought her down in three seconds. As he lowered her to the pavement. The last flicker of consciousness left her eyes.

The trunk lid of his car was unlatched but resting on the lip of the opening. He got the girl into the trunk and quickly bound and gagged her. A last glance around, as he got behind the wheel, revealed no sign of any other person on the street, or in a window. He drove away.

Silent Sight

The location for the second part of his murderous activities involved a bit of genius as well as luck. The abandoned warehouse was less than two miles from where he captured and incapacitated the young woman. Having to drive only a short distance, with the girl in the trunk, lessened his exposure to discovery.

Walker turned off his headlights for the last block. He could see well enough without them. He pulled into the warehouse and parked in a particularly dark corner. Beneath the roof of the building, even the wan starlight of the cold, December night was blotted out.

The gigantic building was so torn apart that even the bums moved out. There was apparently enough structure remaining to hold up the roof, but that was all. The walls and windows played a woodwind symphony, the noise covering the sounds he made. The cold wind whistled and moaned, passing through small openings and large.

He sat and waited for his eyes to adjust to the darkest of shadows. A tiny movement of the car and a small muffled sound broke the spell of the welcoming gloom and stirred him to action. He hadn't anticipated that the target would awaken so quickly. The other girl – his only frame of reference – had taken much longer to rouse from the sleeper hold that he used on her.

Walker quickly went to the rear of the car and opened the trunk. At the sight of him, the girl screamed into her mouth gag. The sound blended perfectly with the rising and falling howls of the wind. She kicked and struggled as he lifted her out of the trunk. She struck her head against the metal lip of the trunk opening, creating a bloody gash.

The excitement of the struggle and the sight of the blood fed his strength. Kneeling down, one knee on top of the girl, he drew the synthetic fiber scarf from his pocket. He made two quick turns around her neck. He looked into her eyes. The eyes that looked back were the laughing eyes of Katie Spahl, not the tear-filled, terrified eyes that were actually there. He turned the scarf, knotting it against her throat. He turned it harder.

The girl kicked and scraped her shoes against the concrete floor of the building. The pressure of the garrote, and her thrashing caused her head to bleed profusely. He scooted away from her to avoid being bled on. She tried to throw her body from side to side, weakening with every movement.

The end came swiftly, her vain efforts at battling her attacker used up far more oxygen than simply letting him throttle the life out of her. The last tiny glimmer of life drained from her eyes. Poika held the scarf tightly for at least a minute longer. The girl had surprised him once, awakening far too soon. He would make sure she was dead.

The tension within him eased. Walker looked around, blinking, as though awakening from sleep. The hate had taken nearly full control of him during the murder. He remembered seeing Katie Spahl's laughing eyes in the face of his most recent victim. The thought of it confused him. No such apparition had accompanied the first kill. Worry tugged at the edges of his mind.

Even in the deep gloom of the warehouse corner, he could see the gash in the girl's head. He removed the scarf from around her neck and went to his car. The lip of the trunk opening was smeared with blood from the girl's head. He used the scarf to wipe the blood away.

He took an empty coffee can from within the trunk and stuffed the scarf into it. Walking to the narrowest part of the building's corner, he lit the scarf with a lighter. The synthetic material burned quickly. He shielded the light of the fire with his body. The rising smoke was acrid and stung his eyes.

After half of a minute, the fire was out, nothing but ashes filled the can. He turned and tossed the ashes into the wind. The wind still sung its late Autumn lamentations, now a dirge for the recently deceased. The ashes scattered upward and outward, spreading over the floor of the empty space; becoming just so much more dirt and dust.

***

Walker had departed the scene of his murder without so much as a glance back at his victim. It was a done thing; something in the past. Fully composed, after the excitement of the kill, he drove home. He had that feeling again. It was existential pleasure, the pleasure he derived from becoming what he was: a stalker, a taker of lives.

Earlier in the day, he knew where he was heading, and what he intended to do. The rising anticipation of the coming kill led him to forget a few simple things at home. He checked himself and reminded himself to not let that happen again.

The door to his apartment was unlocked. He had neglected to pick up his mail. They weren't big things. They were out of the ordinary, enough to demonstrate that he had been in a different state of mind that day. What a small fact such as that could lead to was anybody's guess. He knew it would be better, in preparation for a kill, to never let even the slightest thing seem to be out of order. This thinking, driven solely by the hate inside of him, seemed as ordinary as whether the milk was likely to be spoiled, or not.

He tossed the pile of mail onto his dinette table. One letter caught his eye. The letter was very official looking. The addressee was his full name; first, middle and last. The sender was even more impressive: United States Department of Justice. Below that was: Federal Bureau of Investigation.

TWENTY-TWO

Detective Benjamin Beckestone sat across from Lieutenant Dukasko. As he had promised, he turned his reports in on time. "So, Detective, now that you're fairly sure who it was that made at least one of the phone calls, what's next?"

Beckestone shifted around in his seat, trying not to look nervous. The Lieutenant's summons to his office surprised him. It put him off balance. The Lieutenant had never taken so much interest in him before. "I'm going to treat him like a source – a confidential informant. He hasn't committed any crime, so being confrontational and accusatory might ruin a potentially beneficial relationship."

Dukasko thought, *If he had said "fruitful", I'd have already thrown him out of my office*. Beckestone missed quoting the basic criminal psychology lecture by one word.

172

He decided to give the lower grade detective a little more rope.

"You've used up a lot of time on this, uh – investigation. If all you're going to get from four days' work is an informant, I'm going to have some explaining to do to the Captain." He eyed Beckestone carefully.

Now Benji was nervous. Mention of involving the Captain made this whole thing much more serious. The Lieutenant might as well have said God. In the Department, Captains were really only subordinate to the Chief himself. All of the intervening ranks were middle management, with esoteric responsibilities.

Beckestone decided that if he was out on a limb, he might as well go for it. "Lieutenant, I've got a feeling about this. The whole thing is strange. I'd be willing to bet that Cary Lang made both of these calls and is somehow a lot more wired in to these situations – these crimes – than the average informant. The really striking feature is that he made the calls with no hope of reward, like our usual stoolies. That means he's a citizen, an upstanding guy. At least I hope so."

Dukasko chewed on his cigar a bit and blinked. He was disused to spending so much time talking to his detectives. He was not at all accustomed to listening to a Second Grade Detective for such a long time. "Wrap this up, Beckestone. You're in danger of not pullin' your weight around here. I don't need to tell you that another less-than-glowing performance review will send you back to uniform duty."

There it was. Beckestone knew he was against a wall. The Lieutenant had just spelled it out for him. He managed to do it without actually sounding threatening but the devastating results of poor performance were there to do all the threatening for him. He left the Lieutenant's office trying desperately to not look like he was leaving with his metaphorical tail between his legs but that's exactly where it was.

***

"It was basic investigative leg work that led me to you. It took a lot of talking to people to finally get a line on you." Beckestone was trying to be as forthcoming with Cary Lang as he could afford to be. He needed to get Cary 'on his side.' They were in Cary's apartment, Lennie was due home in a couple of hours.

"What I don't understand is: How did you come to be in possession of such detailed knowledge about the crime – the crimes – that you reported?" he had kept the interrogation – the interview – as matter-of-fact as possible. Whatever he did, he had to avoid turning this potential source off, at least until he found out how he got his information.

Cary looked at Beckestone. The detective was a head shorter than he and not very well dressed, for someone supposed to be a professional. He understood that the detective was trying to make a friend, or at least a non-enemy of Cary.

In that moment, Cary realized that he could count the number of his friends on one hand. They were old schoolmates who could be counted on to help with an apartment move, but he really didn't spend time with them. If Detective Beckestone wanted him as a friend, that was alright with him.

174

"This is really gonna sound strange…" Cary explained in detail how he had come to be able to see people's auras – auras which represented their emotional states. He pointed out how solid barriers did not interrupt the sight of the auras and that distance was only a small impediment to picking up detail.

He finished his explanation by sharing the "silent movie" experience of watching people go through their everyday activities – and their not-everyday ones as well. He explained as much as he could about what he had viewed during the Sharon Manning murder, and the upstairs burglary.

Cary tried to convey how much of what he witnessed was interpreted from really only seeing pantomimes. He explained that making sense of the emotional content made a huge difference in how well he could interpret things.

Cary went to the length of staging a demonstration. He had Beckestone hold up fingers while standing behind a wall, in the bathroom. No matter what combination he came up with, Cary gave the correct count. He then told the detective about reading his emotional state during the demonstration.

When it was all done, Detective Beckestone could only say, "Wow." He rubbed his head, trying to incorporate this body of strange new knowledge into his mind. He looked incredulously at Cary. "You can really do this?"

"Yes."

***

The next day, Beckestone tracked Cary down, in the break room for employees at Vander & Beste. He spoke with Cary only briefly, suggesting that he could help with an investigation. It had been under way for some time but was stalled by the lack of credible witness information.

Cary agreed to help. Beckestone offered to pick him up that night at his apartment at eleven o'clock. Cary came up with a story about problems at the store to keep Lennie from asking too many questions. He really did not like being untruthful with her. He didn't have a better plan.

When the appointed hour arrived, so did Beckestone, in a Dodge Polara sedan that looked like it had seen better days. The car's maroon paint was worn through to the metal in several places. Some of the chrome trim was missing.

One of the car's wheel covers was missing, completing the mournful presentation. In stark contrast to all the wear, the tires all looked as though they were brand new.

Cary opened the back door for Wheels to get in, closed it and got in the front seat. He noticed the car idled very roughly, as though the engine was misfiring. The exhaust system didn't seem to be doing its job very well. The rumble and thrum of the muffler sounded like thunder.

"You're bringin' a dog?" Beckestone looked around at Wheels and back at Cary.

"If Wheels can't go, I don't want to." Cary tried to look at Detective Beckestone evenly, but a small smirk turned up the corners of his mouth, spoiling the moment. As he landed on the front seat, Cary noticed that the car had a stick shift. He thought that was unusual for a four-door.

"Alright, let's just get goin'." He put the old beater in gear and they headed off. The noise from the exhaust system probably woke half the people on the block. Cary hoped they made it out of the neighborhood before the entire city was alerted to their passing.

Benji Beckestone was straight. He was straight enough to be largely unaware when non-straights were around. Being aware of this about himself, he asked Cary, "Look don't get me wrong. I don't have anything against anyone for what they like, but you're always dressed like a department store mannequin." He paused before asking, "Are you one o' them?"

Cary was confused by Beckestone's roundabout way of asking whatever the hell he was asking. Finally, it dawned on him what the point of the whole circumlocution had been.

"Oh, hell no." He kind of chuckled. "The mannequin thing isn't far off, though. I'm a buyer and I get major discounts on all the best clothing lines. A lot of times, companies send me clothes just so I can see their quality. Mostly, they manage to send things that fit perfectly, that's just fine."

After a fifteen-minute drive they were in an area of town, west of downtown, that was home to blocks and blocks of warehouse buildings. The five-, to seven-story brick edifices dominated the streets around them. During the day, little direct sunlight made its way to the pavement. At night, it seemed as though the world was made of brick.

Beckestone parked a car-length back from a corner. The absence of the car's thundering exhaust note was like the end of a headache to Cary. The parking place allowed them to see the side and vehicle entrance to one of the warehouses. When he turned the motor of the car off, Wheels whined, eager to get out and go.

Cary reached back and stroked him. "Not now, buddy." Beckestone quietly fumed about having the animal in the car in the first place. They waited.

Cary couldn't resist asking, "What are we waiting for?"

Beckestone pointed to the building in front of them. "Just exactly what, I'm not sure. The man that runs a business out of that warehouse has been investigated for years for everything from drug running to gambling and prostitution. No one has ever been able to get any evidence on him."

Beckestone looked around at Wheels in the back seat and frowned. "We're here to see whatever we can." He thought for a moment. "We're here so you can see whatever you can."

At just after one in the morning, a van approached from the far end of the block. It was one of those ubiquitous, supposedly commercial, panel vans. The only windows were the windshield and the windows in the driver's and passenger doors. The only markings on the vehicle were the state-required minimums. As it neared the rolling steel door entry, the heavy metal door began to rise. The van turned and began to enter the building.

"There are seven or eight people in that van." Cary sat with his eyes closed. Beckestone watched Cary, sitting there, with his eyes shut. He was appalled and thrilled at the same time. Being able to report on the number of people in a closed van was weird – really weird.

The van disappeared into the building. The rolling steel door closed. Cary began a long narration of what he was viewing. "The people are getting out of the van. It looks like four – no, five of the people have their hands behind their backs. The three other people are escorting them. Two of the captive people are women, all of the other people from the van are men."

Cary opened his eyes. Detective Beckestone sat there with his mouth hanging open. "Something bad is going to happen, isn't it?"

"Keep viewing, or sighting, or whatever it is you call it." Beckestone stared at the blank brick walls of the building, almost as though he could see through them, himself.

Cary fixed his attention on the warehouse building again. "The eight people from the van are walking up a stairway. They're all very scared – terrified." He could see the auras of the apparent captives, stark white with fear.

The three 'escorts' are all holding their right hands upward. They seem to be angry. Yeah, angry, and scared too."

"Pistols." Beckestone filled in a detail that Cary, in his naiveite, wouldn't get.

Without opening his eyes, Cary nodded. His heart was sinking. He wasn't sure he wanted to be any sort of witness to more violence and crime. He thought that this little adventure was something he agreed to out of fear of – he didn't know what. His respect for authority was a strong part of his character. It had steered him in this direction. He began to question the whole thrust of it in his life.

Beckestone realized that Cary had become lost in thought. His eyes were open, staring blankly ahead. He nudged Cary with his elbow. "What's happening now?"

Cary closed his eyes and focused on the second floor of the warehouse. Even from the low angle, he could make out quite a lot about what was going on.

"The people with their hands behind them are all kneeling down. There's another person, a man. He's really angry." Cary could see the angry man's aura. It was deep crimson, shifting over to oxblood. The edge of the aura was such a dark red that it appeared black. The black edge crept toward the center of the red taking over more and more of it.

"The angry man is stalking back and forth, in front of the kneeling people. He is yelling at them. The more he yells the angrier he gets. He keeps making these wild movements – gestures, with his hands. None of the kneeling people are looking up at him, just down at the floor."

Cary was getting a very bad feeling about what was going to happen next. His mouth was way past merely being dry. He feared for the people he was viewing, honestly, deeply, feared for them.

"The three men with pistols are getting the kneeling people up." After a minute, "They're all going down the stairway again. Wait. They're going down again, to a lower level."

The main floor of the warehouse was a half-story above the sidewalk outside. The lower level was a ground-level floor. The nine people remained within Cary's line of sight of their auras. Instead of a view from below, it was a view from a higher vantage point.

"They're walking toward the back; their auras are getting smaller." Cary tried to lick his lips. Nothing. His mouth was so dry that it was becoming hard to speak.

"Now the five people are kneeling again." The angry man's aura was now almost completely black.

"The angry man is walking around behind them. Oh!" He watched as the aural silhouette of one of the kneeling people toppled forward with a sharp initial jerk. The intensity of the white aura faded. It disappeared.

"I think he killed one of the... Oh!" Cary reeled from the violence, squirmed in his seat. "He killed another – and..." Cary winced and twitched three more times.

A minute passed before Cary could say another word. "All five of the kneeling people's auras are gone. I think that means he killed them. The angry man killed them. Shot them. They're gone. Dead."

Cary silently began to cry. He had never expected to be any sort of part or witness to anything like what he had just seen. It was too much.

TWENTY-THREE

Beckestone realized that Cary was losing it. He put his hand on the clothing buyer's arm and said, "Just watch for a little longer."

Cary managed to get a little bit of a grip on himself. "The angry man is going back upstairs. The three other men are lifting things, putting them into something else."

"Bodies. They're moving the bodies." Detective Beckestone knew that the thing that the bodies were put into was, no doubt, another truck. He turned to Cary. "Look, I'm gonna have to let you out, but not here. Just wait a minute."

Cary was confused. He had no expectation of being stranded in this part of town after midnight, by a cop, no less.

Benji Beckestone figured that what he had just said was like a slap in the face, to a gentle soul like Cary Lang. "It's just that you can't be here, or with me, when I call this in. There would be way too much explaining to do. For both of us."

Just then, the rolling steel door of the warehouse started going up. A low, stake-bed truck, with five barrels on it, exited the building. It turned and headed away from where the Dodge was parked. The truck was headed west on Locust Street.

Cary said, "There are only two people in that truck."

Beckestone started the engine of the car. The sudden thrum of the loud exhaust startled Cary. Beckestone shouted over the noise of the car's engine. "There's a quickie-mart a block over. You can use the payphone there to call a cab!" He put the car in gear and accelerated away from the curb.

The Dodge Polara made the corner of the next intersection at about forty-five miles per hour. Cary thought that the old car had covered the quarter-mile block length in about a nanosecond. He had been pushed back in the seat by the enormous g-force, as though by a giant hand. Wheels was laying down on the back seat, trying to be as flat as he could. As the car screeched to a stop, he stared in wonder at Beckestone.

"Hemi. 426. Time for you to go. Don't forget your dog." He revved the engine for emphasis. Cary piled out of the old Polara and opened the back door for Wheels to hop out. The dog's tail was just clear of the door, when Beckestone stood on the accelerator.

The old sedan spun one hundred, eighty degrees, and shot down the street like a bullet, in the same direction that the flat-bed had gone. Cary had no doubt that Detective Beckestone would catch up with the truck. He could obviously run down anything with wheels. He could probably outrun more than a few aircraft. Sheesh.

***

True to his nature, Wheels stood at Cary's side while Detective Beckestone disappeared into the night. He finally whined a bit to let Cary know that he needed to go. Cary snapped on his leash and found a spot for him. The two walked the hundred yards farther down the block to the Majik Markit. A pay phone hung outside, under the awning, over the entrance to the store. Cary hoped that it worked – and that nothing disgusting had been done to it.

The one redeeming quality about being left in mid-town, this late at night, was that cabs came quickly. Without hesitating, Cary let Wheels jump in the cab, ahead of himself. As the cabbie turned to protest the dog in his cab, fishing for a bigger tip, the sound of sirens, from every direction, filled the night.

"Dang! What's that all about?" The cab driver stared at Cary.

"I do not know." Cary effectively put finality in his voice.

"Where to?" The cab driver had forgotten all about jackin' the tip for the dog's ride.

***

"Detective four-eight-five, detective four-eight-five. Officer needs assistance. In pursuit of flat-bed truck! Multiple homicides. Repeat, multiple homicides!" Beckestone yelled into the radio microphone, over the roar of the huge engine, and the cut-out exhaust. The sight and sound of an old Dodge, blasting down Washington avenue at more than a hundred miles an hour was enough to wake every bum for miles around.

Beckestone had a dashboard fireball up, but it really was just for show. By the time anyone realized that the old Dodge was a police car, he'd be long past. He caught up with the truck on Jefferson Avenue, just after making a turn to the north.

Detective Beckestone intended to pass the flat-bed and turn into its path, blocking it. What he managed was to flash past the truck going so fast that when he got into the turn, the car spun one hundred, eighty degrees and stopped directly in front of the flat-bed.

The truck driver was so startled by the sudden appearance of the car in front of him that he had to slam on his brakes to keep from hitting the Dodge. By the time the truck came to a full stop, Beckestone was already out of his car, behind the driver's door, pointing his service revolver at the cab of the truck. The flash of the red fireball, on the dash of the old sedan, momentarily hypnotized the two men in the cab of the truck.

Police academy training kicked in as it never had before. Beckestone controlled his breathing. He kept his eyes centered on the middle of the truck's windshield, sensitive to any movements the two men inside made.

"Police! Hands where I can see 'em! Now!" His voice was rock steady. His aim was steadily fixed on the center of the windshield. He knew he could get off four or five rounds before either of the two men could bring a weapon to bear on him.

The two men in the truck were surprised by the cop's appearance. They had been expecting a simple delivery run. Now they were staring down the barrel of a gun. Neither of them moved.

"Hands! Now!"

Slowly, the two men raised their hands. The sound of sirens – a lot of sirens – was growing in the distance. Beckestone waited. He had to do something before one of these guys got nervous and did something stupid. He cleared the Dodge's door and headed for the passenger side of the flat-bed truck, keeping his eyes, and his aim, on the occupants the whole time.

Beckestone looked at the passenger. "You! Right hand only! Open the door!"

The passenger did as he was told. The door swung open. "Hands!"

The passenger's right hand shot up. Beckestone stepped back. "You. Out of the truck!"

The passenger started to swing out of the truck. Beckestone shifted his gaze to the driver, who sat frozen, hands in the air. "Down on the ground! Hands behind your head! Cross your ankles!"

The passenger did as he was instructed. Beckestone now had him in his field of view, as well as the driver. "Okay, now you! Slide over this way!"

The driver did as he was told. He turned in his seat and started to slide across the seat toward the passenger side. As he let his foot off of the brake, the truck suddenly lurched forward. It banged into the front end of the old Dodge.

It was enough distraction that the driver thought he could reach a pistol in the open dash tray. He brought the weapon up to aim at Beckestone.

Bang-Bang-Bang! Beckestone pumped three shots into him. The intervening distance was only twenty feet, his aim was true enough to put all three slugs into the driver's chest. The driver's hand loosened on the pistol; it fell from his hand. The light of life was gone from the man's eyes.

The driver's pistol clattered out of the cab of the truck and slid across the pavement. It came to rest within inches of the truck's passenger who eyed it intently. The dead driver slumped over and crumpled onto the floor of the truck's cab.

"You wanna pick that up?" Beckestone's breathing had become heavy. He drew in a deep breath. He had his pistol aimed between the eyes of the man on the ground. He turned his head away from where the pistol lay. Beckestone remembered that he needed to have his badge out in plain sight. He withdrew it from his vest pocket of his coat and hung it from the breast pocket.

The sirens that had begun in the distance and grown louder, now cut off. Multiple police cars converged on the intersection. Detective Benji Beckestone let out a huge sigh of relief. Within minutes no fewer than fourteen police cars occupied the intersection. The flash of so many red lights gave everyone headaches, but department rules said that they had to be on.

Beckestone quickly spoke with the area commander, who sent a couple of units to the address on 17th Street where the murders had taken place. He reminded the commander who it was at that address. The commander looked at him incredulously.

The investigation of an officer-involved shooting took well into the next morning. Traffic in that part of town was disrupted until the last of the police vehicles left the scene. The area around the murder scene was cordoned off. Days of investigation at that location would follow.

Detective Beckestone knew he would be spending the rest of the day writing reports. Missing a night's sleep for a career-boosting coup, such as the one he just pulled off, was small price to pay for the product. He was exhausted but knew he had probably saved his future as a detective from ruin.

The real trouble would start the next day. He would have to interview with the Lieutenant. If that didn't go well, he would be talking to the Captain. He did not want to talk to the Captain. Captains made big decisions – like "You're fired!" decisions. Beckestone wanted nothing to do with any of that. He would make sure that his reports, and his interview with the Lieutenant were good enough.

TWENTY-FOUR

Indianapolis was so boring that it was interesting. Nothing could have prepared Walker for the interstate theft and bank-robbery detail of his first assignment. Always arriving after the excitement was over, the FBI was resented by nearly everyone. The big newspaper headlines always went to the Bureau.

Being thoroughly disliked and even hated by the people he was made to work with suited him just fine. There was enough hate to go around. Inside of him, there was enough hate for the whole world. Most of the theft cases were little more than daylight burglaries carried out with no show of force or threat. They blended together well with the amazingly humdrum investigations of robberies of banks that were little more than "Mom and Pop" operations.

The National Academy, as it was officially known, had been a revelation. The types of people let in to be FBI agents were a surprising assortment of lawyers, accountants, and former local lawmen. He was a notable exception, a candidate accepted as a human experiment in broadening the Bureau's applicant pool. The FBI had been given a vastly broadened charter to increase its efforts in areas such as counter-espionage. It needed a lot more people. The tortured and teased boy from Terre Haute was one of those people.

Knowing that he might be more poorly prepared, he tried harder. He memorized the content of everything he was given to read. His notes, from lectures, read like dictation. His grades reflected his effort. One of hundreds of new agents graduated by the Academy every year, he finished at the top of his class.

Field training exercises were something that his Army training prepared him well for. He excelled in everything thrown at him. The firearms courses were mere reminiscences for him. He performed better than any other trainee on the target ranges. Just as it had been in the Army, the hate inside of him perfected his aim and sharpened his reflexes.

All of his glowing achievements in the Academy came to nothing when his lack of any political connections sent him to his first posting in Indiana. The ways of the Bureau were revealing themselves to him, one sad fact after another. Unless he outshined his contemporaries, he was just another agent, a body, doing the bidding of the masters, in Washington.

At first, the frightening aspect of being so close to Terre Haute gnawed at his mind like a rat, chewing its way through a wall to get at some food. The thought of his hometown was couched in painful, shrieking memories. His mind and soul roiled. He fought to keep himself calm; to think of other things. He began to feel the need to kill again, rising in the back of his mind. It slithered like a serpent, from the black depths of his all-consuming hate.

Terre Haute was a place he hoped to never see again. He knew that if someone robbed one of the tin-box banks there, he would be assigned to investigate. The out-of-the-ordinary cases such as kidnappings would be given to more experienced agents.

His partner in his first posting was, predictably, a long-time veteran of the Bureau. Tom Breeden was a survivor. He was a man who knew that the policies of the Bureau changed. They blew back and forth with the winds of political change. His experience taught that it was foolish to latch onto one viewpoint of the Bureau, thinking that it would persist.

Breeden had twenty-five years of experience in the Bureau. Joining just after the war, he became part of the buzz saw of the House Un-American Activities Committee. The persistent witch-hunt investigations and prosecutions ruined more lives than he cared to remember. It was all part of being an FBI agent and doing what he was told. He considered his attitude toward the latter as enlightened, in view of everything he learned from the Nuremburg trials of the preceding decade.

One of the first lessons for a new agent was that if you were not working furiously at your desk, typing or writing reports, you were expected to be out in the field, working on your assigned case. Breeden and his new charge spent a lot of time in coffee shops that were not near the office. They always sat near the back, away from windows where they could be seen from the street. After a short period of time, it became evident from the comments of the waitresses that Tom Breeden had been the mentor for more than one new agent.

The first half-dozen investigations were all relatively straightforward. Over an eighteen-month period, there were robberies of six small banks in southern Indiana. Three were carried out by a notably brazen man-and-woman pair who modeled themselves after Bonnie and Clyde. The three robberies were all carried out with a number of smart-aleck remarks, intended to demonstrate a devil-may-care attitude towards authority.

The robberies carried out by the mouthy duo featured the firing of weapons. No one was ever injured in the heists. The gunfire was an intimidation tactic only. It gave a clue that the man and woman were not truly violent. Their judicious aim with their weapons contrasted with the fact that they were young.

A brief investigation, after their third robbery, followed a mile-wide trail to a small country motel. The pair were cornered by Breeden, his young partner and several local sheriff's officers. The young couple surrendered with no smart-mouth at all.

***

As he began to get into the rhythm of his work, the other shoe dropped. A kidnap case came in from Terre Haute. His Special agent knew he was from there and assigned him and Tom Breeden to the case. Breeden had enough experience to handle a kidnap and the new agent needed the exposure. The two set off for Terre Haute with only short notice.

It was normal to leave quickly for a kidnap case. Time worked against the investigating team. Both agents brought their ready-bags: a change of clothes and several pairs of socks and underwear. The drive to Terre Haute took only a couple of hours. They checked in with the Terre Haute Police Department as soon as they arrived.

The local detectives had already been working from an advantageous point. The kidnap victim was a child, reported missing the day before. The parents contacted the police as soon as they were contacted by the kidnappers. The criminals made the mistake of using a telephone to call their victims with a demand for ransom.

The victims were a wealthy couple. The husband was president of a bank, the kidnapped child was an only son, seven years old. As difficult as it was to tell their story a second time, the frantic couple went through their entire experience for the benefit of the two FBI agents. Interviewing the victims was rote policy for the Bureau, even though in this case, it would turn out to be unnecessary.

The ransom call information was, like all phone calls, listed by the telephone company. A standing local, federal court order, covering kidnap cases, gave the Bureau access to the information with only a telephone call to the local office. It was just one of the ways in which the Bureau was able to move much more swiftly than local law enforcement. The ransom call originated from an exchange in Vincennes, Indiana, two hours south of Terre Haute.

A couple more telephone calls had the Vincennes police alerted and sent to the area where the ransom call originated. Instructions were given to not approach the location without the FBI present. Tom Breeden and his protégé set off on the road again, Terre Haute detectives trailing behind.

They were met in Vincennes by the Chief of Police. He began to give an explanation of their situation before Tom Breeden cut him off. "Just get us out there. Ride with us." Doing as he was instructed the Vincennes chief told another officer to bring his car. He got in the agents' car.

On the ride out of town, the police chief explained that the telephone call was made at a store, out on the road to Monroe City. The storekeeper told the investigating officers about the pair of squatters living on the abandoned Prusselle farm. The man had been the most recent user of the payphone at the store. The storekeeper had editorially included the comment that the "fool squatters didn't think people were smart enough to figure out where they were staying."

Three miles outside of Vincennes, on one of the numerous tree-lined roads, a ram-shackle farmhouse stood. It was a hundred feet back from the road that led past it. Within, a nervous man paced back and forth. His stained bib overalls were pale blue from being washed nearly to extinction. The tee shirt beneath the suspenders was even dirtier. The man appeared to not have bathed or washed within recent memory.

The dirty man paced the floor of the kitchen, pistol in hand. He peered out each of the windows of the farmhouse, toward the road, as he passed it. His step-stop-peek, step-stop-peek, traversing of the kitchen had caused his companion to flee to a back room of the house. She couldn't stand the constant movement. It only highlighted the tension of the present situation. With her was the boy. He was scared. So was she.

The room in which the woman waited with the boy was an unused storeroom. Empty shelves lined all four walls. They sat on the floor. The woman sat side-saddle on the dirty linoleum. The boy huddled in one corner, his knees drawn up in front of him. The room hadn't been used for anything in years. Its disuse preceded the farm's abandonment by only weeks.

The couple who now occupied the farmhouse were squatters, they thought that they had kept their presence from being known to anyone. They stopped here only long enough to use up their last few dollars-worth of food. When that was gone, the decision to do something about their pennilessness was made.

The dirty man told the woman to wait for his return. When he did return, it was with one hand on the steering wheel of the car, the other firmly gripping the shirt collar of the boy. The woman had never been part of anything like what they were doing now. She would not utter a word of protest. She would not make any kind of move that was not co-operative. Those sorts of behaviors had been beaten out of her.

At the limit of discovery from the farmhouse, the FBI waited. The Vincennes Police and the local sheriff's office were also present. There was no doubt who was in charge. Everyone looked to the FBI agents, specifically Tom Breeden for guidance.

The strategy for this arrest was going to be simplicity itself. The ransom demand was for the specified amount of money to be delivered to a location in a Vincennes park. When the kidnap party was separated, the authorities would move in on the location assumed to be where the boy was being held. Another group of police were in place to arrest whoever might appear to pick up the ransom money.

As if given a cue to do so, the car in front of the abandoned farmhouse drove off. Two minutes later, the two FBI agents, followed by the police moved on the house. Tom Breeden entered the house through the front door, followed by his young partner.

The farm house floor plan was unusual. The kitchen and living rooms sat opposite each other at the front, astride the entry. Once inside, the agents took a moment to let their eyes adjust to the diminished light. The place was a mess. Empty food packaging was everywhere. The agents crossed to the hallway that separated the front rooms of the house from the rear. Tom Breeden went to one side; his younger partner went to the other.

As Tom crossed into the opening of the door to the storeroom, a single shot rang out. Tom Breeden ducked low. The bullet went through the doorframe above his head. The clatter of a pistol striking the floor of the storeroom followed. Tom stepped into the room at a crouch. The woman, still side-saddle on the floor, was crying, the pistol next to her feet. Keeping aim at her head, Tom Breeden entered the room and kicked the pistol away from the crying woman. The boy still sat in the corner of the room, clutching his knees, tears streaming down his cheeks.

The arrests were both functionally unremarkable. The dirty man gave up with less of a fight than the woman. At the Vincennes police station, the FBI agents got their first close-up look at the man who had apparently hatched the kidnap plan all on his own.

Tom Breeden saw just another criminal, his younger partner stared at him for some time. The dirty man sat, eyes down, in an interrogation room. The one-way glass allowed for viewing from the other side surreptitiously. The dirty man occasionally looked up at his surroundings, then cast his eyes downward again.

It took a long time to get the Vincennes Police Department to get through the necessary paperwork. The two FBI agents were not able to return to Indianapolis until well after midnight. The federal paperwork would wait until the following day. Justice had been served.

***

Percy Hamble stepped out onto his front porch with the smug satisfaction of a man recently retired. Under his arm was the morning paper, the Terre Haute Morning Star. Sitting down to read, his morning cup of coffee awaited him on a table next to his chair. The large headlines on the paper's front page screamed about a kidnapping, solved by the FBI.

The articles went into tedious detail about how the arrests of the man and woman responsible for the kidnapping came about. The arrest photographs showed the two good-for-nothings with their names and prisoner numbers in front of them. The sidebar story about the FBI agents was expectedly short. It too was accompanied by a photograph of the agents.

Percy almost missed seeing the photo. He was ready for more coffee and set his paper down. Rising from his chair, he stopped and picked up the newspaper again. A close look at the FBI agents' photograph revealed what he suspected: He knew one of the agents.

The retired Court Probation Agent couldn't believe his eyes. There on the page before him was a picture of one of his former probationers. The violent little boy from across the railroad tracks. What was it that the other children teased him with? Oh, yes, they called him Poika.

Percival Clarkson Hamble drank his second cup of coffee that morning with the special knowledge that the Family Court system had evidently done its job most excellently. A youthful offender had been transformed into an agent of society. A positive contribution had been made to the world in general.

***

The whole thing had gone much more smoothly than he anticipated. His Academy training gave him all the information he needed to operate almost as though he didn't actually exist. The crime lab techniques were so advanced. The Academy instruction concentrated on the laboratory's limitations. There couldn't have been a more perfect learning scenario for someone like him. He marveled at how his previous kills went as well as they did. Now, knowing exactly what to avoid doing, prepared him for nearly perfect performance.

The great hatred in his mind leapt with joy at learning that he would need to be out of the office, more than in it. If he was not at his partner's side, that was incidental. It was easy to "assign" himself to look into some small detail, or lead on his own. The stalking and hunting progressed rapidly. Wherever he went, or whenever, it didn't matter if the local police intercepted him. He had the credentials to explain away anything he was doing.

He found his most recent target almost at once. The petite brunette worked an evening shift at a suburban clothing store. Her departure from the store put her at a remote bus stop, alone, at eleven o'clock. The take and kill had been almost anticlimactic to being able to commit the crime in a way that would leave no discernable traces of his presence.

The one troubling aspect of this kill was the appearance of Katie Spahl's face, on the face of his victim, as the light of life left her eyes. The young woman had been so accommodating, wearing a scarf of her own. He decided that the scarf must have been the trigger: It reminded him of the scarf around Katie's neck, on the night of the dance, so many years ago.

He shook his head at the thought of hallucinatory images interfering with his activities. He needed to do it. He wanted to do it. The next time he would need to be more aware of how he felt. He would try to not loose himself so completely in the moment of the kill.

TWENTY-FIVE

Cary's shirt was snug. It was a new experience for him. He never had one of the fine-fabric shirts from this manufacturer shrink. He pulled another one from the closet. Same thing. He stood in the darkened bedroom and thought for a moment. He could hear Lennie's soft, low, even breathing. He looked in her direction. She lay with her eyes closed, sound asleep. Her soft brown hair, due for a cut, was tussled over her forehead and one eye.

It took a moment for Cary to remember that he had been eating more than normal. The sex made him ravenously hungry. Even though he and Lennie had backed off of their multiple repetitions of lovemaking, they still made love daily, or nightly. They had almost every meal together. Even their poorly overlapping work schedules didn't interfere with that.

The more he thought about it, along with not missing a meal, there had been more pizza, and trips to the ice cream shop. Their lives for the last few weeks had become a continuous celebration, so joyously infatuated with each other they were. There was more wine, as well. Much more wine.

Cary figured he better get a grip and stop eating like there was no tomorrow. He swapped out a polo shirt that was new enough, and sharp enough to get away with as work apparel. He pressed a cup of coffee for himself and set a small pot to perk for Lennie. He liked doing small things like that for her.

With Wheels out for his morning walk, Cary said, "We'll spend a little extra time at the park today, buddy." Vigorous tail wagging indicated that Wheels thought that was a good idea. Returning to the flat as quietly as they could, they found Lennie still asleep.

The coffee had perked and Cary poured a half of a cup for the ride into work. It was about as much as he could manage driving a stick shift. He only took the extra coffee on mornings that he felt he needed a little boost. He had gotten in late last night. He was totally terrorized by what he had witnessed but emotional exhaustion led him to fall asleep quickly.

The ride into the downtown area was just the usual stop-and-go. Cary finished his coffee, parked his car, and headed in. About an hour and a half into a very routine morning, it hit him: A wave of combined grief and fear washed over him. It was as though he was back in the detective's car, watching the murders all over again.

Standing on his own two feet, in a stock room, Cary felt as though he was falling. The floor seemed to just fall away from his feet. The falling sensation quickly became whirling. He grabbed the edge of a shelf to steady himself. A cold sweat enveloped him. He could feel it soaking into his shirt and slacks.

Cary stopped what he was doing. He left the stock room and went to the employee break room. Cary was grateful that there was no one else there when he arrived. He poured a cup of coffee and sat at one of the melamine-topped tables. He looked out one of the windows.

***

Lennie walked into the break room at ten thirty. Cary was still there, staring at one of the dirty windows of the break room. The store was in one of those buildings that was so old that it seemed like the dirt encrusted upon every exterior surface somehow contributed to the building's ability to remain standing. The windows hadn't been washed in decades. The light that they allowed to pass through was so heavily filtered by the built-up layers of dirt that they seemed to be a greyish- brown milk glass.

Lennie put her hand on Cary's shoulder, breaking his reverie. He looked up at her. No words came from his mouth. His eyes were red and puffy. The tracks of tears were dried on his face. Lennie sat down next to him. "Jennine said I would find you here. She said you've been in here for a long time, just staring at the window."

Lennie was aware of Cary's leaving the night before being predicated on a very flimsy story about some problem at the store. She was overly tired from work and drank just one too many glasses of wine with dinner. Even at that, she saw through his story immediately.

Lennie played along with the lie and let him go, without comment or protest. Cary was hers and she was his. Without the banns of matrimony, they had become one, already. The trust between them was implicit and nearly absolute. She would let him live his life. Cary was unusual – very unusual. His ability was unlike anything Lennie had ever heard of. If she had to give up a bit of time together, she would.

"I went out last night to help someone – again." Cary halted in his speech, swallowed a dry swallow and continued, "It wasn't the store." His voice was just above a whisper.

"I know. Was it the detective again?" Lennie began to get a sinking feeling in her gut.

Cary nodded. He looked downward, feeling a tiny spike of shame work its way into his mind, for having lied to Lennie.

Lennie knew that being with the police detective again probably had something to do with his "silent sight" and, no doubt, something really bad happening. She cradled Cary's face in her hands, leaning in close to him. "Let's just go home. There are plenty of people who can cover for me. The store can spare you for a day off. Wait here."

The balance of their morning was spent together, in each other's arms, on the couch. At first no words were spoken. Slowly, Cary was able to get the words out, about what he was feeling and why. Lennie listened. She said very little. She did most of her talking with her eyes, and hands. She held Cary tight against her trying to give some of her strength to him, by force of will alone.

By midafternoon, they decided to walk in the park, with Wheels. Arm in arm, they walked along the park sidewalks. Around them, the city and its daily life wore on. Wheels kept pace. Somehow, he knew that the visit to the park that day wouldn't include chasing the frisbee, or a ball. He was content to be with his people.

***

"Detective Solves Multiple Murders." The newspaper laying on Lieutenant Dukasko's desk was one of a pair. Both local dailies had he story on their front pages. The story was all over the radio and television as well. Dukasko wasn't happy with all the press. It didn't matter that it was all casting his bureau in a positive light. He perceived the media as an unpredictable thing. The focus of the news agencies was the most capricious of all. Good news could become bad news in an instant.

Lieutenant Dukasko was on the telephone. He had summoned Detective Beckestone to his office before the Medical Examiner called. Beckestone simply sat and waited patiently while the Lieutenant ignored him. At the best of times, John Dukasko was phlegmatic, if generally unfriendly. Today, he was, by comparison in an emotionally revelatory state. Beckestone could tell that far from being praised for his outstanding arrests, there were "issues" to be dealt with.

Lieutenant Dukasko stared at the ceiling. The voice on the other end of the line held his attention. "Yes, it is an unusual case. Five bodies in barrels. I've never heard of anything like it around here." He glanced at Beckestone.

The stone-like glare from his immobile face had a chilling effect on Beckestone.

Confusion began to creep in. He had busted a major homicide case, almost "in the act." The man in the warehouse turned out to be Hamor Drubedta, head of a gang that was a collection of refugees from the Middle East. Among other sobriquets, they were known as "the Arabs." They were in the process of trying to take over narcotics distribution in St. Louis. They had a lot of competition. That meant a lot of killing from time to time.

Arresting Hamor Drubedta and connecting him with these murders would break the gang's back and render them ineffective for a long time. This was the sort of thing that could permanently change the structure of the drug trade in town. It would certainly stop the inter-gang killing for a while.

"Yes, I agree it is very unusual that the bodies were all still warm." He listened. "No time for any lividity or rigor. Wounds still bleeding. Yes." He looked at Beckestone again. There was no mistaking the hostility in his eyes this time. Benji Beckestone was beginning to hope that he could just melt down, through the cracks in the floor and simply not be right here, right now.

"Doctor, I'm going to have to ask you for a favor. Please don't mention any of these observations in your report. Or to the press. The detective came upon the bodies almost immediately after the killings." Dukasko looked blankly toward the ceiling. "Yes, it's very lucky. And unusual. But still, it's not something that needs to be in the public record right away. The prosecution of the responsible parties will be difficult enough without – uh –

205

untidy details cluttering up the report." One last glance at Beckestone, as the response to his request came back. "Yes, thank you. Thank you very much." He hung up the phone.

After a moment, Lieutenant Dukasko addressed Beckestone. "Detective, I can't wait to read your report about how you came to be where you were, and how you managed to ascertain that the truck was loaded with dead bodies. Your probable cause for the arrest better be rock solid."

Dukasko looked around, out through the glass that enclosed his office. He thought for a moment. "That mook you arrested is telling everything he knows about everything. If half of what he's saying can be verified, Hamor Drubedta is gonna just disappear. He'll have a hard time dodging a visit with the gas chamber. If he does, he'll spend so much time in prison that he'll have time to get to like it."

Beckestone was beginning to feel a bit less threatened. It sounded like Lieutenant Dukasko was honestly enthusiastic about his arrests. He relaxed his hunched shoulders a bit and sat up a little straighter.

Beckestone's change in posture was all the sign Dukasko needed to start in on him all over again. "Do you think I like taking calls from the Medical Examiner's Office like that one?" Before Beckestone could answer, "No. I don't. If you think I like asking favors from the corpse patrol, you are also sadly mistaken. I don't have the slightest idea what that one is gonna cost me. Whatever it is, it won't be pretty."

Beads of sweat, perpetually present on Dukasko's hypertensive forehead, formed little rivulets that dripped down his cheeks. He chewed his ever-present cigar a bit, "Get this straight: Bustin' a case is a good thing. But if you have to have every minute of in the papers and on the television, you and I are going to come to a parting of the ways. Is that clear?"

"Yes, Lieutenant." Beckestone rose from his chair, certain that the tone of voice just used on him was one of finality.

"Now, get outta here, and write that report."

TWENTY-SIX

Words. So many words passed between them. The faraway look in Cary's eyes belied his profound emotional disconnect from his surroundings. When Lennie looked into his eyes, she saw not just detachment but pain. There was fear there as well. When Lennie spoke to him she wasn't sure how much of what she was saying was registering.

A torrent of soul-sharing followed the return from the store. On the couch in their little living room, Cary began the process of actually feeling what had happened to him. Talking about it gave structure to the emotional muck welling up within him. Before all this started, his life was uncomplicated to the extent of his hardest decision being whether or not to advance his relationship with the girl that he knew he wanted to marry.

The act of witnessing multiple murders went through his heart like an arrow. The arrow took tiny bits of him with it, as it passed right on through. The parts taken were fragments of innocence he would never regain, without deluding himself. He did not yet realize that the Cary Lang of yesterday was gone – forever. He was becoming someone new. That was the part he felt intuitively. He wanted Lennie to be part of this becoming. As she held on to him, he clung to her like a child, if only for a short time.

The walk in the park worked for them – for him. Lennie wound her arm around him, and steered their path through the park. She also took charge of Wheels who intuitively tagged along peaceably.

Cary shared his experience – about the aural viewing – and about his mental state in general. He literally disassembled his emotional state and laid it bare for Lennie to receive and become part of. He wondered aloud if the new ability that he had was actually some sort of a curse, or an affliction. He had never thought of it that way but it had brought him some awful experiences.

Lennie's welcoming reaction to his giving-of-self fed his heart and encouraged his willingness to impart as much of himself as he could. The evening stretched long into the night. The lost, faraway look in Cary's eyes faded. He began to see his fiancé and his surroundings again. The ground was once again firmly beneath his feet.

For her part, Lennie felt an existential joy welling up within her. She knew that she loved him for a long time, much longer than they had been together. She never expected that love with another person could involve such an intertwining of psyches. She gave herself over totally, not wanting any barrier between herself and the man who had become her world.

Lennie's childhood was rich with the experience of being in a home founded on the love of two very committed people. Her parents taught her all she needed to know about marriage and true inseparability. Except for her father's job, they almost never went anywhere alone. It didn't matter: The hardware store, the grocer's, the farm supply, were all places they would go together.

Lennie's mom and dad even scheduled haircuts and hairdresser sessions at the same time. Lennie, at first, accompanied her father to the barber shop. Not for her haircut, but just to see the goings on. When she was old enough, her mother would bring her to the hairdresser for her cuts.

The importance of the lives of family members outshone everything else. She learned that a mother's love is encompassing. It welcomes even the heartaches of family life. She learned that a father's love is abiding. It is tolerant of all things that originate with the family.

The hours of listening to Cary finally enabled Lennie to bring in comments that rung like tiny chimes against the ears of her lover. The sound of her voice brought healing and calm with it. More than any physical act between them, this night's conversation bound them together as one.

Later, the quiet conversation on the couch became the whispered endearments of the bedroom. The lovemaking that night brought Cary and Lennie to a new plateau of caring and wanting for each other. Surcease was the gift that Cary received from their union. The pain and sorrow were, for at least a while, gone.

The next morning came in what seemed like only moments after falling asleep. Cary arose and shook the cobwebs from his head. He padded into the flat's little kitchen and set a pot of coffee to perk while he showered. As he toweled himself off, Lennie came in and pressed her naked body against his. Cary wrapped her in the bath towel with him. He kissed her for a long time.

The small talk over coffee made the morning beautiful for both of them. Lennie walked with Cary and Wheels. She showered and dressed quickly so that she could ride to work with Cary. They had discussed doing this very thing previously; now seemed like the time to do it. Happy chatter in the car, going through morning traffic, was new to Cary. He liked it. He began to think that they should have started doing this earlier.

No hauntings bothered Cary the day after having to leave work. During the lunch break, he painstakingly shared everything that he was experiencing during the day and evening. Lennie listened carefully, fully involved in his telling. He wasn't entirely free of the feelings. They still hung about the back of his mind like so much decoration, left over from a very grim party. Still, in all, he was able to get through the day uneventfully.

It was easy for him to fill the extra time after work, waiting for Lennie's shift to end. His work as the store's head buyer was a continuous flow from one season to the next; from one sale to the next. There was never really a stopping point that he didn't make for himself. The work was truly endless. With regard to it being a form of job security, Cary was grateful.

211

It was a different experience for Cary to drive home after Lennie's shift. The traffic was a lot lighter. On the way, he asked her, "So, is this you babysitting me or what?"

Taking a cue from Cary's light one, Lennie let the lame characterization go. "We're together. You and me. A team. This is going to work out."

They exchanged glances, as Cary drove. Lennie went on. "If you're going to be called on to help the police, I want to be there. Somebody has to be there for you: somebody who gives a damn what's happening to you."

Cary drove the rest of the way home. Wheels was more than ready to go out. Taking care of him got Cary and Lennie back to their flat just before eight o'clock. They cobbled together a small dinner and spent the balance of the evening relaxing. They each had reading to do. A bit of conversation crept in, here and there. For a while they spoke of how their new partnership would make things better, if more complicated. The day wound down easily and gently.

***

Three days after the warehouse killings, Detective Beckestone completed his report on the arrest of the truck passenger, the shooting of the driver, and the killings in the warehouse itself. His explanation for having entered the warehouse was that he saw the white panel van, driven by a known gang member, enter a completely darkened warehouse building.

As probable cause, he knew that it was flimsy. He also knew that the prosecuting attorney's office could make it work. He had seen weaker examples of probable cause turned into convictions before. His report along with the volumes of information they were getting from the truck passenger, would seal the fate of Hamor Drubedta.

Taking a deep breath, he got up from his desk, crossed the squad room and knocked on the door of Lieutenant Dukasko's office. The response from the other side of the door was, "Yeah?" It was still the morning. Visits from higher-ups usually came after lunch, so his answer was typical.

Beckestone entered the office. Lieutenant Dukasko glanced up, only to see who it was, then looked back to the work in front of him. Again, Beckestone recognized the typically brow-beating approach: Don't give your subordinates the courtesy of acknowledgement. He stood next to the visitor's chair and waited. The ritual of needing to be invited to sit down had to be adhered to.

"Sit." Dukasko finally looked directly at Beckestone. He saw the paperwork in his hands. "Is this your arrest report?" He held out his hand. Beckestone passed the papers over the desk.

A minute went by. Beckestone tried not to stare directly at the Lieutenant. The animal-eye-contact thing held true here: aggressive species considered it a challenge. Beckestone wouldn't make the mistake of putting a challenge before the man who controlled his fate.

"Really?" Dukasko looked into Beckestone's eyes. His challenge was apparent. "A 'known gang member' enters a darkened building, and you end up killing a man, finding five fresh bodies, and bringing down one of the biggest crooks in St. Louis."

213

Beckestone sat immobile, not looking at Dukasko's eyes. He stared at the Lieutenant's necktie, loosened at the collar. Beckestone couldn't remember if he had ever seen it snugged up.

"Well, it'll fly. Maybe not high, but it'll put Hamor Drubedta away. Along with the gobs of stuff the mook is telling us about, I doubt if his former boss will ever even see the light of day again. I understand the feds want to prosecute Drubedta after we're done with him." Dukasko dropped the report on his desk. Remembering his mistake from their last meeting, Benji Beckestone sat perfectly still. He wouldn't move a muscle. He wouldn't give the Lieutenant an excuse to tear into him again.

A faintly quizzical look crossed Dukasko's face. Beckestone's lack of response took him off guard for just a second or two. "So, all of a sudden, you're a flippin' genius, huh? Catching big-time criminals with their pants down."

"No sir." Beckestone continue avoiding eye contact.

Police Lieutenant John Dukasko shifted gears seamlessly. He began with a disarmingly conciliatory tone. "You've closed a pair of very notable cases lately. Your name is definitely becoming well-known upstairs." He jabbed upward with his right thumb, indicating the direction of the command offices.

Dukasko picked up a folder from the desktop. Before Beckestone could react, he tossed the folder into Beckestone's lap. The young detective opened the folder. A photograph of a young woman – a very beautiful young woman – was the top item.

The file bore the name of a well-known local mover and shaker: Victor Forsyth. He was the current head of the Forsyth family and chairman of the board of a conglomerate called The Forsyth Group. The family businesses covered everything from finance to transportation and manufacturing. The manufacturing companies mainly fulfilled Defense Department contracts. Describing the Forsyth family as wealthy and important did them a crushing disservice.

"The young woman is Shelly Frankel. She's nobody, but she's missing. Her parents say they haven't heard from her for three weeks. They say that she has never been out of touch with her family for more than a day. Until now." Dukasko looked at Beckestone intently, searching for any sign of reluctance.

Pointing to the photograph, "She was last seen in the penthouse apartment of the man whose name is on the file." Dukasko waited for some of the color to drain from Beckestone's face. "That's right, you're gonna be investigating Victor Forsyth."

TWENTY-SEVEN

Walker thought to himself, Gadfree. How do they do it? Even the coffee is the same.

When he was transferred from Indianapolis, he looked forward to the change. What he got was anything but. The Kansas City office was almost identical to the office in Indianapolis. It had to be exactly the same number of square feet. The only difference was that the office of the Special Agent-In-Charge – the SAIC – was to the left of the door, not to the right.

The office was on the same floor of the building that the one in Indianapolis occupied. The light fixtures were the same. The desk and office furniture were the same. The pens, paper, typewriters, office supplies were all the same. The coffee maker was the same, resulting in the same, barely-palatable, goo. The realities of mass purchasing by a federal government agency were present, evident, and tiresome.

Kansas City itself was turning out to be remarkably similar in its crime statistics. The rates of bank robberies and kidnapping were nearly identical to the Indiana office. His partner was, once again, an older, more seasoned agent. At least he wasn't as close to retirement age as his former partner. The age difference between himself and his first partner wore on him after a very short period of time.

The transfer to Kansas City was ostensibly a reward for the initiative he showed in handling the kidnap case in Monroe City, Indiana. He only followed Tom Breeden's lead. Following Breeden into the farmhouse supposedly showed courage and ambition. This was the outcome.

All the same basic expectations were in place: agents needed to spend more time out of the office than in it. He could begin anew, hunting for the sort of girl he hoped to find. Being taken out of his environment shortly after a kill left an empty place in his heart. It was like the last kill almost hadn't happened. The urge to take another target was there, nearly as strong as it was before the last time he made a kill.

A few months of wasting time in the coffee shops that his partner showed him went by. A robbery case every ten days or so kept things busy enough. In Kansas City, crossing state lines in the process of a robbery got you FBI involvement in your case. This happened all the time. The Missouri-Kansas border split the metropolitan area down the middle.

He set out to make scouting passes through the entertainment and university neighborhoods on his own. An hour or two, taken during every other day, or so, was a good addition to the time he spent in the evenings. Most day scouting gave him good leads for places to watch after dark. The year was once again, growing old. The days were shortening noticeably.

In a couple of weeks, he had identified a possible target. The petite brunette was probably a student at UMKC. She shuttled back and forth from the campus to the Country Club Plaza area, where she worked as a waitress in the evenings.

The path that the young woman took from her job to the bus stop went through an alleyway that served as a mid-block shortcut for pedestrians. The alley was dimly lit at best. Parking near the entry to the alley would pose only a small problem. Getting a car there for a "take" would be complicated by the high volume of traffic in the popular entertainment area.

He assessed the plan as being sound. He knew he was hurrying through the process but the urge to complete another kill was definitely there, now. Over and over, he watched the patterns of pedestrians in the immediate area. He checked the best times to leave a car, parked in just the right place.

The girl – the target – worked four nights each week. Tomorrow would be her last shift until next weekend. The gap would allow for her to be missing with fewer people looking for her to be present. A student could miss a couple of classes with no one being concerned. The target's place of work might institute an inquiry or investigation in a shorter period of time.

Tomorrow would be the day. He would leave the car early in the day. A bus ride back to the office after dropping the car off would make sure that his work routine seemed in no way unusual. It would seem like just another errand, checking an investigatory lead.

He would ride back to the Plaza area after work. He already knew where he would spend the time waiting for his target to leave work. Splitting his time between two or three locations would reduce the chances of anyone remembering him to nearly zero. Practiced at being "invisible" in a diner or café, he could pass unnoticed through the throng of people that regularly filled the streets of the Country Club Plaza district.

***

It all went as smoothly as it could have. The girl made a bit more noise as he wrestled her to the ground during the initial attack. No one was around to hear. She was unconscious, limp as a dishrag, before he bound, gagged and put her in the car.

The route he chose for his drive to the kill site worked just perfectly. The mid-west city was closed and quiet, traffic was negligible. He drove to the kill site in a little under eighteen minutes. There was no sign of anyone around the North Kansas City warehouse he selected. The building was empty and unused for more than a decade. The open floorplan allowed for finishing his task while being able to see around him in all directions.

Even before he removed the unconscious girl from the car, the face of Katie Spahl was beginning to appear in front of him. As he worked, it was a thin, faint, ghostly apparition that hung in the air, always in sight.

219

The girl began to awaken as he knelt next to her with the polyester scarf in his hands. She whimpered and struggled against her bonds. Already, Katie Spahl's face lay over hers, taking over her appearance completely.

He placed the scarf around her neck. The girl struggled mightily, attempting to thrash her body away from his grasp. She screamed and snorted, the gag doing its job of stifling her. As he tightened the scarf around her neck, the scarf that Katie wore, or the ghost of it, replaced the polyester one he was using.

In just over a minute, it was done. Katie's face faded, as did her scarf. He left her body slip to the ground. He wondered how he was now accustomed to the presence of the hallucinatory images. Before, they had surprised and bothered him. They were now just part of the scenario.

He took the scarf, policed up any foot prints, and left. He drove the car out of the warehouse and stopped on the concrete roadway. He carefully brushed away his tire tracks, all the way out to where he was parked. The route back to Kansas City was different from the approach route, of course. Once back at his apartment, he melted down the scarf in a pie plate and threw the pile of plastic goo into a dumpster behind the building across the alley from his.

***

The order was waiting for him the next morning. South Dakota. Unrest was being caused by a group that called themselves AIM – the American Indian Movement. Protests were drawing attention, and more protestors. The local Bureau office needed agents rotated in for six-month assignment.

220

Walker knew from the news that Wounded Knee was a powder keg of tribal and Indian hatred for anything remotely connected with white men. Historically, it had been so since 1890. That was the year of the Wounded Knee Massacre. Hundreds of Sioux men, women and children were killed by U.S. Army soldiers gone berserk. If there was a place where the conflict between Native Americans and the invading white peoples was represented in its total, heart-breaking misery, Wounded Knee, and southwest South Dakota was it.

Lately, the location was a touch-stone for Native American activism. Members of many clans of the Sioux, as well as other tribes came to the region to give voice to their hatred of the government. Apparently, the feeling was that the government treated them no better now than before.

This was more than a ready-bag trip. Their plane would leave at four. Six months of off-site work required packing nearly everything he had. He could leave his car in the Federal Office parking lot. He drove home and packed. He cleared out his refrigerator and the little bit of trash. He left instructions for his landlord to not do anything with his apartment.

As he drove back to the office, pangs of regret for not being able to carry out his plan for this evening crept into his mind. Six months in a strange environment would probably mean that he would be unable to take another girl. He would not make another kill and assuage the tide of hate, and need for revenge, welling up within him.

***

Pine Ridge, South Dakota was as lost, desolate and barren a location as he had expected. The wind howled across the prairie grasslands constantly. The population explosion, brought about by the numbers of federal agency staffers, only made things worse. There was little or no contact between anyone who lived here and anyone from the government. Everywhere you looked, hate-filled eyes stared back at you.

He wasn't ready for the lack of comradery between the various agencies. The key word was competition. Civil talk among the various federal agency workers was the rule of thumb. Going out of your way to help another agency wasn't. As a result, the coordination of federal government agency work was non-existent.

After a time, the competition between agencies became overt hostility. This was the environment he walked into: Everybody hated everybody else. He could relate to that. If at your very core, hate ruled every moment of your existence, the hate of others seemed to be quite matter-of-fact. Adopting an attitude toward other agency employees based on hostility was just a new exercise to participate in.

Inter-tribal and inter-clan killings were taking place regularly. The suspicion that a tribe member was informing for any of the law enforcement agencies was a death sentence. There was a lot going on that could be informed on. Untaxed cigarettes and alcohol made it through the toughest set of roadblocks and checkpoints he had ever seen. The trade in these contraband items, as well as the importation of a large number of weapons grew, despite all efforts at limiting it.

The local, tribal police were the first-called to every crime scene. They were utterly untrustworthy and under suspicion for aiding the smugglers. Next came the South Dakota State Police, the Bureau of Indian Affairs, the Alcohol, Tobacco, and Firearms Bureau, the National Guard, and the FBI. The Bureau of Land Management was also there. No one knew what they did.

If there were any unrepresented authoritative agencies, he didn't know of them. There were more investigative minds working on every single case than had ever been arrayed against anything since the Kennedy assassination. Crimes still went unsolved. No one in the community ever had a scrap of information to offer.

Month after month, the agency in-fighting and unproductive investigations continued. At the end of his six-month assignment, he went back to the Kansas City Bureau office, older and certainly no wiser about anything, save inter-agency sniping.

***

Getting back into the routine of Bureau activities in Kansas City took its toll. The hate within him had risen to a pitch that he could hardly contain. It was as though had not completed his last "taking" of a target. With each of his first two kills, the hate subsided for a time, left him alone. Now it was just there, always.

Weeks of scouting new areas for potential targets passed. At last, when he settled on a target – a petite, brunette, Rockhurst co-ed, who took evening classes – the hate within him eased a bit. It was easier to think, without the constant roar of hate in his mind. He could assess more realistically whether or not he was rushing through his preparations.

It was a minor risk to scout the area immediately adjacent to the campus. He worked harder at trying to blend in with a younger population. He knew it was a busy area. The foot traffic around potential "take" locations was highly variable, at all times.

He finally chose an area for his attack. East 53rd Street, a couple of blocks off campus, sported an area with a broken street lamp. The block was east of the campus, where the street crested a hill. The sidewalk abutted a stone wall, four feet high, topped by a short iron fence. Across the street was an unoccupied house. Its for sale sign had been there so long that it was showing weather-wear.

There were no parking restrictions. He could place his car in exactly the right spot, at the "take" point. He could time his approach from the opposite end of the block so that he and his target were alongside his car when he incapacitated her.

The "kill" location was the same one he planned for the other target. It was far enough out of town, yet close enough to get to in a short period of time. It was an abandoned food packaging plant, eleven miles south of town. He had recently returned to the site to confirm that it was still as deserted as it was the previous year.

The school year had only a short number of weeks remaining. He would need to make his move soon. He checked and re-checked his preparations. Whatever day he chose, he would be ready. It was a Tuesday. He decided to act before the end of the week.

***

Wednesday morning, he arrived at the office early as usual. Also, as usual, the Special Agent-In-Charge was in his office already. After pouring himself a cup from the every-present hot pot of coffee, the SAIC called him, in to his office. As he entered, he wondered what the summons was all about. He knew his work in South Dakota was all perfectly in order and documented fully. Things here in Kansas City had been as routine as they could have been.

When he heard the words "transferred to a new city," He almost flinched. The hardest thing to do was keeping from wincing outwardly as the hate within him erupted into an inner rage. Remaining calm and accepting the news with apparent ease took every bit of his composure.

He listened politely to the explanation of how the reassignment of agents to South Dakota was interfering with the normal rotation of personnel from one city to the next. They needed more agents in St. Louis. He would be one of them.

TWENTY-EIGHT

I must be a friggin' genius. I got myself a dandy new case to investigate. Victor Forsyth. Sheesh!

Benji Beckestone drove around aimlessly. The case file was on the car seat next to him, along with the dinner he just picked up at Chuck-A-Burger. He filched a French-fry out of the bag and ate it. Sucking down half of his Coke-on-ice, he thought about his passage from high school, through the police academy and making Detective, 2nd Grade, in only three years. He thought about the time at the junior college, getting his minor degree in law enforcement. Already there were people presenting themselves as candidates for the academy with BS degrees in law enforcement.

He decided to head home, to his apartment. He wove his way through the county subdivisions. Benji Beckestone lived in a fairly unique location. His apartment building was within the limits of the St. Louis city proper. It was only approachable by way of first leaving the city and driving through a suburban neighborhood. There was talk of changing the department's policy about officers living in the city itself. Beckestone thought that it was all just talk.

The Chevy Biscayne was his department-assigned vehicle. The stripped-down police-fleet version was already a rat trap. Being the newest member of the Detective Bureau, Beckestone was given the honor of driving the vehicle that no one else would take. When he first saw the sticker in the trunk that described the car's color as "Bronze Metallic," he laughed out loud. A better name for the color would have been "Shinny-Turd."

The sixty-thousand miles on the odometer belied the condition of the car's interior. A lot of meals had been eaten – and spilled – inside the car. The stains on the front seat were one thing. The back seat looked as though it had been occupied by bears. He tried to not think of what-all might have gone on back there.

The condition of the Chevy was the reason he used his Dodge Polara in the evenings. He parked the department car next to his own car in the parking lot of the apartment complex. There were enough extra places on the lot. No one complained about his two vehicles. He took the Fireball – the red, rotating light that rode the dashboard – out of the Chevy and locked it in the Dodge.

The apartment complex was typical, people stacked vertically, even though the suburban model limited the rise to three floors. A faux-brick exterior gave the newer construction a look that resonated with the miles of brick houses in the city. The chief design acquiescence to being a suburban location was a fair bit of space given over to landscaping. The sidewalks curved back and forth between trees that were just a few years beyond sapling status.

Beckestone walked across the parking lot and decided to eat his burger before going into his apartment. He wouldn't admit to himself how badly he didn't want to go into his lonely little home-on-a-shelf. He sat on a bench provided by the apartment complex. The bench provided a lovely view – of the parking lot.

Beckestone bit into his Chuck-A-Burger Deluxe. The barbeque sauce ran down his chin. He wiped his face with a paper napkin. He thought of all the high school classmates he left behind. Some accompanied him to the police academy; some became involved in illegal activities and went to prison. A few managed to do both.

Five years ago, the opportunities for public high school graduates were limited – if you didn't want to join the military. At the time, he had the ultimate protection for a 1-A draft enrollee: Not only was his only brother in the Army, he was in Viet Nam. The draft board wouldn't touch him.

The war economy was going strong, but decent jobs were hard to get. Benji Beckestone wasn't "connected." He didn't have family or friends who could hook him up with a good job. That was how he ended up in the department. He was smart enough to go to college but didn't have the money. Joining the force was a good move for him.

Finishing is meal, Benji Beckestone looked up at his apartment window and knew what he had to do. He knew all along. Coming home was just a dodge he was running on himself. He was trying to not admit to himself that he was going to pursue the help of his new "friend," Cary Lang. Frustrated with himself, he rose from the bench, stuffed the remainder of his dinner in a trash can. He got into his Dodge and headed back into the city.

***

The rumble of Beckestone's car announced his presence. The noise preceded him down the block and accompanied his efforts at parallel parking. It was just before sunset. The neighborhood hadn't quite yet settled for the night but was well on its way. A few curtains were drawn back, here and there. People wanted to see who, or what, was disturbing the peace.

Cary recognized the sound of the detective's car as it came up the block. He had time to steel himself for a confrontation with the policeman, before he opened the door. Cary was waiting for Beckestone and opened the door to the flat even before the detective could knock. His expression was as dour as he could make it without forcing a deep scowl. "I had no idea that I'd see you again so soon."

"Yeah, I'm sorry. I know the last time we met, you had a rough go. I didn't realize how violent things could get. I also forgot that the average citizen doesn't know anything about how criminals act. I…"

Lennie appeared at Cary's side. She entwined arm around his, held his hand, and spoke to Beckestone. "You're going to have to leave us alone. Cary's still not over the last time you…" She looked into Cary's eyes. She needed to choose her words carefully. She turned back to the detective. "…the last time you left together."

229

Benji Beckestone knew what he wanted. He also knew that he was going to have to do some fast talking to get it. He looked and spoke to Lennie. "Please. Just give me a few minutes to explain."

He held up the file on the Forsythe case. He knew there was big trouble for him if he was discovered sharing investigatory information with people outside of the department. Still, he persisted. "You gotta give me a chance to explain."

He looked from Lennie to Cary. "At least give me a chance to really say how sorry I am for what happened – for what I dragged you into."

Lennie eased her grip on Cary's arm. Cary looked at her. The question in his eyes was plain. She stepped back and let Cary open the door all the way.

***

The conversation that followed was interesting. Benji Beckestone had no sales experience whatsoever. Even at that, he sold his goods. He spent a long time alternately apologizing to Cary and Lennie for dragging Cary into the violent underworld of St. Louis, and explaining how Cary's help was putting away the top drug kingpin in town.

After getting to the point where everyone seemed at peace with the situation, Beckestone brought up the topic of the Forsythe investigation. He leaned heavily on the parts about the missing girl and how distraught her family was. He deliberately left out details about the young girl's profligate life style. He made no mention of her flinging herself at any man she thought was worth real money.

Beckestone drove home the fact that the parents were nearly at their wits end, dealing with their daughter's disappearance. He sold it long and sold it hard. He used every word he had. At the end of it all (and the end of two bottles of white wine), Cary was in a decidedly receptive mood. It was time to close the deal, ask for Cary's help.

There was, at last, a look in Lennie's eyes that Beckestone recognized: resignation. While it wasn't the acceptance he was hoping for, it would do. Benji decided to make his move. "The place the girl was last seen was the penthouse apartment of Victor Forsythe." He hoped the name-drop alone would seal the deal.

Cary and Lennie looked at each other. Their world had nothing to do with the multi-millionaire world of the Forsythes. What lay before them was a connection. It was one they had never dreamed of. Yet, it was about something that was not good. The taint of wrong-doing felt out of place lodged against the name of St. Louis' most eminent family. The look of bizarre quizzicality arose on their faces. Beckestone knew he had them.

"The thing that's needed is to get a look at the Forsythes in their most relaxed, natural state." (He avoided saying 'habitat.') He looked at Cary. "If you'll join me, we'll go look at their home; see what's happening."

Cary spoke before Lennie, "We'll go together, or not at all. Lennie, me and Wheels. You either agree to take us all or it's no deal."

Beckestone leaned back in his chair. Without thinking, "Jesus Christ Katz!" escaped his lips. He had no idea this kind of development was possible, much less likely.

"Okay, okay. It's a party. You guys, me and the dog. What the hell. This is all absurd anyway, right?" He looked from Cary to Lennie then, involuntarily, at the dog. None of them answered.

TWENTY-NINE

The drive out to far western St. Louis County, where the Forsythe estate was located, was uneventful. The whole time, Cary thought that riding in the over-powered Dodge was a good way to go deaf. Beckestone's old car was a reminder of why he bought an economical car like his Volkswagen.

The header pipes settled into a loud drone of engine power on the highway which lulled Wheels to sleep. His two humans in the car, unaccustomed to the roar of the huge engine were not as fortunate. Benji Beckestone was in a trance, induced by the noise of the huge V-8 engine and the opportunity to drive for a while without shifting.

The winding, hilly roads around the part of St. Louis County known as St. Alban's let Benji Beckestone become one with his hot-rod, if only for a little while. The twists and hills let him feel the results of the changes he made to the car's suspension, stiffening it. Everything he had done to the car was to make it go faster and still be street-legal. The work was done on a tight budget, while he was in the academy, and in night school.

The loud car finally came to a level stretch of road, straight for about a half-mile. Beckestone eased the gas pedal to reduce the noise of his engine. Between the trees lining the road, a large house was visible, set back from the road several hundred yards. The car cruised past the iron-gated entrance to the large estate. Each of the gates was twelve feet tall, with an enormous, gothic 'F' emblazoned upon it.

Bingo, thought Beckestone, We're here. He drove on to the next driveway. Turning off the road caused Wheels to waken. He whimpered once, anticipating a chance to get out of the car and run.

Cary Turned from his front seat position and said, "Not yet, buddy. In a little while."

Lennie, in the back with Wheels, draped her arm around the golden retriever and stroked his fur. The driveway that Beckestone chose was just a dirt track that disappeared over the hill in front of them. A short coast along the drive brought them to a break in the trees that revealed the Forsythe house.

Beckestone looked at Cary, "Anybody home?"

Cary, not understanding the request, stared blankly at the detective. He began to answer, then stopped himself. He realized that Beckestone was asking him to use his silent sight to view the large house. Their vantage point was just a bit above the plane on which the house rested. A look straight and level across the intervening ground would meet the second-floor windows of the building. Both men got out of the car and walked to the fence line.

Closing his eyes, Cary could see the auras of at least five people in and around the house. One, a female form, was in the back of the house. Her movements revealed that she was involved in food preparation; slicing and cutting things on a surface in front of her, waist high.

Another aura was at the back of the house. This aura was in the shape of a man. His pantomime of actions reminded Cary of a gardener, reaching up, cutting parts of plants and placing the trimmings in a basket, at his feet.

The third person that Cary detected was a small form, probably a child, in a second-floor room. Cary guessed from the size and shape that it was a pre-teen girl. The small aura was seated and still. The tilt of the small form's head suggested that she was reading.

The three auras were all nearly the same indefinite salmon color. Cary's experience told him that this was the color of an emotionally balanced state. From time to time, each of the salmon-colored auras would drift into a pale yellow. This was a color that Cary recognized as the result of concentration. He knew that the more intently a person concentrated on a task or object, the more intensely yellow their aura became.

The other two auras in the house, a man and a woman. They were farther away from Cary – and from the other people in the house. They were near enough to each other to figure out that they were together in the same room. Both of their auras were red, the color of anger. One of the two auras was intensely and deeply redder than the other. As the two people moved about the room they were in, their auras took turns intensifying and diminishing.

"There are two people in the house. I think they are arguing" Cary opened his eyes and looked at Beckestone. "They're in the other end of the house, farther away."

Without a word, Beckestone walked over to his car, opened the passenger-side door and pulled a pair of binoculars out of the glove compartment. He walked back and handed them to Cary.

Cary looked at the cop with confused wonder in his eyes. He had never thought to find out if he could view auras through a telescope, or binoculars. He took the field glasses and turned toward the house. He lifted the glasses to his closed eyes.

He opened his eyes and looked at the detective. "I got nothing. I can't see the auras through the binoculars." He had hoped for a moment that the field glasses could make a difference. He realized that he had discovered something about his newly acquired ability. It was not anything useful. His disappointment was real.

"Okay, so what's going on with the two who are arguing?" Beckestone nudged Cary's elbow to get him to look toward the house again.

Deliberately calming himself, Cary focused on the two figures at the other end of the house. Although smaller because of the distance, his concentration enhanced the sense of detail in the two auras. The red aura of the woman was not moving but Cary could see her head tracking the movements of the man as he moved back and forth in the room, occasionally gesturing with wide sweeps of his hands.

The man's gesturing reminded Cary of the wild gesturing he witnessed just a couple of days ago, before the murders. He began to get a sinking feeling in the pit of his stomach. He opened his eyes and looked toward Lennie, in the car.

Lennie didn't miss the obvious pleading glance from Cary. She opened the door of the car and got out. With Wheels in tow, she sidled up against Cary without a word. She knew that anything she said, just right now, would probably be way off base. Her focus was on just being there to be supportive of Cary. Somehow, Wheels took the cue and sat quietly at her side.

Detective Beckestone looked at the trio of his surveillance team members and thought, What a bunch. Nobody would ever believe this. Not in a million years.

Cary continued to focus on the pair of auras. The man stopped for a moment, arms-length away, in front of the woman. She was obviously speaking. Suddenly the man reached out and slapped the woman in the face. The violence of what he had witnessed sent a shudder through Cary. Lennie, who had entwined her arm with his, tightened her press against him.

The woman's aura briefly lightened. Cary was afraid it would fade out, like the one's in the warehouse. It didn't. After a moment of diming, the woman's aura brightened and became a deeper shade of red. It began to darken. As the man's aura stalked away from the woman's. Her red aura of anger deepened into the deep, dark, nearly-black of hate and rage.

237

Cary related what he saw, haltingly, more or less as it happened. He watched as the shape of the man walked down a stairway. His movements took him farther and farther away, the red of his anger diminishing only slightly. After a bit of undecipherable movements, the man seated himself and began to move across Cary's field of view.

The sound of a car caused Cary to open his eyes. "That's the angry man, in the car."

Beckestone knew the car. It was Victor Forsythe's Mercedes-Benz. The gigantic black sedan was known all around St. Louis. Most times – but not all – it was driven by a chauffeur. Evidently, Forsythe had driven himself to his country home.

Cary watched as the figure of the man topped a hill and disappeared from view. Returning his special sight to the house he found the woman, more or less in the same area of the house she was in when the man struck her. Her deep red aura had lessened somewhat in intensity but was still deep, dark, oxblood red. She was sitting. Her arm was draped over the side of something; Cary guessed a chair or sofa. The aura of the woman sat motionless for a long time.

Wheels whined, signaling that it was time for him to go. Lennie stepped away from the two men and let him take care of business. Cary opened his eyes at the brief disturbance. He blinked once or twice letting his eyes adjust to the afternoon light.

Beckestone took the clue and decided that they had seen enough. The three people and Wheels got in the car and drove back to St. Louis. As he drove, Beckestone wondered what the knowledge of what had just transpired

in the Forsythe country house would do for his
investigation.

***

    The last thing that Benji Beckestone thought about
Cary Lang, as he left the southside neighborhood last night,
was that he was glad that nothing more violent than a face
slap had occurred. He recognized the fact that civilians
weren't as inured to violence as police officers were.
Before working with Lang, he was unaware of the huge
difference. The world that most people lived in was very
much unlike the world that needed the police department to
keep under control.

    Going into the office this morning, things were
notably different than they were before he broke the
Drubedta case. Passing the receptionist, he received a clear
"Good morning, Detective Beckestone," from Rita. There
had been an absence of hushed conversations in his
presence in the office, and the break room. For what it was
worth, he had earned acceptance into the very exclusive
membership of the Detective Bureau.

    Beckestone picked up his messages from Rita's desk,
and thanked her. At his desk he briefly thumbed through
the stack of messages. Near the bottom – a place that
indicated the message came in a while ago – one message
caught his eye. He read the short little message over and
over.

    Holy crap! Beckestone shot up out of his chair. He
walked the slip of paper back to Rita's desk and found out
the message had come in late last night. It was taken by the
central message desk. Thanking Rita, he looked at the

message, reading it over again, as he walked back to his desk.

After a half hour of considering the implications of what the note said, Beckestone decided it was time to involve the Lieutenant in the investigation. In this particular case, a written report wouldn't do. He knew he was walking on thin ice, investigating the most powerful family in the city. He also knew that not telling anyone about Cary Lang and his unique talent was heating up the ice that he was on.

If nothing else, reporting in person would stroke the Lieutenant's ego. Not a lot of that went on, so even that was a dicey call to make. He knocked on the Lieutenant's door.

"What is it?" Beckestone didn't know how a voice could smell like a cigar, but the one coming through the door definitely did. He went in.

THIRTY

Certainty. Beckestone was sure that the look on Victor Forsythe's face was the look of certainty. He was certain who he was and what he could do. He was probably certain of the kind of person that he could crush like a bug: 2nd Grade detectives. Beckestone imagined that if he looked in the dictionary for certainty, he'd find Victor Forsythe's image staring back at him.

Beckestone sent a request to Forsythe's office to interview him about the disappearance of Shelly Frankel. He expected little more than a nice letter from Forsythe's lawyers stating precisely how and why Mr. Forsythe would not be allowing himself to be subjected to any such interview.

Instead of a refusal, his secretary called the bureau and set up a time for the interview. The response was the surprise of the young detective's life, recent events notwithstanding. He had to change mindsets from thinking how he would work around not getting a chance to talk to Forsythe. Now he had to gear up for a challenging exchange with the most influential man in town.

Benji Beckestone had little experience with interviewing suspects in the bureau's offices. Most of his interviews were in the field, with witnesses that were usually compliant. Interviews with perpetrators typically featured guilt that was already determined beyond any explanation that they might offer.

In this case, he would be faced with a subject that he couldn't even overtly label as a suspect. He thought that Victor Forsythe would not only answer his questions unsatisfactorily, but find a way to ruin his career as an outcome of the conversation.

It was 9:00 AM, on Wednesday. Beckestone thought to himself, *With any luck, I'll be cashiered out of the department before the weekend.* He had arranged the interview with Victor Forsythe over the objections of Lieutenant Dukasko. Dukasko had promised not to back him up one bit, if it came to a showdown with Forsythe. Along with what Forsythe could do to him, that was two strikes against him already.

One thing registered clearly with Beckestone: The business magnate came to police headquarters alone. Here was a clear indication of hubris, the self-confidence that reached far beyond what it deserved. It amounted to an unintentionally revealed flaw in the otherwise shining armor of the man's public persona. Beckestone had no idea what it would add to the outcome of the interview.

***

The day before, on Tuesday, detective Beckestone had arranged with Cary Lang to be at headquarters when Victor Forsythe presented himself for the interview. He made sure to have Cary come early, in order to get him settled where he needed him to be. He also set aside times for two rooms for Wednesday at 9:00 AM: Interrogation Room One, and the office next to it.

Interrogation Room One was a windowless room with a table and two chairs in it. The office next to the interrogation room was also windowless. It was a flexible-use space sometimes employed to keep multiple witnesses or suspects separated. For Wednesday, Beckestone arranged for the office to be equipped with a multi-line phone, on the headquarters trunk system.

Beckestone explained to Cary that he needed him to view Victor Forsythe's aura during the interview. He only needed to know one thing: when Victor Forsythe became nervous or fearful. It would be his clue to use in guiding himself to answers that the man might not otherwise be willing to give.

Beckestone showed Cary how to signal him whenever Forsythe was starting to feel fear: Cary simply had to dial one of the multi-line phone's numbers from the other one. If Victor Forsythe was fearful, Cary would let the phone ring twice, then hang up. If a period of time went by and Forsythe's aura revealed happiness, Cary would ring the phone only once. Beckestone would be able to hear the phone ringing from the interrogation room.

Benji Beckestone knew that his system could only be described as crude, but it was all he had. He tried not to

243

think about how much he was hanging on Cary's ability to stay with it, remain focused, and come through for him.

***

Coming into the police headquarters this morning was a strange experience for Cary. Detective Beckestone met him at the front door, but he was still uneasy. He guessed his edginess was all the 'crime and punishment' that went on in and around the police station. They crossed the vestibule to the elevators and stepped into one that came almost immediately. Just before the doors of the elevator closed a hand stopped the doors and the automatic mechanism reopened them.

A tall woman stepped into the car. As she turned to face the front, she glanced at Cary and stopped in mid-turn. It was Detective Harding, the woman who had confronted him at the courthouse. Cary involuntarily flinched at recognizing her.

The tall woman detective looked back and forth from Cary to Detective Beckestone. She looked as though she was about to speak, then stopped. She continued her turn, toward the front of the elevator car, without a word. The elevator doors closed and the car began its ascent.

Stepping off the elevator at the third floor, the woman detective couldn't help but notice the audible sigh of relief from Cary's side of the car behind her. On its further way upward, Cary briefly related his prior encounter with Detective Harding.

Beckestone got Cary situated in the small windowless office in short order. He had only a brief period of time to prepare before Victor Forsythe arrived.

***

After establishing that both he and Victor Forsythe were aware of how many times Shelly Frankel had been seen together, Beckestone got to the heart of the matter.

"Are you aware that the last time Shelly Frankel was seen, it was at the building in which your penthouse apartment is located?"

"No, I was not aware of any such thing." Victor Forsythe's tone was even and smoothly modulated. "I haven't seen Ms. Frankel for some time."

Forsythe looked calmly into Beckestone's eyes. "It is perhaps possible that Ms. Frankel was visiting someone else in the building."

"Were you at your apartment on the night of her disappearance?"

"Disappearance? Who's calling her absence a disappearance? From what I know of Ms. Frankel, she could traipse of to anywhere, for any period of time, without warning of any sort."

"Shelly Frankel's parents reported her missing ten days ago." Beckestone became aware that he had been maneuvered into answering questions from the person he was supposed to be getting answers from.

"Do you know…"

Ring, ring. He heard the phone in the office next door.

"Do you know who else she might have been visiting in your building?" He's lying about seeing her in his apartment. *That's one.*

"Absolutely not, Ms. Frankel and I were only acquaintances. We only met at parties." It was an obvious lie, but one that Victor Forsythe carried off with aplomb. He actually inspected his fingernails to show a sense of distracted impatience.

Ring, ring.

Some time was spent talking about which clubs he and Shelly Frankel "ran into" each other. Beckestone decided to change the subject. "How are things at home? Everybody happy?"

He knew that it had been only a few days since the argument at the country estate. It was a weaselly approach, but he needed to prod his subject a bit. Victor Forsythe didn't answer. He decided to push harder. "Is everything okay at your home in St. Albans?"

"Why, yes. Everything s fine at home. Why do you ask?" Victor Forsythe was deflecting again, asking questions instead of answering.

That's two.

"Your wife, Sarah, isn't it? Is she happy?"

Forsythe's calm, steady voice lowered just a note or two, minutely slipping in its near-perfect modulation. "Yes, it is. Sarah. Why is she in the conversation now?"

Ring, ring.

"Just trying to cover all the bases, Mr. Forsythe." Beckestone knew he was on a track toward making Victor Forsythe very uncomfortable.

"You have help with the house? It's very large." The Forsythe estate was well known. It had even been the subject of a televised tour on the local PBS channel.

"A housekeeper."

A deliberately short answer, and only a partial answer. Another attempt at hiding facts. *That's three.*

"You also have a gardener, is that right?"

Victor Forsythe paused before answering.

Ring, ring.

"Yes, that's right, there is a gardener."

"There must be a lot of work to keeping up the grounds of the estate, the garden." The rhetorical question was just another prod.

Ring, ring.

The middle-aged business man looked at his watch. "Is there a point to this questioning?" He looked toward the door of the room. Beckestone didn't miss the glance, Forsythe's desire to leave revealed itself, if ever so briefly.

"Just one more thing. What's the name of your gardener?"

Ring, ring.

THIRTY-ONE

4:01 AM.

The multiline telephone in Victor Forsythe's bedroom blinked. The ringer was deliberately silenced. The Forsythes still shared a bedroom, although not for the last few days. The silenced ringer was an accommodation to not awaken someone else in the room. Business went on at all hours, so did management of that business. The tiny switch in the base of the telephone made a faint noise which, after a minute or so, woke Victor Forsythe.

Mentally complaining to himself about who would be calling him at this hour, he picked up the phone. A dial tone greeted him. He focused his eyes on the base of the telephone. It was the 'special' line. He pushed the button to switch lines.

Of course, it is. No one would call the house at this hour – for any reason. Only a handful of people knew the number for the 'special' line. They all had specific instructions for when and what to call about. Quietly, he answered. "Yes?" He listened to the person on the other end of the line.

After a minute, he hung up the telephone without saying anything else. *So, I find out at this hour, so that I can't do anything about it. Whoever is orchestrating this thing really knows what they're doing. No time to arrange travel, no time to make moves of any sort. Very clever.*

Victor Forsythe was being played by one of the best in the business. The prosecutor for the City of St. Louis was nobody's fool. He made sure that no word could get to Forsythe before it was too late. He also made sure that word got to Forsythe when he wanted it to. It would constitute a message in a message to such a shrewd and canny businessman.

6:01 AM.

The intercom from the gatehouse beeped in the kitchen. Victor Forsythe was there, waiting to answer it. The groundskeeper sounded nervous. "Mr. Forsythe, there's an awful lot of policemen out here. They say they got a warrant."

"It's okay, George. Let them in." The housekeeper finished making the coffee. She poured a cup for her employer. The alteration of the normal household routine was enough of a clue for her to find somewhere else to be; something else to do. She went there and did that.

7:01 AM.

249

A very bright, sunny Friday morning greeted the St. Alban's area of west St. Louis county. The number of police vehicles lining he Forsythe estate driveway was impressive. Detective Beckestone saw vehicles from the city police department, the county police, and the state. There were several unmarked cars present, brought by the District Attorney's office. It was unusual for the prosecutor's office to be here but this was a very special case.

The number of cars and utility vehicles could easily have included uninvolved jurisdictions. The planned search of the Forsythe estate was a big deal. The community of law enforcement agencies was like any other. Word of the impending search had gotten around. People were curious. They wanted to know. Beckestone was fairly sure there were people here acting as investigators on only the flimsiest of justifications.

There were many people on the grounds of the estate. Beckestone imagined that a reporter could just waltz in and go unnoticed. It was no great leap to imagine a reporter getting word of the search from a friend in any of the involved agencies. It was also not impossible that a reporter could have seen the long parade of law enforcement vehicles, known something newsworthy was about to occur, and followed along.

He started looking for familiar faces among the suits worn by investigators from the other departments. If a reporter were among them, he would likely recognize him. While searching the faces of the other agencies, he got a few quizzical looks in return. So far, he had seen no one that he knew to be a reporter.

***

9:01 AM.

Evidence technicians were concentrating their efforts on the area in and around the estate's garden. It was the area of the house that got the greatest emotional rise out of Victor Forsythe, during the interview. Beckestone was able to corelate a lot of the interview contents with Cary, in a debriefing after the Forsythe meeting.

He gained a lot from interviewing Victor Forsythe. He also had information from the telephone message he picked up in the office. When he first read the message, he wondered at the timing of it, coming just after his trip to the country estate with Cary – and Lennie – and the dog. He still wondered.

Armed with everything he had, getting the prosecuting attorneys to obtain a search warrant for the Forsythe estate was a cinch. He imagined the high entertainment value for the judge who signed the warrant. The prosecutor's office insisted on moving very quickly. The interview of Victor Forsythe was only two days ago.

Beckestone was confident that significant damning evidence would be revealed during the search. What he was unsure of was how much he had left Lieutenant Dukasko out of the investigation. Dukasko promised to drop his Detective, 2nd Grade, like a hot potato if anything went amiss with the Forsythe interview. Since then, Beckestone had not updated his lieutenant on any of the investigation activities, including today's.

11:01 AM.

Investigators from the prosecutor's office interviewed the gardener. Quite a long time passed while they obtained a lengthy list of the most recent renovations done to the garden. The gardener led the investigators from one place to the next, pointing out what had been done, and when.

The little knot of investigators moved about the garden grounds in a haphazard manner. At every stop, questions were asked and answered. After an hour of this wandering tour, one of the investigators stepped away and directed evidence technicians to search in the earth at one of the spots indicated by the gardener. After a short period of digging, a crowd of investigating officers grew around the spot. Beckestone knew something was up and joined them.

***

Victor Forsythe could only sit and wait. Even the morning sun, beaming into the sitting room as brightly as it could, did not ease the cold grip of fear on his heart. He only drank half of his coffee. The rest was cold; it had been for some time. The police investigators seemed to be swarming over the entire estate, like so many ants. How did the young detective get anything out of that pointless interview?

When word came this morning of the impending search, he called his lawyer to be present. He wasn't here yet. All that money spent on retainers, and this is what I end up with: nothing.

He took note of the fact that Sarah was strangely absent. She was usually puttering around the kitchen this time of day. This morning, she took her tea in her bedroom. Victor Forsythe suspected her complicity in the whole search warrant affair. He had no proof. What would I do with proof, confront her?

The front door of the house opened. Detective Beckestone and three investigators from the prosecutor's office walked in. They looked from room to room, on the first floor. They found Victor in the sitting room, a blank stare on his face.

The three other investigators stood in the doorway to the sitting room, effectively blocking any hope of exit. Detective Beckestone crossed the room and stood before the wealthy business man.

"Victor Forsythe, you're under arrest for the murder of Shelly Frankel." He looked down on the middle-aged man, now seemingly much more vulnerable than just two days ago. *The certainty's gone.*

After a minute of staring blankly at the detective, Victor still did not move. Beckestone directed him to stand, and turn around. He began to place his handcuffs on Forsythe's wrists. Looking over his shoulder, "Is this really necessary?"

"You bet it is, Victor."

The magnate of industry winced at the sound of his first name, used so familiarly, by a nobody, a junior detective, at best. He began to suspect that there were going to be many new experiences to get used to.

***

12:01 PM.

Sarah Forsythe conveniently appeared at the front door of the palatial home, just as her husband was being guided into an unmarked car. Still in her dressing gown, she held a teacup in her hand.

Benji Beckestone stood two steps down the front stairs, looking up at her. "Did your husband call for legal assistance yet?"

The response was leisurely and apathetic. "I don't know." The look of total disinterest in the plight of her husband suited the answer perfectly.

After a sip of her tea, Sarah Forsythe pointed with her chin, toward the car carrying her husband away, and asked, "He gets a phone call, doesn't he?"

Turning back to the house, she continued her thought, "He can call them." She re-entered the house, the front door closing behind her. She left Beckestone standing alone on the steps, shaking his head.

Thinking about how it was a tip from Sarah Forsythe that gave him the probable cause he needed for a search warrant, Detective 2nd Grade Benjamin Beckestone thought to himself, *That was one costly slap in the face.*

***

5:01 PM.

Late on Friday afternoon, the Detective Bureau office was quiet. The week's business was winding down, shift workers were preparing to start their weekends. Benji Beckestone walked across the office to his desk.

He had stayed in 'booking,' just to watch Victor Forsythe be fingerprinted. By the time Forsythe was led to his holding cell, his facial expression had changed. The blank look of denial was now the brow-knit look of an angry man. The extent of the problems he faced were beginning to sink in. He was not happy. Beckestone wondered how much different this was going to be for a man who was so used to getting his way all of the time.

As he slid his pistol into the drawer of his desk, Beckestone saw that Lieutenant Dukasko's office door was open. The Lieutenant was looking directly at him. He didn't look happy. Beckestone began to suspect that leaving Dukasko out of the loop for the last two days was about to catch up with him.

Unseen, from behind the wall of the lieutenant's office, the Captain emerged. He turned toward Beckestone and left the lieutenant's office. Beckestone was unaccustomed to being around the Captain. He didn't even try to read his facial expression.

The Captain walked over to Beckestone's desk. Even before Benji could rise to his feet the Captain tossed a badge onto the desk. Benji, now on his feet, looked at the badge on his desk. 'Detective 1st Grade' decorated its face. Beckestone looked from the shiny new badge to the Captain.

"Good work, Detective." He turned away.

"Thank you, sir." Beckestone called after him. The Captain was already across the office. He left without another word. Beckestone turned back toward his desk. He saw that the Lieutenant's office door was closed.

THIRTY-TWO

The sudden reassignment from Kansas City to St. Louis left Walker's mind burning. There was a constant struggle to behave as normally as he could during working hours. There were frequent triggers for his mind to erupt into a rage. He concentrated as hard as he could, focusing on his role as an agent of the Bureau.

The SAIC in Kansas City assured him that this was a long-term assignment. The Bureau's woes, in dealing with the South Dakota mess, were finally being addressed. Fewer agents were going to be shuffled around. The Bureau was, supposedly, now building a corps of agents who were meant to be assigned to various locations, as needed.

He found an apartment in a mid-town location suggested by the Bureau. While he was moving his belongings, he reflected on how his entire military and

Bureau experience had never sent him farther afield than the Washington, D.C. area. All of his working life centered on the Midwest. Pittsburgh and Kansas City were the limits of his travels. He considered the whole South Dakota experience to be just a weird aberration.

There was nothing for his warped mind to do, but make the best of the situation. Having to start anew – scouting locations and finding a target – was just something that he would have to do. He used the distraction of planning his next kill to calm himself. Ideas for how he would approach his next kill began to float through his mind. He became ever calmer. Determination began to replace the sense of panic he was feeling. His new city posting would work out after all.

Once again, he began the process. The local colleges were spread all over town. Each had its own little area nearby, where students gathered to drink away their stresses. The downtown area was still vibrant, if a bit in decline, like so many other cities. The two large department stores in town kept their headquarters stores there. As anchor businesses, they kept hundreds of other stores busy with clientele of their own.

All of these retail operations needed store workers. The majority were female. The majority of those were young. Along with the college campuses, the St. Louis area was a target-rich environment for a hunter such as himself. The fire in his mind settled into a bed of smoldering coals. The contumacious needs within him would be sated, eventually.

Soon. He hoped, very soon. There was a duality to his thinking. He realized that the last time he made a kill, he rushed through the process. He knew that if he couldn't keep his mind focused on the necessities of avoiding capture, he would ultimately undo himself. Still the core of his very being cried out to kill again – to rid the earth of every manifestation of Katie Spahl.

***

The news of Victor Forsythe's arrest filled the St. Louis airwaves, and occupied all of the press coverage for the weekend. Cary and Lennie Spent the two days, acquiring newspapers and watching the televised reports. The talk between them was of little else. Unlike his previous experience with helping Detective Beckestone, there was no direct exposure to the violence in people's hearts.

By Monday morning, the television and radio news reports were starting to include less of the Forsythe story, and more of other news. The story was still on the front page of both daily newspapers. It would stay there for a long time. Other news was starting to occupy the print space that was once solely occupied by the sensational arrest.

As they did before, Cary and Lennie rode in to work together. The business of the store went on, regardless of the hoopla raised by the events of the weekend. For Cary, there was reassurance in having the demands of the job to deal with.

Lennie looked forward to the lunch 'date' they had arranged to visit the store's jewelry department to look at engagement rings. Cary didn't give Lennie a ring when he asked her to marry him. His practical German side kept him from guessing at Lennie's ring size and plunking down a wad of money on a design he wasn't sure that she would like.

Lennie wasn't at all disappointed by not getting a ring at first. Her Teutonic heritage was, likewise, practical almost to a fault. She intuitively understood why Cary would wait to have her pick out her own design. She was pleased to be able to get exactly what she wanted. It also appealed to the young couple that the store would allow them to combine their considerable employee discounts and get a lot more than they otherwise could.

***

The return to more-or-less-normal, and the happiness over picking out a ring, were short-lived. In the middle of an otherwise perfectly ordinary Wednesday morning, two men appeared at Cary's office door. Both were dressed in dark suits. Both wore white shirts. Their solid-color ties matched their suits. Cary quickly assessed the quality of the suits as straight-off-the-rack purchases; not tailored at all.

Both of the men had very short hair. One was a crew cut, the other a flat-top. They were muscularly built – so much so, that it was readily apparent. The men were so nearly the same height that Cary was unable to detect a difference at first. The crew-cut man spoke before Cary had a chance to greet them.

"I'm agent Denny. This is agent Rosse." Both men simultaneously pulled flat wallets from their jacket pockets. "We're from the FBI."

Both of the men held their wallets open in front of them for exactly the same five-second interval. The gold badges were small, compared to the size of the wallets.

Clearly emblazoned on the identification cards were the three large letters, leaving no doubt about the source of the credentials. Both men closed their I.D. wallets with an audible "snap." It was a very practiced method of punctuating their introduction.

For a moment, Cary was speechless. Neither of the two agents reacted to this response. They had seen it before. Involuntarily rising to his feet, Cary said, "What…" He pushed his chair back from behind himself. "What can I do for you?"

***

A short time later, Cary found himself being escorted through the entrance to the Federal Building. It was a dozen blocks from the store, downtown. Going through the doors, he was certain that he saw Detective Beckestone walking away from the same building. It was the shortest of glimpses. But, he was sure who it was.

The three men rode the elevator. Cary was surprised that they only ascended one floor. Stepping off the elevator, he realized that there was no stairway adjacent to the elevator shaft. The purpose of that kind of design eluded him. It seemed out of the ordinary.

They walked to the end of the second floor, where a door, marked "Federal Bureau of Investigation" awaited them. Once inside the offices, Cary's escort led him to an office with the sign S.A.I.C. on it. They passed through the door so quickly that Cary didn't have a chance to read the small lettering explaining the acronym.

Inside the office sat a man behind a desk. The sign on his desk read: "Arne Ingmarsson." Below that was the title

"Special Agent in Charge." As Cary was led into the room, the man behind the desk did not look up from the work in front of him.

The obvious size and dimensions of the man were poorly concealed behind the desk. The man's shoulders were every bit of double the breadth of Cary's. He seemed to be literally jammed up under the desk, although he did not look uncomfortable. Cary momentarily thought of the furniture in a kindergarten classroom, the kind that made you feel out of place because you were so much larger than anyone who could use it.

Special Agent Ingmarsson also had a crew cut. His white shirt was starched, and wrinkle-free. A black neck tie – a bit narrow for the current fashion – was knotted tightly at the absolute center of the collar. Cary noticed the man's hands. In keeping with the size of the man, they were huge. Cary realized that his experience with such people in the world was extremely limited.

The room wasn't very large. Special Agent Ingmarsson made it seem smaller than it actually was. Other than the desk, there was a table behind agent Ingmarsson, stacked high with computer print-out papers. The stack of papers took up so much of the table top that they were threatening to topple off of one end. Cary wondered at the bewildering amount of information that so much print-out could hold.

Above the table, the wall of the office was covered with a large map. The area of the map was the midwestern United States. Stick-pins with various colored heads were stuck in the map. There were a lot of pins, perhaps more than a hundred. Cary had a vague understanding that the different color pins might represent different categories of crime. The clustering of pins around the cities seemed to be a very normal thing.

After only a momentary wait, Ingmarsson looked up from his work. Cary took his short wait to have been only a cursory attempt at exerting authority. He guessed that a Special Agent in Charge didn't have to make a show of the power that he had. Enough people around him knew what he was and that was all he needed.

The look in Agent Ingmarsson's eyes was another thing. It was serious – deadly serious. The intense look did all that it had to: convince Cary that there would be no polite banter. There would be no conversation without a decided point to it.

"You've been helping the police with solving crimes." Ingmarsson's statement was not just rhetoric, Cary knew that this interview would be tough. It could easily go on a lot longer than he wanted.

"Yes," He hesitated, "Yes, I have." He was unsure how much information he should share, at first.

For the balance of the day, the interview between Special Agent Ingmarsson and Cary Lang had two areas of focus. The first was Cary's unique ability. The FBI man was as calm and unsurprised as he could have been, given what he was hearing. Nothing that Cary said got a rise of any sort out of him.

Ingmarsson was completely patient. He listened carefully to everything Cary told him. Cary got off the subject a few times, talking about how he felt. Ingmarsson didn't interrupt him, or try to redirect his story. He simply let Cary say whatever he wanted.

The second thing that the Special Agent got Cary to talk about was loyalty to his country. At first, Cary thought it was odd. The Special Agent approached the topic in many different ways. Each method of discussing Cary's loyalty to his country was designed to bring out a different side of Cary's character.

After a long discussion about voting and civil rights, Cary decided it was all more about how risky it was to be around someone with Cary's ability, if you didn't trust them. If the FBI needed to trust Cary, it was because they had work for him to do.

It was after five PM. Cary was tiring of the interview. He decided to move the conversation along. "Just what do you want me to do?"

"It's not entirely clear what the Bureau wants from you. Right now, I think that someone other than Detective Beckestone should have some idea of how your particular talents can be utilized."

THIRTY-THREE

Cary spent the afternoon considering the course that his life had taken. While answering questions and responding to leading rhetoric, his mind drifted to thoughts of how his life might otherwise be, if he had never developed his special sense.

Before all this business with his new-found ability, he really felt like he had a grip on the way his life would progress. All of that was gone now. Sitting in the FBI office, he wondered how much of his life he would ever be able to return to.

Two and a half hours of interview passed before the Special Agent suggested a break. Cary took care of business and availed himself of the office coffee service that was offered to him. Special Agent Ingmarsson was gone from the office for a few extra minutes.

Cary took advantage of the opportunity to look around the room. One wall of the room was decorated with a colorful, large map of Iceland. A coat of arms adorned one corner of the map. The name Ingmarsson was emblazoned across the bottom of the map. Cary imagined Arne Ingmarsson as a Viking, on one of those long low ships, dressed in a large cloak and wielding a gigantic sword.

Next to the map of Iceland was a framed display of military badges and insignia. There was a set of stripes with so many chevrons that Cary couldn't imagine what the rank might be, other than sergeant. In the center of the stripes was a star with wings around it. There were also several battle ribbons displayed. Just as his interest in the military was beginning to focus his attention, Ingmarsson came back into the room.

He saw that Cary was looking at the framed military memorabilia. "That all seems like it was so long ago."

"How long was it?" Cary couldn't resist the impulse to be the one asking questions.

Not missing the turnabout, Ingmarsson answered anyway. "I was in the Army until four years ago."

"That's a lot of stripes." Cary left the rhetorical statement lie there, the way his interviewer had been doing all afternoon.

Ignoring the timid attempt at a tease, Ingmarsson explained, "Command Sergeant Major. Even with all that, it was just Army life. I guess I got tired of it." He finished his sentence with a slight smacking of his lips, as if to indicate some unspoken emotion.

Cary didn't try to figure out what the unspoken part might be. There was enough going on without worrying about trivial matters. He took the terse explanation at face value. It was evident that more than just working-life changed for Ingmarsson when he separated from the Army. He realized that Ingmarsson wanted to continue the interview.

In short order, Special Agent Ingmarsson got to the core of the matter at hand. "Everything I have been able to glean from your file suggests that you will be willing to help." He looked intently at Cary. The look in his eyes that Cary took for seriousness that bordered on hostility was gone. In its place was a look of expectation.

Cary realized that somewhere along the line, Agent Ingmarsson had gotten on his side. The transaction between them had become much less confrontational. The thought that maybe it was he who had gotten on Ingmarsson's side began to form in the back of his mind. It was pushed aside by the stark awareness that the FBI had a file on him.

"There's a file?" Cary blinked in confused curiosity.

"Don't be concerned. The biggest job f the Bureau is to collect information. All kinds of information." Ingmarsson gestured vaguely toward the pile of computer print-outs, behind him. "What's done with that information – how its organized and used – is its own science."

Special Agent Ingmarsson attempted a smile. It faded from his face almost before it appeared. He knew he had managed to put the younger man at ease, at least a bit. What he did next and how he did it would make or break the plan he had in mind.

The FBI man stood behind his desk. "Let's continue this outside." He led Cary from the confines of the small office. Together they walked to the elevator and rode down the one floor to the lobby. At the street, they crossed to the park area that ran across the largest part of downtown. The trees were still heavily laden with leaves but Autumn had begun in earnest. The rustle of leaves on the ground around them mixed with the sounds of the city.

As the walked long the sidewalk, Ingmarsson continued. "The fact that there is a file on you is really of small consequence. There are files on everyone that has ever come into range of Bureau scrutiny. As I said, the Bureau collects information. Your new – um – ability, your new sense, can help with a new investigation. Your ability will contribute a new kind of information to all of the others that we collect. I've already gotten approval from my superiors.

"Your name and what we have found out about you are simply another small portion of the vast amount if information that the Bureau has at its command."

He let Cary digest the new understanding about how he was known to the FBI. He hoped that Cary understood that it was not necessarily a thing to be worried about. Cary guessed that a file of information about him probably meant that people he knew had been spoken to. He wondered if Lennie was one of them. He shuddered to think that his fiancée had been interviewed by the Bureau's agents. What would she think?

Before he could spend more time diving into a state of worry, Special Agent Ingmarsson refocused the conversation. "As I said, back in the office, your file information suggests that you would be willing to assist the Bureau in an investigation."

Cary was really out of his element, now." I wouldn't know how to go about getting time off from work." He continued to walk along with the FBI man, but began to slow his pace slightly, causing Ingmarsson to slow and turn toward him.

"We've already taken care of that. As it turns out, your employer is really eager to make sure you can assist us. Sometimes the reputation of the Bureau – whatever that might be – begets a willingness to cooperate that is truly refreshing." He smiled broadly at the young store employee at his side.

Cary could only stand and wonder. What did they think? What would happen when he returned? Would he even have a job? He never thought of anyone in the management echelons as being anything but store functionaries. The notion that FBI men had walked in and somehow arranged for an extended absence for him caused his head to spin.

He realized that they had stopped in the middle of the sidewalk. Ingmarsson touched his elbow, to guide him back into walking. "There are a few documents to sign – confidentiality, and all that – then we can get you back to work. We'll begin tomorrow."

***

The ride home that evening was interesting. After he and Lennie had both gotten into the car, Cary was unsure how to begin. Lennie let him off the hook. Rather she dragged him off the hook. "Well? How did that go?" She smiled a beatific, knowing smile at him. Cary got her to explain that an FBI agent had interviewed her, about him.

Happy that Lennie not only knew about the FBI but was pleased and eager to learn more, Cary launched into a long story about his afternoon. The story continued until they got home. He picked Wheels up from the apartment and headed for the park. Using play with the dog to blow off a little steam of his own, Cary launched into a vigorous round of frisbee catch-and-chase with the golden retriever.

When the dog and Cary were all tired of play, they started to head home. That was when Cary noticed the dark sedan parked next to the area where they played with the dog. Inside were FBI agents Denny and Rosse. Cary wondered briefly why they were there. He watched his rearview mirror as he drove off and saw the FBI car following. Evidently, I'm special. The thought didn't make him feel anything but more concerned about what he was getting himself into.

***

On the street outside the four-family flat where Cary and Lennie (and Wheels) lived, FBI agents Denny and Rosse settled down for a long wait. Their relief would come at midnight, they would have a short night to rest and start back up in the morning. This assignment was chiefly theirs. They would bear the greater share of the time commitment to the work needing to be done.

Quiet conversation passed between the two men from time to time as they observed people in the neighborhood going about their routine activities. Later in the evening, the conversation focused on their immediate charge, Cary Lang.

Denny, looking straight out the windshield of the car, yet not really seeing anything, said, "This really is a different sort of a case. Isn't it? I mean, what is it that we're going to do with this guy? Ingmarsson said we're going from town to town with him for some reason. If what Ingmarsson says about Cary Lang is true, this is going to be one unusual case."

Rosse, equally focused on nothing in particular, responded, "Yeah, strange is the order of the day with this case. And we've got to keep tabs on Captain Strange." He pointed with his chin toward the apartment building.

Beginning to chuckle quietly to himself, Denny answered, "Yes he is, isn't he? The Wizard of Odd."

Both men had to cup their elbows to their mouths so the sound of their laughter would not be heard outside the car.

THIRTY-FOUR

He awoke in the morning. For the first time in his life that he could remember, Walker had overslept. He didn't remember switching off the alarm clock. It was only fifteen minutes. It was still very much unlike him to do that.

Since he was a boy, he had set the determination for himself to be in command of those parts of his daily existence that he could. Training himself to rise at the sound of the alarm was one of those things that he could control. It had never failed him before.

The storm of confusing thoughts in his head raged on. Since being given the case file yesterday afternoon, he had to deal with the fact that the killings they were investigating were ones that he had committed. Part of his mind read each case report with detached fascination. It was truly

271

remarkable to see so much effort spent in describing the nothing-at-all that he had left behind.

Part of his mind heaved and roiled with the need to kill again. It had been a lot longer than he ever would have wanted. He considered whether being in the Bureau was a good idea after all. That part of his mind was also close to being unthinkingly afraid. It was not afraid of discovery. It was afraid of not being able to keep killing; to keep destroying the living reminders of Katie Spahl, and all that her memory meant to him.

He quickly went through his morning ablutions and skipped the cup of coffee he usually made for himself. There would be coffee at the office. Crossing from mid-town to downtown a little more quickly than usual made up for the lost time. His arrival at the Bureau office was, as usual, a few minutes early.

***

Cary received instructions to pack for a week of out-of-town travel. When he arrived at the downtown federal building, he had his suitcase in hand. He was shown through to the elevator without interruption. The walk down the long hall to the FBI offices seemed longer than the day before. Cary barely realized that it was the change in his routine, making him anxious.

Having to say good-bye to Lennie for a week was difficult. He no more wanted to leave her than he could fly. She had been such a great help while he struggled with the emotional impact of the violence that he had been exposed to.

Cary steeled himself for his new commitment by telling himself that he was just going to have to grow up, and completely participate in the investigation. He had agreed to assist with it. He needed to make sure that he was not a hindrance, but a real contributor to the effort.

The morning session in the office of Special Agent Ingmarsson consisted of a lengthy briefing. As such, it was just the outline of the information that the two FBI agents would have to work with. They would have all the file information at their disposal while they investigated. Cary was not given access to the files, but all of his questions were answered more than adequately.

The investigation briefing centered on a number of murders. They had taken place in several different cities. The FBI was looking into the possibility of a relationship between the cases. The victims of the killings were all young women. They had all disappeared at night. The scant available evidence suggested that they had each been taken from a carefully selected, public area. There were no witnesses to the kidnappings in any of the cases.

Each of the murder victims was strangled to death with a knitted scarf. The murder scenes in each case had a common quality: a paucity of available physical evidence. The fact that each of the murder scenes had so little evidence was a chief factor tying the cases together. It was a very thin thread of relationship, but it was real. It was also part of the very little that they had to go on.

At eleven o'clock, the briefing concluded. Special Agent Ingmarsson sent the three of them on their way. Bag lunches awaited them in a Bureau car in the garage. The car was fully fueled and ready to go.

The drive was uneventful, at least as far as the two agents were concerned. For Cary, other matters arose from a casual survey of the auras of the two FBI agents with whom he was traveling.

It was an almost perfectly unlikely thing. Cary had ridden along in the back seat of the Bureau car for more than seven hours and felt himself beginning to tire. Conversation in the car was sparse at first. It dwindled to nothing after a couple of hours.

They were in mid-Ohio. The scenery was, to say the least, not stimulating. As they continued eastward the specter of the coming night loomed high above the horizon. Cary let himself begin to doze a bit.

For no particular reason, he let his aura-viewing sense run free. His head was initially turned to the side. In the sparsely populated Ohio farmland, few auras presented themselves. He turned his head toward the front of the car. The auras of the two FBI agents startled him.

Without paying attention to the fact that he was doing it, he shifted to a more upright position in his seat. He opened his eyes briefly to see Agent Rosse driving and Agent Denny in the passenger seat. As he did so he noticed Agent Rosse glancing at him in the rear-view mirror. He let his eyes close again, feigning sleep.

The two FBI agents' auras were what had startled him. Both were completely different from what he anticipated. Expecting to see the yellow color of someone paying attention to what they were doing, he saw bands of intense red, sometimes shifting over to the oxblood-dark-red that again darkened to black. It represented intensifying anger, becoming insane rage. As he viewed the auras, both shifted back and forth: anger and rage.

After a time, he saw that agent Rosse's aura revealed the green of happiness right next to the black of hatred. This was intensely confusing for Cary. He thought of the two FBI agents as the typically rock-solid, stoic go-getters of crime prevention. The display of a roiling emotional state was the last thing he expected.

Denny's aura showed fear and the blue of sadness more often side by side. It made little sense to Cary. The trouble was that he now had reason to doubt both of his companions. These were the men leading the investigation. Apparently, neither was the utterly reliable G-Man of the movies.

Eleven hours after leaving St. Louis, they checked into a motel in Pittsburgh. It was nothing special, but it was neat and clean. Cary was provided with a room to himself. The two agents would share a room. Their investigative work would begin in the morning.

Cary called St. Louis to say good-night to Lennie. He was careful to reverse the charges. He didn't want to have any extra room charges screwing up the motel bill and potentially making the FBI men unhappy with him. He and Lennie talked for a short while. Most of the conversation was devoted to sharing endearments and promising to make up for lost time when Cary returned.

After trying to sleep for about an hour, Cary heard the door of the room next to his close. The sound was just loud enough to suggest that the person who passed through the door didn't care that it was well after midnight. Cary viewed the aura – unmistakably one of the FBI men – walk down the colonnade of the motel building. He turned to see the other man's aura evidently making a telephone call. Both of the auras were still roiling in an elevated state of emotional arousal.

Neither man had yet exhibited behaviors that Cary could relate to their aural displays. The way they presented themselves was entirely consistent with Cary's expectation of them as calm, dispassionate investigators. Both of them appeared to be the rock-solid, stoic, manly type. The aural displays of highly elevated emotional states belied their calm exteriors.

A few minutes later, the telephone call was still in progress when the other agent returned. The agent in the room quickly hung up the phone when the other man started to enter the room. Cary had no idea of the significance of any of it. Neither of the men's aura showed unusual emotional coloration.

Everything he saw was grist for a mill of thoughts and doubts that turned and ground away at Cary's mind. He forced himself to cease his aura-viewing. His head still swam with residual images of the surprising auras he had seen. Sleep only came after a couple hours of trying.

***

The next morning, a very tired and sleepy Cary Lang accompanied the two FBI agents to the Federal Building in downtown Pittsburgh. He was able to rise and be ready on time, but the meal at the motel diner was working against him now. He poured an extra cup of coffee for himself from the FBI office pot.

After a short organizational meeting with the Pittsburgh Special Agent in Charge, Cary was sequestered in a room adjacent to an interview room that was part of the FBI offices. A loudspeaker, which would enable him to listen to the interviews, rested on a table in the center of the room. There was a legal pad and pen for him to use in making notes.

It was unusual for him to hear people he was viewing, since he almost always viewed auras from a distance. It was just something else he was going to have to adapt to. He actually thought it was unfair to listen in on people he was viewing. It was like reading minds…

Cary caught himself with the thought: Reading Minds. He really never thought of it quite that way. Obviously, the FBI thought of it that way, very early, after hearing of his new-found ability.

The other thing the FBI had thought of was putting Cary in relatively close proximity to a viewing subject, just the way Detective Beckestone did. The ability to pick up on nuances of body movement and posture greatly enhanced and influenced his interpretation of what he viewed.

In the course of the morning, four different people were brought in and interviewed. The interviewer was a member of the Pittsburgh FBI team. Agents Denny and Rosse were using the time to pore over the case files in order to see if they could come up with any new approaches to solving the cases. They left, to speak at length with detectives from the Pittsburgh Police Department.

All four of the interviewees had one thing in common: They all lived near the place where the victim was last seen. Three of them had criminal records. All of them were afraid. From what Cary could read of their posture and movement, they all responded as though they were under a lot of pressure.

As the interview questions got more pointed, the interview subjects all became more fearful. Slightly different questions produced different levels of emotional responses. In a general sense, none of the subjects was reacting differently from the others.

Cary's overall impression of the interviews was that none of the subjects was unusually more fearful of discovery than the others. None of the FBI agents seemed to react to the lack of a conclusive result of the morning's work. They had all experienced the same sort of dead ends in investigations before this morning.

Agents Denny and Rosse returned from their conversations with the local police. They achieved the same inconclusive outcome. After a short debrief with the SAIC, the trio left the offices and headed out.

Over the dinner table, plans were made for the next leg of their journey. They would drive to Indianapolis the following day. The drive was a shorter drive than the one from St. Louis to Pittsburgh. They would leave in the morning, check in with the local Bureau office, and work the case.

***

Special Agent Arne Ingmarsson slogged through the pile of computer print-outs.

As he did so, a thought began to form in the back of his mind. Still incomplete and not fully structured, it didn't have the requisite strength to nag at him – not yet.

Faith. Belief. He knew that the facts he needed were probably in the stacks of print-outs. The strength of his belief drove him on, hour after hour. He had been at it for more than two weeks already. He read ream after ream of printed information trying to pick out some small shred of information that would actually contribute evidence to the investigation.

Every moment he had, that was not dedicated to running the Bureau office, was committed to this search. He was attempting to prize the small bits of data out of this daunting pile that would come together and point them in the right direction. His long time in the Bureau taught him the value of turning detailed facts into evidence. Grinding the information down to its essence – what the computer operators called crunching the data – would eventually lead to a solution.

Ingmarsson collated times of the three different murders: the time of day, day of the week, day of the month. There was no sense of connection there. The months and years seemed to bear no relationship to each other as well. He made a note of one tiny thing that he noticed: The interval between the second and third murders was shorter than between the first two. He didn't try to attach any significance to the fact. It was just one piece of information; a data point.

Leaning back in his chair and stretching, he looked at the huge stack of unread computer print-outs. He looked at his watch. There were still a couple of hours left in the day.

He rose from his desk, and left the office. A minute later, he was back, cup of coffee in hand, ready to get back at it. He grabbed a stack of print-outs, sat down, sipped his coffee, and resumed reading.

THIRTY-FIVE

The long, bench seat in the back of the government car was big enough for him to stretch out a bit. While the road noise hummed and thrummed along, Cary read. He bought a paperback book from the place that they stopped for gas. It was a sensational fictionalization of a real murder story. He kept his eyes down, and his attention on the book.

What he learned about the two men he was traveling with bothered him in more than one way. He knew that being intimately aware of people's emotional states on a personal level was fraught with problems. He already had a few close calls with Lennie, interacting with her without her knowing that he was reading her aura.

Cary felt as though he was being forced to be in the presence of two men that could be very dangerous. Both were physically powerful. They were both fully enfranchised federal agents. They both carried pistols. Neither was acting in a way that reflected their apparent inner turmoil.

Cary knew he was inexperienced in understanding human psychology. With his "silent sight," he knew that he was in over his head. He now knew that he was in the middle of something that was much more complicated than he originally thought.

The drive from Pittsburgh to Indianapolis would take another three hours. Cary already decided that if he needed to rest his eyes, he would refrain from any aura viewing. For the moment, he needed to just be normal. He needed to not be gifted with any special ability. He was grateful for the fact that he had achieved the ability to turn his new sense off voluntarily. He wondered at what torture it would be, if that were not the case.

***

After arriving in Indianapolis, the three men checked in at the Bureau office. Plans were already set for a case review and a single subject interview. That would take place the following morning.

The evidence collected in Indianapolis was even more scant than in Pittsburgh. The lone interviewee made the mistake of being a vagrant found in the vicinity of the murder scene. The murder was already two days old at the time of its discovery. The sense of the subject's likelihood of being involved extended to the point of understanding that he was in the wrong place at the wrong time – two days after the murder took place.

The scene of the murder was a city park. The park had the curious existence of a place that served no purpose whatsoever. The city government established it amid the numerous commercial properties in the area, with the thought that it would be used by workers on their breaks and lunch hours.

The truth was that the property occupied by the park was too small to use for commercial purposes. Rather than see the vacant lot become an impromptu dumping ground, a park was established. If it ever was used, no one knew. There was never sign of anyone in the park.

At night, with all the businesses done for the day, the little park was even emptier. Someone decided that it was perfect for a murder. They were right. Two days passed before the body of the young woman was discovered.

***

That evening, Cary's attention was once again drawn to his agent-companions. Cary heard their raised voices exchanged in a few short lines of abrupt dialogue. He allowed himself to briefly view their auras. Once again, the sight of highly emotional, angry auras greeted him. Not wanting any more questions in his mind, Cary quickly ceased viewing. Whatever it was with the two agents, it was going to have to work itself out. Cary hoped that his involvement with the two FBI agents wouldn't extend to their problems.

He again called Lennie. They spent a long time – spending a lot of money on long distance charges – just talking. Cary needed her, needed to be with her. She was his safe place now. With her, he was more at peace than at any other time, especially since his new sense developed.

Even though they talked about "everything," Cary didn't mention anything about the agents' auras. He left that out of the conversation mainly because he understood so little about what was going on there. It would be pointless and cruel to burden her with such information.

***

The next morning was a disappointment. The interview subject was an alcoholic vagrant. It was discovered, at the time of the initial investigation, that he was a veteran. In order to keep track of their only person of interest, the police got him into a state-run alcohol rehabilitation center.

The interview revealed a man who was frightened of being interviewed by the FBI, but little else. At first, Cary thought that the man's high level of fear meant something. But after a few minutes, the man's emotional state quieted. None of his reactions to questions were particularly revealing. Cary suspected that the difference in his reactions was the result of years of drinking as much and as often as he could.

Cary had to label the session as being as inconclusive as the one in Pittsburgh. The agents' review of the small amount of case detail available was equally disappointing. Once again Cary noticed how little reaction to falling short of their goal the FBI people demonstrated. He wondered how much disappointment and frustration went along with investigative work. If what they were experiencing was typical, Cary knew he wasn't cut out for it.

The morning's work progressed quickly enough to allow the three men to depart for their next stop immediately after lunch. Cary made sure he had enough reading material for the drive.

***

The evening sky behind them already darkened enough to reveal the glow of the city as it faded in the distance. Driving past St. Louis, without bothering to stop, seemed stupid to Cary. He guessed that neither of the two agents in the front seat had as much reason as he – Lennie – to want to interrupt the trip. He had never met men as focused and determined as these two men. This knowledge gave him a tiny bit of insight into the FBI criteria for agent selection.

These thoughts led him to think, for at least the hundredth time, of how little he knew about the two FBI agents. They had the upper hand in the collective relationship of the three of them. They had access to whatever information was in his file. He had no such information about either of them.

Cary guessed they knew at least something about each other. He also guessed that they had been working together for some time – but not a long time. He wondered at the friction between them that led to their loud, abrupt – argument? – the other night in the motel.

Cary also thought that if all went well, he would be home again in a day, or so. He settled back in his seat, opened the book he brought along, and read. In a few hours they would be in Kansas City, ready to start the whole rigamarole over again.

***

If their work in Indianapolis seemed be unproductive, the trip to Kansas City was worthless. At least it seemed that way to Cary. The frustrations of their largely unproductive work were wearing his patience and perspicacity thin. Even though he agreed to be part of the investigative team, he still felt – at least at this point – like he was being dragged around the country for no good reason at all.

Prior to their arrival, the usual arrangements were made to conduct an interview of a person identified in the original investigation as being of interest. The three men arrived in Kansas City Too late to check in at the Bureau office. The subject interview would be conducted. The case notes would be reviewed. If necessary, they would speak with the local law enforcement people. One more night in a motel would be their last, if all went well.

They arrived at the Kansas City Bureau office only to find that a review of the case determined that the person to be questioned was, in fact, of no possible interest to the case. Their original claim to have been at the scene of the crime was a manufactured claim, presented by a claimant that apparently "had issues."

The discovery of the false claim was made only after the group of three men departed from Indianapolis. There was no particular reason for them to check with the Kansas City office ahead of time. Their entire eight-plus-hours of driving turned out to be a waste of time and resources.

A brief conversation with the detective assigned to the case led only to one notation in Agent Denny's note book: There was an almost perfect lack of physical evidence at the murder scene. It seemed like a very scant finding for all the time and effort put into it.

***

Back to hunting. Getting back to St. Louis meant that he would be able to return to his pursuit of a suitable target. The effort of maintaining a calm outward appearance was becoming way too great. Walker needed to get away, be on his own, hunt alone. Working toward achieving another kill was really the only way to ease his inner turmoil.

It would be only a few more hours. Back to town, unpack, settle in. He would start the next day with his usual routine. Then, he would be able to return to the search, the hunt. Find a target, find a place to take the target down. Find a place to complete the hunt; to make the kill. The thought of actually being able to kill again sent a shiver down his back. He managed to sit perfectly still, although the hair on the back of his neck stood straight and stiff.

He glanced at his passenger and in the rear-view mirror. Neither of the other two men in the car took any notice.

***

Cary deeply felt the absence from Lennie. Two days of his life with her were gone. Even though he would see her tonight, he still felt sense of loss. He was happy to be on the way home. He would see Lennie tonight. Happy wasn't the half of it.

Until now he had managed to keep from viewing the auras of the two FBI men again. It was too confusing. Seeing their inner tumult added too much to what he was expected to do, to see, to try and understand. His own great sense of relief at finally being on his way home caused him to forget, just for a moment that he didn't want any more information about the two agents' emotional states.

Closing his eyes for just a few seconds, he viewed his companions' auras. He expected to see the green of happiness dominating their auras. After all, he was happy to be going home. Once again, he saw the roiling flow of emotions. One of the men was at least partly happy, although his green aura flashed and blinked with streaks of deep red anger, and black hatred.

The other man's aura was bluer – sadder – than green. In likewise fashion, his aura flashed red and black. Whatever was on the two men's' minds was obviously too much for Cary to deal with. He opened his eyes and concentrated on looking at the scenery.

THIRTY-SIX

Cary's return to home came on Friday. Aside from being bowled over by Wheels when he came through the door, he spent the weekend in Lennie's arms. The time passed in an all-too-brief two days of love and laughter, playing with the dog in the park, and growing together. Coffee in the mornings went on for hours, as they talked and talked about Cary's trip.

Cary related is reactions to the cities he visited so briefly. Because of his instructions from Special Agent Ingmarsson, he wasn't able to say much about the investigation. All he could say was that they really hadn't discovered much about what they were looking for. He again avoided mention of his observation of the two agents he accompanied.

The weekend came to an end. Monday morning saw Lennie staying in a bit later, leaving Cary to drive to work by himself. She drove herself to work while Cary was gone, and wasn't ready yet to give up her early morning hours of freedom. She spent the time over coffee, sitting with Wheels at her feet, reading the newspaper. It was a bit more expensive for them to commute to the same place separately, but for at least a while, Lennie wanted her mornings.

Cary found that things at work were as normal as they could be. He checked in with his boss on Monday morning. No mention was made of where he went or what he did. Cary was impressed that the FBI could so completely smooth over an absence such as his. He thought maybe it meant that he thought of himself as being more important than he really was. Either way, he was glad to be back at work.

It took a day or so to get back into the swing of things at the downtown store. His desk was neatly arranged and the "In" and "Out" boxes were empty. Whoever took over his ordering while he was gone didn't alter any of his systems at all. The files were all in perfect order. He was able to pick up the flow of seasonal orders in stride.

The return to sharing lunch times with Lennie was another reassurance that his life was going to go on as usual. It was familiar and new, at the same time. There was left over pizza from the weekend for the first couple of days. They fell into the usual habit of talking about store happenings while they ate.

At the end of the first week after returning to St. Louis, Cary got a telephone call from Detective

Beckestone. The call came in at work, shortly before the end of the day. He was surprised and somewhat suspicious at first. He was relieved to find that Beckestone was only checking up on him. His interest extended no further than his own investigations. From what he said, it was apparent that he knew nothing about Cary's trip with the two FBI agents.

Benji Beckestone thanked Cary yet again for his help with the Forsythe case. He told Cary that he was now Detective First Grade. His promotion came as a result of bringing the big case to a close. He told Cary that the scuttle-butt from the Prosecuting Attorney's Office was that Victor Forsythe would accept a plea deal. This was so that he wouldn't have to spend all of the rest of his life in prison, just most of it.

During their conversation, Cary was briefly transported back to the awful night of the murders in the warehouse. The feelings he had that night filled his mind. He had to end the telephone call sooner than he otherwise would have. Continuing to talk to Detective Beckestone would only remind him further of that horrible experience. He managed to end the call politely, but just barely. He knew that Beckestone would probably pick up on his abruptness. He couldn't help it.

As he sat there in his office, Cary began to make comparisons between what he viewed in the warehouse, and the aura of the two FBI agents he chanced to view. It was not a great leap of deduction or logic to understand that the deep, dark aural reds of hate – so dark that they seemed almost black – were the same in all three men. His new understanding gave him reason to really be afraid of the

291

two FBI men now. He fervently hoped that he would see no more of them.

At last, Cary rose from his seat and straightened the desktop for the next weeks business. He made a stop by the Young Sophisticates department to say good-bye to Lennie, and work out dinner plans. He could get in a good play session with Wheels. He listened to the Doobie Brothers on the way home from work.

***

"Poke-a-Poika!" Wham! The oversized fist of Lon Spahl smacked into the side of his head. With stars in his eyes, and bees buzzing in his head, he fell to the ground. "Poke-a-Poika!"

Ready for the next blow to rain down on him, Walker awoke with a start. His tee-shirt and sheets were soaked with sweat. He never had a dream like that, not even while the physical abuse was happening to him as a child. He recalled that he never really dreamt anyway, not that he ever remembered.

He sat on the side of his bed. The apartment was dark. At three AM, it was quiet in the apartment building. There was no way he would be able to get back to sleep. He went to the kitchenette and started a pot of coffee. It would be an extra-early start to his day.

The Bureau work was light. He would have a lot of free time during the day today. Following the rule of being out of the office more than he was in it, he'd take advantage of the chance to hunt. While the coffee perked, he went down to the lobby of the apartment building and bought a newspaper.

He showered, still trying to shake off the effects of the dream. His mind was overactive, his senses were heightened. A small amount of adrenalin – the elixir of fight or flight - still coursed through his bloodstream. His hands trembled, if ever so slightly. He took a minute or two longer in the shower, letting the water run down his body, to calm himself.

After dressing, he sat down and read the newspaper, front to back. The local coverage of the Forsythe affair still took up a lot of the print space. He found a wire service story about the ongoing protests in South Dakota. He had long ago put that whole experience out of his mind. He was a bit surprised that there was still enough going on to merit national coverage.

Getting to the Bureau office at his usual time, he set out to finish the investigation that he was assigned to. A local trucking company was having more than its fair share of trouble with the unions. It seemed like the sort of problem that would need a long undercover assignment. Making that call was above his pay grade. He made his notes and would turn them in at day's end.

Free, ostensibly for the rest of the day, he set out to track down a suitable target. If that yielded poor results, he could scout for a kill site. Skipping his usual start in the mid-town university district, he headed downtown. He parked his government car in a public garage, and set out on foot. Ground work was almost always done on foot. You could miss too much, cruising around in a car. Walker would seek out the next target, the way he knew best.

He ate lunch in a diner. The small shop was wedged in between two tall office buildings. It had that curious quality of being a one-story affair, dwarfed by the abutting structures. There was no other use for the small wedge of land upon which it stood. Because of its location, it would probably be in business long after every other downtown restaurant had gone out of business.

The diner provided no suitable prey. This was so, despite the fact that numerous young women patronized the diner. He set out to hunt the stores and shops of the downtown business district.

Stores, attended by young women of every type and size were all over the place. He passed through one of the large department stores. Beautiful young women, made up and coiffured to the limit, sold make up, perfume and jewelry. The scents of the center of the ground floor sales area were besotted with a mixture of perfumes dispensed in generous amounts from scores of sample bottles.

Blondes and redheads, brunettes and the infrequent heavy-set young girl filled the ranks of the salesgirl staff. He left the large store and crossed the street to another. The situation here was mainly the same: purses, cosmetics, jewelry. There was one exception. The corner of the main floor sales area was occupied by a women's clothing department. The sign over the sales area said: Young Sophisticates.

He saw her. For just a moment, he thought it was an illusion. Again, for another moment, he suspected himself of hallucinating. The girl behind the counter looked like Katie Spahl. No, she was Katie Spahl.

Watching from another department, he tried not to stare. If he made any eye contact at all, this part of the hunt would be over. Fiddling with a piece of merchandise, as though he was interested in it, he kept his attention on the young salesgirl. He began to calm down, just a little bit. The resemblance was astounding. He heard it said that everyone in the world has a twin. This girl was a perfect match for Katie Spahl. The sight of her caused a steady stream of shivers to course up and down his spine. The anticipation in his mind raced nearly out of control.

He moved away from the young Sophisticates area altogether. He had marked his target. He new where to find her. The name of the store was Vander and Beste. It would be a simple matter to return and follow her, track her. In his mind the pieces began to fall together. Hunt, track, take, kill.

With one part of the puzzle at least partly solved, he left the downtown department store to go to his office. Finish the day, begin again tomorrow. Find the take site. Find the kill site. Prepare, leave no trace, no evidence. The demands of the hunt calmed his mid like nothing else could.

He allowed himself to get ahead of his own planning. It was so long since his last kill that he already knew of a kill site, even with no particular target in mind. Now that there was a target, he would have to make a detailed scouting tour of the area. A state park, twenty-five miles outside of town, would be perfect for his needs. The distance was greater than he usually confined his sites to. The area was distinctly remote, and devoid of human activity, at least at night.

Tomorrow, he would nail down his route to the kill site, mark the time required to get there. If it didn't fall within the time limit – the amount of time it usually took a target to recover from carotid artery compression – he would have to find a location that was closer to the take site.

The need to kill was palpable. He didn't just want to kill the girl who looked so much like Katie Spahl, he needed to kill her. Nothing would be right in his mind until he did.

THIRTY-SEVEN

Two weeks after returning from his unusual cross-country trip with the FBI, Cary Lang was well settled into the routines of his job. The winter seasonal buys were all in-process. He had merchandise in-store, en route, and being prepared for shipment. His stock would be on hand just as the Christmas displays were being set up. Years of repeating this systematic coordination gave him the experience to run things smoothly.

Wrapping up a week of work was all that was on his mind when the telephone rang. The caller was Special Agent Ingmarsson, from the FBI office.

"Would it be possible for you to meet with me on Monday? I've got a few things to discuss with you about your part in the investigation. Questions have come to me about the different cases that you can answer. In fact, only you can answer."

Ingmarsson's tone was matter-of-fact. There seemed to be no particular unusual impression conveyed at all. Cary knew that this was a technique employed by investigators. Perhaps Ingmarsson was just so accustomed to using it that he did it unawares.

Cary was surprised to hear from the FBI at all, let alone just two weeks later. Trying not to sound too excited, Cary answered, "Yes. I'll set some time aside in the afternoon. Can we do this at two?"

"Two o'clock, Monday afternoon." Click. The call couldn't have lasted a minute. Cary leaned back in his chair, drew a deep breath, and let it out.

I'm gonna have to figure out a way to keep from getting dragged into all this crime and violence. Cary was moving away emotionally from the excitement of having his new ability. He actually employed it at work, gauging the emotional states of people he had to deal with. It was a way of being in control of what happened while using his 'silent sight.'

There was an unavoidable up-and-down, busy-not busy, then busy again quality to the store work. With some of the people he worked with, it was easy to tell whether they were stressed out, or not. Other people at the store managed to not wear their hearts on their sleeves. Cary thought that as long as he could "read" their dispositions, it would only make it easier for him to deal with them.

Cary looked around his office. He really was all caught up. Even though it was an hour and a half early, he decided to head out. There were enough long, late days ahead of him. Keeping up with the Christmas rush was never easy. He would more than make up for one short Friday afternoon.

***

Passing through the door of the FBI office, Cary reflected on how short the two days since Ingmarsson's call seemed. This meeting, scheduled as it was, occupied his mind throughout the entire weekend. He knew he was being distracted and detached from Lennie. He felt as though he couldn't help it. He so very much wanted to never be exposed to the hate and violence he bore witness to previously.

Agents Denny and Rosse were both in the office, apparently busy with some work assigned to them. Neither looked up from his desk to acknowledge his presence. Cary didn't know whether to be offended or not. He walked on through to Special Agent Ingmarsson's office.

The afternoon meeting turned out to be a whole lot less threatening, or even interesting than Cary anticipated. Ingmarsson had a sense of exacting thoroughness about him, and he conveyed it to Cary. The questions he asked were all follow-on questions to things that had already been asked and answered. The information he related to the FBI agent didn't seem to be important at all. It was all just a bunch of trivial details.

During the afternoon, Cary took advantage of the odd moment of respite to view the aura of his counterpart. Ingmarsson's very evenly constrained, yellow aura reflected a state of calm concentration on the matter before him.

Unable to resist the temptation, Cary took a brief glance at the auras of the two FBI agents he worked with. The surprise of the afternoon was that both of the men had vivid blue and white bands of color dominating their auras. Sadness and Fear. Cary could only wonder at what was going on. Where he expected to see the men's auras reflecting concentration on their work, he saw that both still were in an aroused emotional state.

Along with the aural displays he had seen during the investigatory trip, Cary was now as worried about the two men as he was frightened of them. Cary didn't think Agent Ingmarsson would like that he was sneaking peeks at his men's auras. He kept his discovery to himself.

The meeting ended. With an internal sigh of relief, Cary left the FBI office behind. All the way back to his own office, he tried to think of other things. The image of the FBI agents' auras kept creeping back into his mind.

***

The Monday afternoon office work was done. He spent the weekend wondering why Ingmarsson brought Cary Lang back. It was another thing above his pay grade. He put it out of his mind as he headed out to resume stalking the girl downtown.

In another hour or so, the girl would finish her shift and leave the department store for the night. Walker headed to the little diner, wedged between the two tall office buildings. It was becoming a regular haunt for him. There, he could waste time, and eat, before the girl left work.

The place was called Irv's. The hot grill was behind a wall with a little window in it. In that cramped, tiny kitchen, a large, overweight, sweaty man prepared all of the food. A good guess was that his name was Irv, but no one ever asked. It was the kind of eatery where you could eat meals for decades, and never know another soul in the place.

As the time approached for the girl to leave work, he finished his meal, paid up, and left. He was aware of each and every single person in the place. All were regulars, no new faces this evening. He was also aware that none of the people in the place paid any attention to him at all. Staying constantly aware of who might take notice of you was a well-honed survival skill.

Right on cue, the young woman he waited for emerged from the employee entrance of the great department store. Turning up the block, she walked to the corner and waited for the light to change. The throng of evening shoppers was not too large. Everyone was busy with what they were doing. He could maintain visual contact with her indefinitely under these circumstances.

Two blocks from the store, his target walked into a pay-by-the-day parking lot. For store workers, the rates were still just low enough to be affordable. The young woman put a hand full of change in a numbered box, mounted on a steel pole. Being not totally unfamiliar with what he was seeing, he knew he would lose contact with the girl.

He moved slightly to get a better look at the car that the girl would get into. A red VW coupe. He read off the license number, repeating it over and over as the girl drove out of the parking lot.

There was nothing for him to do now, but write down the number. He would go about his normal evening business. Tomorrow would be the day to follow her home. He hoped for a take point near the girl's home. The downtown area was much too busy for it to happen here.

As he planned, the next day gave him the chance he needed to follow the girl home. She appeared at the parking lot, right on time. She paid her daily fee and drove off, oblivious to his pursuit.

Weaving through traffic, and finding her way to the southside residential neighborhood, Lennie pulled into the car park behind their building. Watching from the end of the alleyway, he instantly knew there was a serious complication. An oath escaped his lips at the sight, "Jesus Christ Katzenjammer." He never swore. The curse words came on their own. He only knew that they were words he heard hundreds of times in his youth.

He very much wanted things to be different from what he knew they would be. He found a parking place down the block from the four-family flat that he knew so well. Revealing how complicated things were likely to be, the girl appeared at the front window of the apartment where he had kept watch over the strange young man, Cary Lang. The likelihood that she was somewhere near when he was here before had the sense of bitter irony about it.

That night, he drove back to his mid-town apartment seething with rage at the set of circumstances he was now facing. He was provoked. The girl was the target. No, she was THE target. The moment he saw her, fate intertwined their life stories. In a sense, she was already his, in his clutches, nearing death.

He imagined over and over the sensation of strangling the life out of her. He saw the light of life in her eyes fade to nothing. He heard the last breath lazily escape her lips as he finally loosened the scarf around her dead neck. He felt her limp form slip from his hands when he was done with her. In his imagination, he killed her, over and over.

Danger. There was so much danger of discovery. His heightened emotional state finally triggered a self-aware calming of his mind. He would have to work much harder at being unnoticeable. He would have to stalk the girl much more carefully. The strange young man was a real problem. There was a dog to worry about as well.

He thought a bit more calmly about his dilemma. Somehow, it was appropriate that the girl who so strongly resembled Katie Spahl should be living with someone that he knew. A more complex plan, with more effort put into the final outcome, would make this a great memory.

That night, sleep came to him amid thoughts of his previous victims. For the thousandth time, he went through each kill, trying to recall as much detail as he could. The memories quieted his roiling mind.

***

That night, in the little apartment, Lennie was cold. She wasn't ill in any way, just cold. It was as though an icy cloak wrapped itself around her. She clung to Cary for warmth. She took a hot bath. Still the cold would not leave her. An extra glass of wine helped her off to sleep, still so cold that she felt as though she might start to shiver.

THIRTY-EIGHT

The office was stuffy. Normally the small confines of the SAIC office didn't bother him. Today, with all of the extra piles of computer print-outs, it seemed like a tomb. He had stacked them everywhere, even on the guest chair, across from his desk. The amount of paper on his desk barely left room for a coffee cup. There was no window that he could open. Getting fresh air meant going outside. He didn't have time for that.

Special Agent in Charge Arne Ingmarsson had a pile of notes on his desk. The half-page note paper looked almost out of place, compared with the dimensions of the 18-inch computer paper. The handwritten notes – some his, some from other agents – were the core of his understanding of the case that he was trying to put together. The notes were a mess. So was his grasp of the case.

The time-course of the case was unusual: over more than a three-year period. That alone ensured that the information set would be enormous. The Bureau prided itself on collecting information – data. There was a lot of data.

Sipping at his coffee, now more room temperature than warm, he put down the case notes. The unhatched idea in the back of his mind still rested, not quite ready to assert itself. It nestled right alongside the aggravation that Ingmarsson felt.

Repeatedly going over the case notes, going back to the source material, and rereading everything wasn't working. The was just too much data. He looked from one print-out stack to another. Somewhere in the stacks were the one, or two, bits of information upon which the break in the case would turn. Until he could isolate those facts, things would remain the same mess that they were.

He decided to change gears. He put down the print-out in his hands and pulled a file from a stack on the corner of his desk. The file was work schedules and assignments. It included a schedule of vacation times that various agents had been given.

Bureau personnel vacations were scheduled through a central directory in Washington. This was so the Bureau knew who they could assign to new locations without interfering with vacations. There was a core philosophy within Bureau management that time off was important. Rescheduling a vacation was a rare event.

There was supposed to be local oversight of each and every vacation awarded. The "supposed to be" part was his responsibility. There had been a mix-up. It had occurred within the last couple of years, but had caused a ripple-effect in the normally non-overlapping vacation times. There were going to be problematic agent absences if Ingmarsson couldn't fix the snafu.

He read through the SAIC instruction guide, reassuring himself of what he dreaded. The only way to solve the problem was to find out precisely when and where the mix-up had occurred. The only way to do that was requesting data from Washington. In order to make sure that the point of error was included in the data set, he requested three years' worth of information. More print-outs. Just What he needed.

Ingmarsson filled out the data request form. The usual procedure was to call the data processing room with the specifics of the request, and then send the written request through inter-office mail. Right now, hand carrying the request to the processing room would be a good excuse to get out of his office. Rising from his chair, he tried to think of where he was going to put more computer print-outs. An answer to that question would not come.

The data processing room was so warm that it made his stuffy office seem like a nice place. The data processing machines lined three walls. The recording tapes on all of the machines were spinning, stopping, spinning again. The combined low noise of the machines created an uncomfortable hum. Along with this, a large printer churned out long sheets of print-outs. Its print head made a machine gun-like noise. Arne Ingmarsson wondered how anybody could work in a room like this every day.

The two men in the computer room were casually dressed. They were surprised to have a visitor. If they had worn jackets and ties to work, they were nowhere in sight. One of the two long-haired men started rolling his shirt sleeves down at the sight of the FBI man. Ingmarsson's neatly knotted tie, and crisp white shirt contrasted sharply with the paisley shirts and flare-leg slacks worn by the two computer operators. The men were federal employees, but not Bureau employees. The dress code difference was obvious.

The man who was apparently the leader of the two stepped forward and spoke with Special Agent Ingmarsson. He took the request form and looked it over.

"Two days." He spoke loudly, so he would be heard over the noise of the computer machinery. He looked at Special Agent Ingmarsson for some acknowledgement.

The short response was all Ingmarsson needed. He nodded and started back toward his office. He avoided trying to thank the computer man verbally. He disliked the thought of having to yell indoors. Neither of the two computer operators turned a hair at the lack of a thank-you. They were accustomed to the type of behaviors that the environment of the computer operations room fostered.

There was nothing unusual about the turn-around time for his request. Even though the request could be transmitted electronically, the information would have to be sorted out of a much larger data set. Some number of man-hours of work would be involved. The print-outs would be in his office in two days' time.

He didn't look forward to slogging through another ton of information. That was just the way it was going to have to be. He would find the mistake, and sort out the problem.

307

Arne Ingmarsson had a habit of distracting himself
from troubling thoughts. He brought his gaze down to his
shoe tops. The anticipation of all the extra work made his
polished brogues seem much heavier. He walked his heavy
shoes back to his office.

***

Cary was giving free rein to his imagination. He knew
that Lennie liked it when he did. He ran his lips along the
side of her arm and atop her shoulder. Continuing on, her
caressed her neck with his lips, ever-so-lightly licking the
tip of her ear lobe. Lennie curled and coiled like a serpent
beneath him, offering the nape of her neck to him.

Cary let his hand wander lightly slide down the center
of Lennie's back. Heated anticipation already caused a tiny
bit of sweat to form just where Cary's hand came to rest.
The feel of it against her silky skin was enough to give rise
to Cary's passion. He pulled Lennie over on to her back
and began making love to her in earnest.

The two young lovers thrashed back and forth across
the bed, making love as though they had been apart for
years. Cary returned a few days ago, but the tension of their
separation wasn't fully erased. One certainty rested on the
two young people: Whatever length of time it was going to
take, to make up for the lost time, was how long they were
going to work at it.

***

On the street, just a small distance from the front
entrance to Cary and Lennie's apartment, a very non-
descript government car waited. It was parked at the
opposite curb of the narrow, one-way street. The location

gave the lone occupant of the car a good view of the front entrance of the building. Part of the side of the building was also in his line of sight. He could see when lights were turned on and off in every room of the apartment that he was watching.

Walker kept his silhouette low and nearly out of sight. After getting over the shock of learning that his intended target was the strange young man's girlfriend, the hunt progressed apace. It was a simple matter to follow the girl around. She was oblivious to his presence.

He already knew about the two-hour difference in their work schedules. That was an obvious choice to leverage as a point of attack. The girl was alone in the apartment for two hours every day after the boyfriend left for work. Sooner or later, she would create an opportunity for him to take her.

With so much of the hunt back in the forefront of his mind, Walker was as calm and steady as he had ever been. The new-found peace of mind even washed over into his work. It was much easier to get his work done quickly, when he could focus on it calmly. Getting his work done quickly left him more time to do what he really wanted: pursue the hunt.

It had been a simple matter to begin checking in at the office a bit earlier than normal. Taking care of start-of-day paperwork took only minutes. Then he would start his day's work outside of the office. The first couple of hours were committed to stalking the young girl. His absence from the office fit well with Bureau expectations. Since his reports were always timely, and in order, it was assumed he was doing his job properly.

Morning hours spent, familiarizing himself with her routines, was going to pay off, sooner or later.

***

The evenings blurred into the nights. The nights seemed to last for mere moments. The love between Cary Lang and Lennie Baerd grew and grew. Sometimes they actually managed doing everything without being more than an arms-length away from each other. Their immense comfort with each other became something else. They were at last one.

Cary thought of how deeply and wonderfully he had come to be as close to Lennie as possible. They had purchased the engagement ring without an idea of a date for their wedding. In their minds, it was a big thing to have to plan, more work than they wanted to take on right away. Their time of growing together was more important than the need for a wedding.

For Cary, the time had come. On a beautiful Autumn day, Cary asked Lennie to marry him, once again. This time he asked her to marry him the next June, on a Saturday. He actually wanted to spend time looking at the calendar with Lennie, volleying the dates, back and forth, coming to a choice together. It was a truly sappy way of doing things. Sometimes love is sappy.

***

The park. That was it. He would take her at the park. The young girl, the Katie Spahl doppelganger, took the golden retriever to the park on mornings when the weather was clear. The neighborhood around the park was known as St. Louis Hills. It was home to working-class people, although these working-class people generally worked later hours than average. Lots of white collars. The area was the largest upscale neighborhood in the city proper.

The timing would be critical. The window of opportunity would be very narrow. It was risky to plan a daylight target acquisition. Risky? It was crazy. He knew that, but the morning hours were a gift of time he couldn't pass up. If he timed his take-down correctly, the fewest number of people would be about.

With any luck at all, no one would be about. Walker decided that luck needed to be removed from the equation. Any attempt at a take-down would have to come when all of the other factors were in order. The "make or break" on whether to proceed with the attack, would be the absence of any other people. It didn't seem at all unlikely that the morning hours would cooperate. It could be done.

Rain that fell for the last few days would have been an interference. He thought that he remembered that it would be clearing for the next week, or so. He decided to check the weather reports and move at the next opportunity.

Having let his need to kill again steer him in the direction of a daylight kidnapping felt wrong. Walker knew that his exposure to risk was enormous, but need drove him on. It had been truly painful for him to go so long without ridding the world of girls like Katie Spahl.

THIRTY-NINE

"What did you want to see me about?" Detective Beckestone leaned back in his office chair. Now that he was Detective First Grade, his desk was no longer jammed into the back of the squad room. He also no longer had to work from a straight-back chair. His desk was notably one of the five large desks in the room. Small perquisites came the way of those who were promoted. Better office furniture was one of them.

For Benji Beckestone, no one ever thought of calling him that any more. He was now an official ball-buster of the St. Louis Police Department, his slightly shorter than normal stature notwithstanding. Even Rita, the squad secretary, avoided nearly addressing him informally at every opportunity. Among the changes that his new status brought him, that one far exceeded the others.

"I've been having trouble sorting out some of my recent experiences. Most of my problems started with the killings in the warehouse – the Hamor Drubedta case."

Cary sat in the interview chair, next to Beckestone's desk. "I thought there would be someone – in the department, or a referral – who could help me."

"Bad dreams, huh?" Beckestone smiled thinly at his own attempt to lighten the conversation. He thought of Cary as more of a friend than anything else. He was truly sorry to hear that Cary was experiencing problems – problems that he caused. He dragged the kid into the Drubedta case without thinking about things like psychological trauma. He compounded the mistake by involving Cary in the Forsythe case – more than once.

"Let me see what I can do." Beckestone looked through a thin book, labeled Police Department Directory. He picked up the phone and dialed a number.

Cary listened as Beckestone spoke to whoever was on the other end of the line. Apparently, an opportunity to speak to someone was available this same afternoon. When he hung up the phone, Detective Beckestone said, "Let's go."

Cary had no idea that he was going to be escorted to wherever he was going, but followed nonetheless. Beckestone led Cary on a path through office after office. Finally, they came to the end of a long room that Cary thought must be another detective squad room, but this one was much larger than the one they left.

A door in the end of the room led to a small anteroom where a receptionist sat behind a desk. A tiny plastic easel sign on her desk read, "Sheila Barnes, Receptionist." Beckestone spoke first. "I'm Detective Beckestone. We just spoke on the phone."

Without a word, the slender young woman rose from her desk and opened the door to the office behind it. The door was lettered with the words "Department Psychologist." Cary entered first. As he passed the receptionist, she started to close the office door. Beckestone stopped her, and pushed his way past her into the tiny office. Still silent as a sphynx, the receptionist stepped back into the doorway, and closed the door. The comment of a raised eyebrow was all she cared to share as she did so.

The occupant of the office was a woman, dressed in a very business-like style. She rose from her seat in a wingback leather chair and greeted the two men., "I'm Dr. Thornton." She extended her hand a shook both men's hands. "Tamara Thornton."

Introductions went around briefly. Cary thought that Dr. Thornton's maiden name must have been Hispanic, for she looked very much the part: raven hair, golden-brown skin tone. Cary realized that Dr. Thornton was aware of him sizing her up. He involuntarily blushed.

The psychologist waved Cary toward another leather wingback chair. Cary took a seat. Addressing Detective Beckestone, Dr. Thornton said, "I thought I was seeing Mr. Lang. Having both of you in the room isn't going to work."

"There are some very unusual facts about this session that you are going to find hard to believe." Beckestone glanced at Cary. "I am only here to vouch for his sincerity and truthfulness. Even if what he tells you seems impossible, Mr. Lang has helped solve several crimes with

314

his special abilities. His assistance has helped to clear no fewer than seven homicides."

Dr. Thornton drew a deep breath, let an arched eyebrow of her own settle down. In her time with the Department, she had already heard the most outrageous stories from every rank. She was honestly taken aback that one of her previous clients thought she needed warning. She looked from Beckestone to Cary, and back again. "Okay, then. Can we begin?"

Beckestone took the cue, and let himself out of the office. Dr. Thornton began, "What would you like to tell me?"

An hour later, Cary exited the small office with Dr. Thornton at his side. "Department rules only let me see you this one time. Sheila will give you the particulars about Dr. Bannon. He will be able to help you." She waited while Sheila wrote out the requested information.

After Cary thanked both Sheila, and Dr. Thornton, he left the office. With the door to the anteroom now closed, Tamara Thornton looked wordlessly at Sheila Barnes. She silently pointed to a drawer in Sheila's desk. Taking the hint, Sheila opened the indicated drawer, pulled a fifth of Wild Turkey, and a bourbon-splash glass from it. She handed the two items to her boss.

Dr. Thornton took the bottle and glass into her office and closed the door. Seated at her own small desk, she thought about always having open hours for short-notice consultations. She poured the bourbon carefully into the glass with the outward sloping sides.

She really thought that she had already heard the most unusual and frightening stories. Mr. Lang, however, was in a class by himself. If Benji Beckestone hadn't warned her that it was all true, she would have thought Lang was psychotic. What he had gone through would give anybody problems.

The talk about the terribly worrying auras of the two FBI agents threw levels of jurisdictional complexity into an already convoluted doctor-patient relationship. All she was able to do today was listen, and reassure Cary Lang that it would be possible to solve his problems.

She thought about calling Rich Bannon, and giving him a "Heads up!" about Cary Lang. Then she thought, Maybe after a drink. Maybe two.

***

A couple of blocks away, Special Agent in Charge, Arne Ingmarsson pored over computer print-outs. Late in the day, he was back on the multi-state murder investigation. That half-baked, tiny kernel of an idea, in the back of his mind, was getting to be more of a problem. Ingmarsson looked over the pages of data knowing that he was missing something. There is something that ties this all together, but what.

He spent the morning unraveling the vacation scheduling foul up. Getting that done successfully really boosted his confidence. The whole problem was a double-booked week of vacation one of the agents had taken. The agent involved would be happy to hear that an extra week of free time would now be available to him.

He dove into the morass of facts before him with renewed vigor. Look at it from another angle. What if Bureau agents in the specific cities could look at the whole picture?

He picked up the assignment schedules for the different cities on the list: Pittsburgh, Indianapolis, Kansas City. Quickly scanning the lists of names, two stood out among the others: Denny and Rosse. Both had been assigned to posts in cities that were part of the case. He couldn't imagine the providence that already had them on the case. Ingmarsson double checked assignment dates.

Ingmarsson wondered at how neither of the men mentioned their postings in the cities involved. Was it just chance, or neglect? Then the idea in the back of his head made its presence impossible to ignore. Agents in the cities at the time of the murders? What if…?

He shook his head. Was that what's been eatin' at me this whole time. What a crackpot idea! I guess I'm workin' too hard, these days. He returned to his original notion. Agents in the cities where the killings took place could at least provide some local background for the case.

It was the only thing resembling a breakthrough in the case. He decided to follow up on it as soon as possible. He wanted to personally debrief the two agents. He had a catalogue of questions for each of them. Still, that nagging, half-baked thought in the back of his mind wore on. He couldn't shake it.

Arne Ingmarsson didn't believe in instinctive detective work. His time in the Army's Criminal Investigation Division taught him otherwise. If an investigator experienced "gut feelings," they were usually just distractions from what they should be concentrating on. Letting emotion and unprofessional behaviors influence an investigation were becoming things of the past.

The Bureau wanted hard, scientific analysis, not conjecture. More and more, the Bureau looked to culling and analyzing huge volumes of information – data – to provide the answers to questions. He looked around the room at the mountains of computer paper.

There ought to be a better way of doing this. The thought was almost instantly lost as he went back to his reading. Similarities. What are the most notable similarities?

***

Alone in his apartment, Walker felt physically ill. Sitting on the side of his bed, he was soaked in a cold sweat. It not possible for him to be comfortable. The apartment was still warm. Its location in the western side of the building meant that the exterior walls absorbed a lot of heat from the sun. Even though he was nearly completely undressed he still perspired heavily.

The inability to satisfy his need to kill again raged and thundered in his mind. The severe tumult in his thoughts manifested themselves in hand wringing. He gave up pacing hours ago. Every thought he had about the danger of a daylight kidnapping were instantly countered by waves of nausea-inducing rage.

He wiped some excess spittle from his mouth. The uproar in his mind also made itself apparent by running his guts like a Mixmaster. There was no chance at all that he would eat tonight. His bodily upset wouldn't allow it. He lay in his bed, the steady flow of sweat making even that seem like torture.

Lying there, he cast aside the foolishness of being the stalker, Walker. There never was a separate persona associated with the identity. It had all just been a game. He knew he distracted himself from the ever-present need to kill with the Walker sobriquet. He said aloud, in his empty room, "It's me, Rosse, Kurt Rosse." Somehow, dropping the game of pretense he played within his own mind helped ease the inner struggle. "It's just me."

The weather for the next morning would be clear and breezy. He went over the preparations for the attack that he had already made: plastic sheeting in the trunk of his car, tape and binding-cord in his jacket. There was Mace for dealing with the dog, if necessary. He mentally walked through every step of the take-down.

He struggled with keeping the cut-out in place. If there were anyone around, he would have to abort the attack; try again, later. Every time he thought of stopping the attack, his mind raged, in a near-frenzy of determination to go through with the murder, no matter what. The battle within himself left him clutching his gut, as it roiled in response to his mental turmoil.

Curled in a fetal position, at long last he slept. It was a fitful, toss-and-turn, sleep.

FORTY

A typical morning in the St. Louis FBI office was like offices all over town. There were people seated at desks, working. There were people coming and going. In his small office, still piled high with computer paper, Special Agent in Charge, Arne Ingmarsson tried to pick up the threads of his work from the previous day. He remembered needing to speak with agents Rosse and Denny.

Stepping to the door of his office, he summoned Denny from his desk. There was no sign of Rosse. Agent Denny left what he was doing and entered Ingmarsson's office. As was usual practice, he closed the door behind him.

Ingmarsson spoke first. "I see agent Rosse hasn't made it in yet."

"He's already come and gone. I saw him leaving just as I came in." Agent Roger Denny looked impassively at his supervisor.

"I know he's working on the same cases as everyone else, but what gives?" It was usual practice for an agent to get their paperwork out of the way first thing in the morning and do out-of-office legwork later in the day.

Denny shook his head. "I don't know. He certainly time-shifted his work. He basically checks in at morning, and returns in the afternoons to clear up paperwork. I guess it leaves things more orderly for the next day. I never thought about doing things that way."

"Well, I've got a few things to clear up about this multi-state investigation. I don't want to let my questions go unanswered for too long. There are things you can both tell me that I really need to know. Before you and I get started, I want Rosse headed back this way."

Ingmarsson rose from his desk and instructed one of the agents in the office to locate Agent Rosse. If he was in the field, the local police departments could be asked to keep an eye out for him. It was a simple matter of sending out a teletype message to the local departments. Flagged as "Important," a call would go out over police radios.

A radio call would enlist hundreds of people in tracking down his agent. In many cases, the large number of municipalities in the county would hinder a search. In this case, it actually could help, if only by virtue of the great number of officers alerted to look out for him.

Ingmarsson decided that, in the meantime, he would look for Rosse on his own. It was a great excuse to get away from the sight – and the smell – of the piles of computer paper he seemed to be buried in. He could drag Denny along and question him while they drove. He collected Agent Denny, and headed for the car parking area behind the building.

***

Coming early to the federal building gave Kurt Rosse an unexpected benefit. He was able to park in one of the few covered parking places that weren't reserved for senior officials. He got one right next to the SAIC's. His parking place afforded him an easy few of who came and went. It was just like a surveillance job: Park back, slouch low in the seat, use your mirrors.

After checking in this morning, he made sure that all of his paperwork was up-to-date. He stayed late at the office yesterday finishing his daily report. Most agents polished them in the morning, looking for errors or omissions as a fresh start to the day's work. He submitted his report, and left before any of the other agents came into the office. He knew the SAIC was there, but they never crossed paths.

He needed to wait before going to the park. If he got there too early, he risked being spotted by someone who could report seeing him. The shorter the amount of time between his arrival and the take-down, the better. Sipping at his coffee, he remembered not to gulp it down. A full bladder at the wrong moment would only interfere.

When, at last, the time came for his cross-town drive to begin, Rosse drove his car out of the federal building car park. He was unaware that a call, to locate him, was going out over the local police departments' radio channels, at that very moment.

**

That's an unusual call. An FBI agent? Detective Beckestone heard the radio call. He glanced at the frequency displayed on the small scanner that he kept in his car. It switched from one police frequency to another, sweeping them over and over for an open call. The radio message was to locate only. It meant that the call was a courtesy to the FBI who relied on local law enforcement for assistance.

The FBI had not yet equipped their own cars with radios. Huge changes were afoot, since the death of Hoover last year, but that still was not likely to be one of them. The Bureau was just another federal agency, perennially asking for funding. The budgeting geniuses in Washington had not yet gotten around to paying for modern communications equipment.

It was in this atmosphere, of the Bureau being more than forty years behind local police departments, that such requests were necessary. Simply locating one of their own was only slightly above being truly menial work. It was certainly not outside the range of requests from the Bureau for support from its local law enforcement brethren.

**

It was, as predicted, bright and breezy. The Autumn leaves heaved and whirled in skeins and masses before the cold winds that drove them. The ground was still wet in many places. Rain from the few days before left a damp leafy mess.

Rosse drove up behind the parked Volkswagen coupe. The license was correct, it was the girl's car. He drove around the parked car and backed up close to it. He turned his engine off. He looked around. No one around, wherever he looked. His heightened sense of self-criticism threatened to ruin his focus. He was breaking so many of his own principles by taking a target in broad daylight. The rage inside of him quickly quashed any intention to hesitate or falter.

Quickly, he got out of the car, unlatched the trunk lid and left it resting just above the latch. He looked at the sign next to the walkway that led into the park. It was a large, brass, shield-shaped sign, atop a cast iron pole. It read, "Francis Park." He mentally joked with himself, Who calls a park 'Francis?'

He got back into the car and waited. He checked his pockets. The binding-cord and tape were there. He fingered the small can of Mace in his other pocket. If the dog was a threat, he'd deal with it. He looked around. No one.

What was her name, again? Lenora. That was it. It didn't matter. If everything went well, she'd be in his grasp within moments. The heat of the anticipation, once again, caused a profuse sweat to break out. He wiped his hands on his trousers.

Watching the open grass area that was adjacent to the street, he quickly saw her, playing frisbee with the golden retriever. He checked his watch. The session would be over soon. She needed to get to work. She would be returning to her car. He looked around. No one. He had been parked there for less than five minutes.

Right on cue, he thought. He watched as the young girl took the plastic disk from the dog's mouth. The dog's look of excited anticipation faded as the girl attached a leash to its collar. They headed toward the cars, oblivious to his presence. He looked around. No one to be seen anywhere.

He slid from the car seat and stooped low, next to the car's left side. His position would enable him to approach the girl from between the cars as she came near. With luck, she'd walk right between the two cars. He would be on her in less than a second. He looked around. No one.

As Lennie, very obligingly, walked between the two parked cars, Rosse struck. With surprise on his side, his arm was around her neck in less than a second. He slid his other hand over her mouth.

Lennie was stunned. Terrified out of her mind, she flailed her arms trying to reach the assailant, behind her.

He began to squeeze. The image of the brown plaid headband worn by Katie Spahl appeared on his victim's head. The sight of the illusory headband caused no reaction at all within him. It was just there.

Lennie felt her strength start to falter, the pressure on her neck… He wasn't choking her…

Behind Rosse, the golden retriever whined and whimpered, confused by what was happening.

Lennie knew that death was coming. Inexorable, relentless death. The sounds around her faded, darkness enveloped.

Just as the dog's whimpers were turning into a growl of impending attack, the girl went limp. With lightning speed, Rosse turned and flipped open the trunk lid. He dropped the limp body of Lennie Baerd into the trunk. The sudden disappearance of his mistress caused Wheels to stop growling, now more confused than ever. The battle in Rosse's mind continued: Stupid, stupid, stupid. It came from the well-trained military part of his mind. No, perfect, perfect! screamed back from another.

The absence of worry about the dog let Rosse concentrate on his prey. He rushed through applying the wrist and ankle bindings. He taped the girl's mouth and closed the trunk lid. He turned to face the dog, grabbing the can of Mace as he did so. A look of confusion on the dog's face told him everything he needed to know.

A moment later, he was driving away. As pointless as it was, he looked around once again. Still no one in sight. A quick check of the rear-view mirror showed him the dog, still sitting in the street, leash dangling from its collar, right where he left it.

Still, the battle within him raged. *Stupid! No, perfect!*

***

Marie Moreland wasn't sure of what she saw. At eighty-three, she wasn't sure of anything. She sat in the front room of her house, looking out the window, at the park. She sipped her tea. She pulled her housecoat a bit more snuggly around her neck. The house seemed cold. It always seemed cold, these days.

Her thoughts were flowing back and forth, as they always did these days. The taste of the tea made her think of her husband Michael, gone now, fifteen years. Wherever we went, people said, "Here come the M&M's!" We were such a pair. A smile danced across her faced and faded, even more quickly than it appeared.

The only light in the room came from the windows before her. She wouldn't waste the electricity, turning on lights. That was the way people of her generation thought of things: Use a little now, save for later. The money left for her would never run out. She still couldn't be frivolous with it.

Even though the daylight outside was bright, it did not illuminate her face. Marie Moreland spent every morning sitting in her living room, looking out onto Francis Park. It was the only use the room got. The house Michael bought for them cost so much more, just because it faced directly on the park. Marie thought of it almost as her duty, to look out onto the park and watch the people there. No longer able to go on her own to Michael's gravesite, she honored his memory every morning.

For a moment, the man that she saw seemed to be hugging the woman. She raised her arms in an odd way. Then she was gone, the man was standing alone by the car. Marie wondered briefly about the odd scene. It was so far down the block. It was so odd.

The thought to call someone about the odd thing she had seen was pushed aside by the flow of her thoughts, again living in the past. Michael would have known what to do, who to call. The tea had grown cold. She picked up her cup and saucer. She rose from her seat, with a last glance at the colorful cascade of leaves flying about in the wind. She walked into the kitchen, reminded of why she had done so by the dishes in her hands.

Marie Moreland went about the rest of her day. Brief glimpses of the strange scene in the park mixed with memories that spun and swirled in her mind. In the afternoon, she napped as she always did. Later, the programs that she followed would be on the television, distracting her from even her most vivid memories, few as they were.

***

Cary's morning was proceeding normally. The Autumn merchandise was moving out nicely. The back areas of the store were already jam-packed with Christmas sale items. When the day came the entire store would transform itself from an Autumn sales haven, into a Christmas merchandising wonderland.

At ten o'clock his telephone rang. The caller was Elaine Rosecranz. She was the floor manager, Main floor. She reported that Lennie didn't report for work this morning. Her absence was causing some problems with reassigning sales people.

Cary shared that he knew of no plans for her to be away from work. He also said he would see what he could do. He called home. There was no answer. He was really at a loss. He decided that something must be wrong, and left the office.

Cary drove from his usual parking place. He noticed that Lennie's car was not in any of the usual car lots that served store employees. He arrived home a short while later. There was no sign of Wheels or Lennie. Everything in their apartment seemed in order. He knew that Lennie took the golden retriever to the park on clear mornings. Before leaving the building, he checked in with Mrs. Roberts. She had nothing to contribute except for a wish that Cary find Lennie soon.

As he drove up to the park, Cary saw Lennie's VW parked at the curb. Encouraged by the find, he raced up to the car, only to find it locked and empty. He looked around. There was no sign of Lennie or Wheels anywhere. His heart was starting to sink in his chest. A knot was forming in the pit of his stomach. Real, bone-breaking worry was starting to form in his mind.

Cary decided that since Francis Park was bounded on all sides by streets that he would drive the entire perimeter and see if he could see Lennie or Wheels. The sixty-acre park revealed most of itself to view from the bordering streets. There were only a couple of areas not directly visible from one or another street. He could cover a large portion of the park from his car.

About three-fourths of the way around the park, he spotted Wheels. The loveable golden retriever was sitting under a tree. He was a good quarter of a mile from where Lennie's car was parked, but he was just sitting there. Cary could make out the leash fastened to Wheels collar.

Cary parked his car. As soon as he cleared the side of it, Wheels spotted him. Running as only dogs can, with his heels flying out in front of his head, Wheels came charging up to him. He disregarded the leash flying in all directions as he ran. The gentle creature had waited patiently in the park, for his master or mistress to come for him.

Wheels seemed no worse for having been left alone in the park. He wagged his tail so frantically that it seemed he would shake himself apart. Cary knew that the animal's overly excited state came from being left, out of his normal element. He hoped that's all it was.

After walking through the entire park, Cary was despondent. He was also convinced that Lennie was not there. He headed back to their apartment, with Wheels in tow. It seemed strange to leave Lennie's car behind, but he had no other choice.

Maybe Lennie had shown up at the apartment. If so, there was probably a doozy of a story attached. The notion of her being at home was Cary's way of dealing with the fearful situation in which he found himself. He wanted her to be there. He was bargaining with reality; hoping against hope that everything was all right.

FORTY-ONE

Cary was sitting on the couch in the living room of their apartment. Wheels was seated at his feet, leaning against his legs. Cary thought of the possibilities. Nothing that came to his mind generated a positive image. He was sick to his stomach. He was way past the sinking feeling. He felt as though all the blood had been drained from his body. A cold sweat formed on his forehead. I'm gonna faint.

Cary started to rise from his seat. His head spun. He clenched his fists. He bit down hard on his upper lip. No, I'm not.

He lurched into the bathroom, grabbing the door frame for support. Wheels padded along. behind him. Leaning on the sink, he ran the water to let it get cold. He put both of his hands under the cold water. Bringing a handful of water up to his face, he literally slapped it against himself.

The shock of the cold water caused him to gasp. He sucked in a bit of water, and choked on it. Spitting and sputtering over the sink, he realized that he had, however gracelessly, gotten out of being on the verge of fainting. Wheels sat in the doorway of the bathroom with the usual adoring look on his face.

Cary's shirt was soaked. He didn't care. He cared that Lennie was apparently missing. He decided to call the one person he knew who could help. After that, he would head out and search on his own. There was no way he could just sit around the apartment and worry.

The telephone in their apartment was a wall phone in the kitchen. It had an extra-long coil cord on the handset. Cary tapped in the numbers.

***

"Yeah, well, you can't file a missing person report before twenty-four hours has elapsed." Detective Beckestone had listened to Cary Lang tell the story of Lennie not reporting for work. He also told of finding Lennie's car, and the unattended dog at Francis Park.

"I'm not sure what I can do from here. Let me get back to you. Are you at home?" Beckestone really was out of his element. Missing persons investigations were typically fruitless searches for people who didn't want to be found anyway. This was a different matter. He knew the people involved, and that Lennie's sudden absence was unusual, if not outright abnormal.

What he knew about the type of police work involved in missing persons cases would barely cover a thumbnail. He rang off with Cary and headed for the Missing Persons desk in the main detective squad room. Maybe they could steer him in a direction that would actually help.

Benji Beckestone left the downtown Police Headquarters building, armed with a couple of very useful suggestions from the Missing Persons desk. The detective sergeant there only gave him straight talk, no off-putting remarks about how difficult searches of this kind could be.

Beckestone left his own casework to sit idle. He was independent enough now, as Detective First Grade, to be able to do that without the Lieutenant breathing down his neck.

***

Chippewa Street was a main drag in south St. Louis. Cary drove the length of it eastward, at least as far as made sense. He turned around and drove west. The late morning traffic was light. He had no idea what he was doing. Somewhere in the back of his mind, he understood that he was just burning off excess energy derived from the increasing fear that he felt.

He drove anyway. He considered a route for a north-south search, still without any plan at all in mind. He wasn't exactly sure what – or who – besides Lennie he was looking for. Was she riding in a car, or truck? Was she out in the open, or somehow concealed? Was she walking along one of the thousands of streets in the city?

The gas tank on the VW was nearly full. He could go on all day and night, if Wheels held out. The golden retriever rode along in the back seat, oblivious to the ocean of worry that buoyed his master along.

Like many urban thoroughfares, Chippewa Street ended and changed names at Watson. Cary decided to backtrack to Hampton Avenue and make his north-south foray. He made a U-turn and sped away, first heading north. He had no reason for going one way or the other.

Cary's foot was heavy on the gas pedal, transferring his anxiety through the throttle to the tiny motor. As his car approached the Oakland Avenue intersection, a patrol car suddenly appeared behind him, lights flashing.

Obediently, Cary turned the VW into a gas station. The speed of the car made it lurch over the sloping entrance. Too fast. I was going too fast. And, I guess, a U-turn, too. Cary didn't know what the officer was likely to have seen him do. He only vaguely recalled the things he saw, and did, over the last half hour.

Cary stopped the car and turned it off. He came closer to his normal senses, as the police officer behind him exited his patrol car.

***

Turning southward on Hampton Avenue, from Oakland, Arne Ingmarsson's eyes were drawn to the flashing lights of a patrol car in the gas station to the left. He saw the VW coupe that was the obvious target of the police officer. He caught sight of the VW's driver.

"Isn't that Lang?" He brought the government sedan to a halt and began a U-turn of his own, to see if he was going to be of any help. He drove back to the gas station and pulled in, behind the police cruiser. The officer was walking from the patrol car toward Cary Lang's VW.

The police officer was surprised and unhappy to find his car boxed in between two other cars. His experience and training taught him to be wary of such situations. He turned toward the newly-arrived vehicle, keeping the VW in his field of view. He unsnapped his pistol strap.

As he exited the car, Special Agent Ingmarsson withdrew his badge wallet from his breast pocket. Flipping it open to reveal the small gold-colored badge inside, he held it before him as he approached the police officer.

Waiting for the police officer to come to the window of his car, Cary was surprised when he didn't. Craning his neck around, turned half-backwards in the car seat, he saw the FBI man, Ingmarsson, talking to the policeman. He could only stand to sit that way for a minute. He turned back in his seat and adjusted his rear-view mirror. He watched the two men talk, behind his car.

The conversation went on for some time. At first the police officer looked like he was angry and not receptive to whatever the FBI agent was saying. Something changed after Special Agent Ingmarsson adopted what appeared to be a less confrontational approach. The police officer put away his ticket pad and walked back to his patrol car.

Ingmarsson then walked over to Cary's car. The driver's window was already down. "Park your car over there. Join me over there." Ingmarsson pointed first to an empty parking place near the front of the gas station office. His second gesture indicated his car, stopped behind the patrol car.

FORTY-TWO

Special Agent Ingmarsson decided that it was time to give Cary access to information he didn't already have. He knew that Cary Lang agreed to accompany the two agents and read auras. He had done so without hesitation. He had done so also without knowing what it was that they were investigating. Ingmarsson thought it would produce a better, more objective report from Cary, if he only knew to watch the auras, and nothing else.

Ingmarsson began an explanation of the unique string of murders that they were investigating. The murders were committed in different states. That was the quality that put the case on the FBI's radar. It was assumed that the killer kidnapped his victims in one place and took them to another to kill them. Another quality of the murders was that the killer managed to leave almost no evidence at any of the crime scenes.

The explanation of what they were doing began to wear thin on Cary. He was worried about Lennie being missing. The details of the FBI case were, by comparison, merely tedious. Then Agent Ingmarsson began describing the victims of the murders: They were all attractive, petite, brunettes.

The Special Agent didn't need to say much more before Cary blurted out, "My fiancée is a petite, brunette. And she's attractive."

Ingmarsson was unmoved by the information and slightly peeved at the interruption. He glared a bit at Cary, hoping that the young man would just get on board with finding Agent Rosse.

Cary reached out and grabbed Ingmarsson by the arm. "Lennie didn't report for work this morning. She took our dog to the park, before work, and disappeared."

***

That nagging idea in the back of Arne Ingmarsson's head popped right back out in front. It wasn't a crackpot notion, all along. The facts were there, in front of me for God-knows-how-long. He snapped at Cary, "Get in the car."

Cary collected Wheels and made for the FBI car. Once there, he and Agent Denny witnessed a truly strange episode take place inside the office of the gas station. Ingmarsson walked in and began speaking to the middle-aged man behind the counter. The man didn't seem to care that he was being spoken to at all.

The obvious effect of the clerk's behavior took no special talent to interpret. Ingmarsson slammed his fist down hard on the glass counter in front of him.

The counter clerk looked up, still exuding a deep lack of interest. As his gaze met Ingmarsson's, the FBI man snapped open his badge wallet. The clerk's look of disinterest disappeared instantly. Cary knew the man must have had some time in the military. He was now clearly standing at attention, or the middle-aged equivalent of it.

Ingmarsson spoke three or four sentences, all the while boring a steel gaze into the eyes of the clerk. Each of his sentences was met with a sharp nod of the head and some verbal answer. When Ingmarsson pointed to Cary's car, the clerk snapped his head to the side for a brief look and snapped his head back to face Ingmarsson. Cary heard none of what transpired between the men, but still understood every bit of it.

As the two men waited there, Cary saw the police officer writing in a notebook. Agent Denny explained, "Special Agent Ingmarsson was arranging for your car to be kept safe. It'll be here, whenever you return." Thinking of how stunned the gas station clerk was, Cary thought, *That clerk will watch my car till hell freezes over, if necessary.*

Special Agent Ingmarsson left the gas station office and headed back toward the cars. Just as he was walking past the police officer, the walkie-talkie type radio on the policeman's belt squawked out a report that a car matching the description of Agent Rosse's was seen near the entrance to Babler State Park.

Ingmarsson heard the radio report. He asked the police officer to have the radio dispatcher repeat the message. The second radio call confirmed the first.

Ingmarsson got into the Bureau car. He blinked at the sight of Wheels in the back seat, but said nothing. Ingmarsson said to Agent Denny, "The radio call stated that Rosse's car was at a place called Babler State Park."

Without waiting for Denny to answer, Cary chimed in, "I know where that is. It's about twenty miles west. We can cover most of the distance on highway 40." He stammered a bit, "Just…just get on the highway, go west."

***

Detective Benjamin Beckestone sat in his Dodge Polara hot rod. The car in front of him, parked alongside Francis Park, belonged to Lennie Baerd. It was unlocked, as though its owner expected to return in a short period of time. An hour of watching and waiting showed no sign of the young woman. He admitted to himself that he was more emotionally involved in the case of Lennie's current situation – whatever that was – than he ought to be. He had accepted Cary Lang as a friend, especially since he owed him so much.

Beckestone knew that Cary was helping the FBI with something. What it was, he did not know. He also knew that Cary was extremely upset about Lennie being nowhere to be found.

Just as these thoughts were going through his mind, a radio call was intercepted by his police band scanner. It was a report that a car matching the description of one belonging to the FBI agent spoken of in the earlier radio call was now at Babler State Park.

Beckestone also heard an officer request the message to be repeated. That was an unusual request. A Department officer wouldn't make a request like that on his own. Something's up.

Beckestone started the overpowered monster of a motor and made a U-turn out of the parking place. The roar of the four-hundred-twenty-six-cubic-inch engine thundered through the normally quiet neighborhood.

Beckestone knew that the route to Babler was going to be circuitous. He could cover a huge part of the distance on the new Interstate Highway 44. He also knew that with the red Fireball on his dashboard, he'd make impressive time. It had been a long time since he had the chance to run the Dodge wide open on the highway.

***

The grounds of the state park were, as he anticipated nearly empty. A mid-week afternoon was likely to work out well, after all. Rose reassured himself that even though he was way out of his normal pattern of behavior, his plans would come to fruition.

His first turn into the park revealed a much greater than anticipated thump from the back of the car. He had driven for more than forty-five minutes since using the sleeper hold to drop the target into his arms. The girl was probably awake, or close to it. He needed to get to his chosen site for the kill as soon as he could.

Rosse needed to avoid the areas of the park where the maintenance people worked. Fortunately, that area was close to where the park office and any staff might be, as well. The route he took wound around sharp curves and climbed steep hills. The bundle in the back of the car – the target – bumped loudly, over and over.

Rosse came at last to the driveway that he was looking for. It was almost unnoticeable from the road. It was old, overgrown with weeds, and only covered with pea gravel. He found it while scouting the location earlier this year. He steered his car into bushes that encroached nearly to the center, from both sides of the driveway.

After a sharp dog-leg turn, the drive went on for another hundred yards, before coming to a dead end. There was a clearing, but nothing else. Whatever was here had been gone for a long time. It was just the sort of spot he required. Finding it with his target in the trunk greatly pleased the part of his mind that was now almost completely in control. Soon, very soon!

***

Bumping and rolling in the trunk of the car, Lennie struggled against her restraints. Her hands were tied behind her. Her mouth was covered with tape. She was now awake long enough to only want to be free. She didn't remember how she got into the car trunk. She only knew that the wrist restraints were a tiny bit loose, so were the bindings around her ankles.

Every turn of the car caused her to roll back and forth. She thought maybe she could wriggle her hands free and…

The car stopped. The engine was turned off.

***

Marie Rader sat in the Conservation Department truck, waiting just inside the entrance to the park. She left the Park Office just minutes ago. She was beginning her tour of the Babler State Park grounds as she usually did. A short time spent watching road traffic was a good way to ease into a normally relaxed afternoon of driving around the park.

As a Park Ranger, Marie was bound to be in contact with the public at some point, every day. Her role as a Ranger gave her near-total control of how much contact there was. She enjoyed the opportunity to teach people, especially children about the wonders of the natural world around them. Having to enforce state regulations was the price of all the benefits of her work.

A slow mid-week day, such as today would be good for sense of fulfilling her need to be outdoors, in contact with nature. With only a few people in the park, she would be able to stop at a couple of her favorite places in the park. She looked forward to not having to interact with people very much at all. Marie was not what you would call a people person.

The training group she was part of accepted her without much rancor. A woman wanting to be a Park Ranger was a new thing – not totally unknown, but still new. Marie Rader was well beyond being smart enough. She breezed through the classroom work. Her love of the natural world helped her excel in all of her courses.

The physical part of Ranger training was also no problem for Marie Rader. At five feet, eight inches, she was just tall enough to make the grade. Her medium build belied her one hundred-fifty pounds of wiry, muscular physique. Few of the men in her training class bested her in the field challenges set for the trainees.

Marie Rader hoped that today would be another beautiful, quiet commune with the world she loved.

***

The FBI car was literally blasting its way through the Highway 40 traffic. Cary told Agent Ingmarsson how far they would be going before they turned off the highway. The St. Louis Special Agent in Charge took the information as notice that they really had a long way to go. He wasn't wasting any time. Another fifteen minutes of so, would bring them to the park entrance.

Cary otherwise was in a deteriorated state. Emotionally, he was nearly drained. Mentally, he was exhausted. Learning that Lennie was missing and might be the target of a killer was driving him insane with fear.

Cary rode with one arm draped over Wheels. The dog was laying low on the seat next to him, made nervous by the movement of the car, as it raced along. Cary drew a deep breath and began to think about the auras of the two FBI agents that he worked with. Both were in extremely agitated states, at least as far as he understood it.

He decided to view Agent Ingmarsson. He closed his eyes and allowed his aural sense to work. It revealed a reassuringly calm, pale yellow aura. Cary understood this to be the color that people exhibited when they were focused on a task or work.

But there was something else. Cary had become aware of being able to detect progressively finer variations in the auras that people exhibited. He thought it was a natural progression in the development of his ability. Now, as he sat with his eyes closed, in the back seat of the car, he not only saw the fine differentiations, he heard them as well. There was a high-pitched whine, that varied in perfect synchronization with the ever-shifting color tones of Ingmarsson's aura.

Cary opened his eyes. The sound vanished. The sound only recurred after he again closed his eyes, and focused his attention on the colors of the aura displayed before him. He guessed that he didn't so much hear the sound, but perceived it. The same mechanism with which he viewed auras was allowing him to detect more and more about the people he viewed.

Cary was surprised by his first experience with his new ability. He was amazed that there was now a further refinement of his skill.

***

Benji Beckestone felt as though he was the very wind itself. The car rode down the multilane highway at one hundred-twenty miles an hour, effortlessly. The race-tuned suspension on the car was built for what he was doing. The header exhaust roared like a lion. The sound was music to Beckestone's ears.

If he thought of himself as the wind, everyone else envisioned a bullet, as he went by. No one he passed had even the least part of a moment to see the flashing red light on the car's dashboard. He came up on the exit to the two-lane that led to the park. Beckestone throttled back and put on his blinker.

The hot rod Dodge careened around the turn on to the two-lane. Beckestone thought to himself, Ten or fifteen minutes.

FORTY-THREE

Wind sang and whistled. It blew huge rafts of leaves off of the trees. From time to time, the masses of leaves blocked the bright Autumn sunlight as though they were clouds. Lennie lay motionless, listening. For a moment there was only the sound of the wind. Then she felt motion, and heard the clack of the car door latch. More motion, the car door slammed shut. Fear welled up inside of her.

Lennie woke in the back of the car, surprised at first that she was not dead. The terror of finding that she was bound and gagged, and in the trunk of a car, quickly replaced the surprise she felt. Sliding and bumping back and forth, while struggling against her restraints only seemed to make her feel worse. Try as she might, she could not free herself.

The sound of footsteps brought her fear to a peak. She froze. The trunk latch was released. The lid lifted. Blinking in the sudden intense sunlight, she looked into the eyes of whoever opened the trunk. The sight of the man in the black suit and tie caused her to begin struggling against her restraints furiously.

The black-suited man lifted her, still struggling, out of the trunk of the car. As she cleared the lip of the trunk, Lennie suddenly stiffened her body, then went limp. The maneuver caused her to slip from her captor's grasp and fall to the ground. She hit the gravel beneath her, butt first. Her head struck the side of the car, hard. Just a bit dazed, Lennie struggled against her wrist bonds. They seemed to be coming loose. She hoped it wasn't just wishful thinking.

She looked up just in time to see the hand of her captor, now balled into a fist, coming right at her. Then, nothing.

***

Rosse was angry. He was angry that he had broken so many of his rules. He was angry that he was exposing himself to discovery by making a kill in daylight. The insane drive within him screamed and raged back from the depths of where it dwelt in his mind. Kill her!

When the girl, the target, the Katie Spahl doppelganger, slid from his hands, he was incensed. He didn't want make a mess of the kill. The careful stalker and hunter within him needed to do a reasonably neat job of executing the kill. The girl wriggling out of his grip let loose the rage in him, and he struck her, hard. The target slumped to the ground. He hoped he had not killed her outright, with the blow.

Rosse stood over the girl for a moment and watched for her breathing. He became worried when, at first, she didn't breathe. As he bent down to check for a pulse, she took a small, rasping breath. Then she took another, and another. She was unconscious, but alive.

Rosse picked up the limp form of Lennie Baerd and carried her toward the woods. He already knew where the kill would take place, where he would strangle the life out of her. Damn! There was no scarf or other garment to substitute for it.

Ever resolute and inventive, Rosse knew that there was one thing he could use: His necktie. The thought of having to use his own clothing to finish the kill made him angry, again. It was just another sign of how badly he had messed up this entire process. Still, the rage inside of him screamed, *Finish it! Kill!*

***

Ingmarsson steered the car through the entrance to the park. He made the turn at an unreasonably high speed. The body of the Bureau car bottomed out in the turn. If he had been going any faster, he would have slid the car through the park entrance, sideways.

He passed the Department of Conservation pickup truck without a thought. He was looking for Rosse's car. Finding that could be the key to stopping another murder from occurring. He continued on into the park, unaware that the pickup truck started up and fell in behind them.

Marie Rader knew a government car when she saw one. That was a government car. What they were doing in the park, her park, she didn't know. Whatever their purpose was, they were in a big hurry. If the government had an interest – apparently an urgent interest – in something in Babler State Park, she needed to involve herself, for certain. She sped the truck up trying to catch up with the car that had passed her.

Ingmarsson saw the truck, larger in the rear-view mirror, every time he glanced up at it. Without any hard information that Rosse was definitely a killer, they were still just trying to locate one of his agents. They came to a fork in the road. He steered to the left. Still going too fast, the car slid a bit in the turn. The Macadam surface rumbled beneath the tires of the car.

Where the hell are they going? The park office is the other way. Marie Rader sped up even more. She now wanted to overtake the car and speak with whoever was careering and racing through the park. Piles of leaves in the roadway acted like ice beneath the wheels of the truck, making it difficult, and dangerous, to try to keep up with the car. She sped on.

**

Cars. The sound of vehicles on the road stopped Rosse where he stood. The small clearing was totally hidden from view of the roadway. Yet he waited, unsure of exactly what he would do, if the cars came down the driveway. He cursed himself again, a fool for committing a daytime crime.

The weight of the girl in his arms brought him back to reality, as the noise of the vehicles on the road passed, and faded away in the distance. With no more distraction, he resumed walking to the point at the edge of the clearing where he would finish his kill.

Carefully, Rosse laid the limp body of Lennie Baerd on the grass. The grass was thin and sparse, still wet from the dew of the morning. The grass grew in clumps, separated by patches of bare earth. The ground around the clearing had gone untended for years – perhaps decades. It was well on its way to reverting to its prairie grassland state.

Rosse unknotted his tie and began sliding it from around his neck. Looking down at his target he began to see the face of Katie Spahl form, from the nearly-perfect match of the unconscious girl's face. The brown plaid headband appeared on her head, topping brown bangs on her forehead.

Still, she slept. He watched for a moment. He would not kill her unless she was awake. He needed to see fear and terror replace the smiles and laughter of his tormentor. He needed to see the light fade out of those two brown eyes. No, those eyes must be open and awake, before I shut them, forever.

**

Rounding a series of curves that rose and fell in the hilly countryside of the park grounds, Ingmarsson was becoming distracted by the presence of the pickup truck. It was too close behind them to be incidental. He glanced in the mirror, and saw the lights of the truck flash on and off several times. It was an obvious signal to stop. Stopping for any reason now seemed like a bad idea. He considered that perhaps he could get help from whoever might be in the truck. Dropping from the crest of a high hill, they came around one last curve in the road and saw the park office building. He decided to stop there, deal with

351

whoever was in the truck, and get some suggestions from the park staff.

The pickup truck was almost a little too close to the government car when it suddenly veered off the road, into the office parking lot. Yanking on the steering wheel of the truck, Marie Rader brought the vehicle directly in behind the car. The car was slightly better equipped to stop on the pea gravel surface of the parking lot than the truck. Park Ranger Rader couldn't keep the two vehicles apart.

Thump! The truck rear-ended the car. As she recovered from the sudden surprise, Marie Rader saw the driver of the car exiting the vehicle quickly. Her training took hold, and she slid from the seat of the pickup instantly.

The suited driver of the car stepped toward her. "What do you think you're doing!"

He stepped Toward her and attempted to pull something from beneath his coat. Dressed even as she was, in her uniform, Marie Rader presented an unthreatening appearance. If a person bothered to look closely, they would actually see a tiny, wiry, very muscular woman. It was a subtle thing that Special Agent Ingmarsson missed.

Marie Rader's self-defense training prepared her well for being a solitary agent of the state government. Having to patrol remote areas by herself kept her constantly in the right frame of mind to protect herself. She flexed her knees slightly to lower her center of balance, stepped inside the reach of her assailant's arms, and tossed him to the ground like a sack of potatoes.

Before her assailant could react to the suddenness of her maneuver, Marie Rader drew her pistol and aimed it squarely between his eyes.

"FBI!" A voice behind her shouted, "FBI!" Marie Rader, still aiming her weapon at the man at her feet, looked up to see another man in a suit holding an open badge wallet. The small badge of the FBI was unmistakable. The large letters on the ID card next to it said everything necessary.

Beginning to realize that she had just manhandled an FBI man, Marie Rader looked back down. The grinning man lying there held out his own badge wallet for inspection. The deep red blush of embarrassment began to fill her cheeks. She holstered her pistol, and reached down to help the man to his feet.

Once on his feet, Arne Ingmarsson had his own embarrassment to reveal. He smiled, his face red with chagrin, too. "That was quite a throw, Ranger. Jiu Jitsu?" He began to shake the leaves and pine needles form his coat.

"Simple Judo, sir. Although I've been told that I'm very good at it." Marie Rader wondered exactly how much trouble she was likely to be in. "I'm sorry, I…"

Ingmarsson held up a hand. "No. It's me who should be sorry. I came at you kind of suddenly, didn't I?"

Yes, sir." Marie was starting to feel a tiny bit less stupid for what she had done.

"I'm sorry, we're trying to move a lot faster than we normally do. We have reason to believe that one of our agents is here in the park. We also have reason to believe that someone's life may be in danger." Ingmarsson paused to let his statements sink in. He didn't want to connect Rosse with murder, absent any hard evidence

"What we have to do is cover as much ground in the park as we can, and locate our agent." As he finished, the loud roar of an overpowered car came over the hilltop, and down into the little valley where they were. The old Dodge was obviously race-built, but there was a Fireball, red light, on the dashboard. In a situation that was already uncomfortable for everyone, the sudden appearance of the car seemed crazy.

The driver of the car turned off the Fireball. He held a badge out the window of the car. Ingmarsson felt that whoever this cowboy was, he wasn't stupid. The neatly dressed driver of the car got out and joined the Rader, Denny and Ingmarsson.

Before Beckestone could say a word, Cary Lang shouted out from the back seat of the Bureau car, "Detective Beckestone!" The back door of the car opened. Wheels dove out, dragging a leash behind him. He ran up to Beckestone and stood there wagging his greeting.

Cary got out of the car and joined the others. As introductions were made, Wheels trotted to take care of business. Being the good companion that he was he returned to Cary's side immediately.

Special Agent Ingmarsson, being the leader that he was, quickly got to the point. He directed Denny to drive the Bureau car, Cary and he would ride along. He suggested to Ranger Rader that she team up with their newest crew member, Beckestone. They would split up, and cover a greater area, more rapidly.

The last thing that Ingmarsson did was to instruct everyone that a shot was to be fired if a sighting of Agent Rosse was made. They really had no other way of signaling each other.

Marie Rader started toward her pickup truck. She turned toward her new co-worker and said, "I know this park like the back of my hand. Let's go."

Having temporarily exorcised his speed demons, Beckestone hopped in the passenger seat of the truck without a word. The two vehicles left the parking lot of the park office. The FBI car went to the left, the pickup truck roared off to the right.

FORTY-FOUR

The afternoon was growing long. It was not yet late, but the steep, high hillsides cast shadows across the valleys between them. The bright, lowering sun shone through the trees into the eyes of the searchers. The shadows of some trees still blocked the sun totally. The on-again, off-again flashes of sunlight made it difficult to focus.

Cary thought it was getting impossible to see. That's it! The frantic journey to the park had made him forget about his "silent sight." Clutching Wheels, he now closed his eyes and scanned the area around them. Every aura, or group of auras was far away. The movement of the car kept allowing the auras of the people in the car to block more distant ones.

Cary asked Agent Denny to stop the car. He got out and continued his scanning. He tried desperately to pick out the detail he needed from distant sightings. Agent Ingmarsson didn't understand at first what was happening. Denny explained. Ingmarsson was impressed that the young man was composed enough to think of it.

All of the far-away auras were too indistinct for Cary to study. Everywhere he looked, it was the same. Except for one aural display. Every time he scanned across it, the high-pitched sound came to him, as if carried on the wind. The more he focused his aural viewing ability on the aura, the more distinct the sound became. He recognized that although it was high-pitched, it had a different quality to it than the one he detected from Special Agent Ingmarsson. The spectral whine was coming from nowhere else.

"There!" Cary pointed in the direction of the aura that drew his attention. Is was a slim thread of a lead to follow, but it was all they had. The two FBI agents in the front seat of the car looked at the map and located the point on the map. Cary got back in the car, and they were off before he got the door closed.

***

Lennie began to awaken. She flexed her fingers behind her. Her hands were pressed into the dirt. She was reluctant to open her eyes for fear of what she might see. When she finally did open her eyes. The cold hateful eyes of her attacker stared back at her. She screamed and struggled against her bonds.

The tape across her mouth all but completely stifled her scream. Her attacker was kneeling astride her, not quite sitting on her. He reached down and slid something around her neck. She screamed and thrashed from side to side

357

beneath her attacker. He tightened the cloth around her neck. His grip on the cloth around her neck was like iron.

Kurt Rosse only saw Katie Spahl, laughing at him. The memory of that night, so long ago, tore through him like a scythe, destroying any semblance of composure. She was there, in the brown plaid, knit skirt that matched her headband, the cream-colored, ruffled blouse. Tears began to stream from his eyes.

"Poke a Poika! Poke a Poika!" He could still here the catcalls of his childhood tormentors. All the memories: the hateful laughter, the taunting, the beatings were there. He was a teen-age boy again, awash in fear and terror, silently cultivating hate. Decades of fear, hate and anger flowed from his mind and became the impossible strength of the madman.

Lennie twisted mightily against her restraints. All at once they slipped from one wrist. With all the strength she had, she pulled her hands from beneath her. Both hands were now filled with gobs of grassy earth. She flung them into the face of her attacker.

Rosse could only do one thing: keep tightening the necktie around Katie's neck. The light in her eyes must go out! Die! He was oblivious to the tears dripping muddily onto his victim's face. His mind raged on, Finish it. Kill her!

Scrabbling against her attacker's arms Lennie flailed and beat. She thrashed from side to side trying to wriggle free of the noose around her neck. She felt her ankles come free of their bonds.

***

The car actually slid sideways around a couple of the turns on the leaf-strewn, Macadam park roads. Cary was certain that they would have an accident before they got to where the auras were. As the car swerved around the roads, he tried viewing the auras ahead of them, but it was nearly impossible. The only encouraging sign was that the high-pitched whining sound increased as they got closer.

When at last, the car was alongside the auras, still at some distance, Cary shouted, "Here! Stop!"

Agent Denny slammed on the brakes. The car slid a hundred feet, or more, on the pea gravel surface of the road. He began backing the car to where Cary stopped them. The nearly-hidden driveway entrance appeared at the edge of the road. With one last closed-eye view, Cary pointed toward the driveway and said, "Down There!"

What he had seen was now clearly one aura physically on top of another. As he made to get out of the car, Wheels' leash tangled around his feet. He struggled with it. Agent Denny was already out of the car and going down the hidden drive.

***

Rosse's car was at the foot of the driveway. Agent Roger Denny had his Bureau-issue pistol drawn. He had never fired the weapon anywhere but Bureau shooting ranges. He was more than competent with it. He didn't like it. He only carried it because the Bureau ordered him to do so.

At the edge of the clearing he could see the back of Rosse's head, low in the tall grass. He was apparently kneeling, his hands in front of him. Denny made out the shape of person beneath Rosse. He shouted out, "FBI!"

Denny's shout got no reaction from Rosse. Agent Denny pointed his pistol toward the back of Kurt Rosse. Indecision crept in. Combined with a lack of firearms experience, it caused him to stop. He did not want to shoot. He definitely didn't want shoot to shoot someone he knew, in the back. He shouted again, "Rosse!"

There was still no reaction from Rosse. Roger Denny knew that his reluctance and inexperience, combined with a loss of objectivity, were going to lead to a bad outcome. He decided to fire a shot over Rosse's head. He hoped it would frighten and distract Rosse from continuing his attack. He knew, in the back of his mind, that Bureau training never directed agents to fire warning shots.

There was the sound of footsteps, behind him on the gravel drive. Denny fired his pistol.

***

With one last surge of strength, Rosse tightened the necktie around Katie Spahl's neck. He hoped to crush the life out of her entirely. He leaned forward and raised his hips, bringing the mass of his weight to bear, driving his victim into the very earth itself. His arms were burning, aflame with the exertion of the struggle and the force of the overwhelming madness within. Still, he tightened his grip, twisting the necktie more tightly.

Rosse's move gave Lennie the one last chance she had. Since he was no longer sitting astride her, she brought her right knee up into his crotch with all the force she could muster. As her knee struck its intended target, the awareness of things around her started to fade. Darkness and silence were, once again, enveloping her. Her last experience was sadness. She felt the pang of loss. Then nothing.

The sudden pain in Rosse's crotch caused him to straighten up, involuntarily. The bullet fired from Denny's pistol struck the back of his head.

In an instant, the boy known as Poika, by his family – and by his torturers – ceased to exist. The fiery oceans of hate were no more. The perverse need to kill, and kill again, were erased. His existence, and all of the existences he brought to untimely ends, vanished together, into the ether of nothingness.

The momentum of the bullet toppled Rosse forward. Blood and brains streamed from every orifice in his head. He lay motionless atop his victim.

Stunned that he had just accidently killed Rosse, Agent Denny stood immobile on the gravel driveway. His right hand, still holding the pistol, dropped to his side. The golden retriever, trailing half of a leash, raced past him. Then the young man, Cary Lang ran past, almost as fast as the dog. Lastly, Special Agent Ingmarsson walked up alongside him.

Ingmarsson put his hand on Denny's shoulder. He looked Denny in the eye. "Good shot." He continued walking past Denny, thinking about how many problems Denny solved by killing his partner. They weren't so much Denny's problems, but his. Denny's problems were just beginning.

Wheels raced to the place where Lennie lay, trapped beneath the corpse of Kurt Rosse. Snarling and growling like some fierce, wild beast, he tugged and pulled at the dead body, defending his mistress.

The motion of the corpse on top of her roused Lennie to partial consciousness. She flailed and screamed struggling to push the bloody corpse off of her. She could hear the snarls and growls. She was devoid of a sense of time, and did not know that it was Wheels. She became terrified that some forest animal was now trying to get at her. Her screaming and struggling intensified.

Cary threw himself to the earth next to Lennie. He heaved Rosse's dead body off to one side. "Lennie! Lennie! It's me Cary! Lennie."

Cary pulled his beloved up into his arms. He loosened the necktie from her neck. Rosse's body was still partially across Lennie's lower half. Cary wiped some of the blood and gore from her face, with his hand. She opened her eyes.

Cradling her ever so gently in his arms, Cary caressed and kissed her. He was totally unconcerned with the ghastly mess on her face. She was alive, still alive. That was all that mattered.

Arne Ingmarsson walked up. He leaned in and finished pushing Rosse's body off of the young girl. Back on the gravel driveway, Roger Denny stood. He had not moved since firing the shot that killed Rosse. His arms hung limp at his sides. The pistol was still firmly gripped in his right hand.

The sound of another vehicle, sliding to a stop on the road, was followed by two door slams. Ranger Rader and

Detective Beckestone came down the weedy gravel driveway. Both cantered and slid along, becoming aware that they were arriving after the important action.

Marie Rader surveyed the scene. She said, "I guess I only thought I knew the park well. I never knew this little clearing was here. Huh."

FORTY-FIVE

Special Agent Ingmarsson's office was crowded. At least with another person, and a dog, it seemed crowded to Ingmarsson. There were far fewer piles of computer paper, but some remained, stacked on his desk and on the other office furniture in the room. In some form or another, computer-generated information was making its way into all investigations. Ingmarsson accepted the notion that his life as an agent would always involve the products of electronic computation.

The whole business with Kurt Rosse, and how he could have become an FBI agent in the first place, was passing into memory. Cary Lang was now an official adjunct contributor to FBI investigations. In this role, Arne Ingmarsson arranged for a stipend to be paid to Cary, every month. He also, somehow, made sure that Cary could leave his work at Vander & Beste behind, whenever the Bureau needed him.

Today, Ingmarsson merely needed Cary's help with finishing a final report about the death of Agent Rosse. The report was going to go all the way to Washington. It described Rosse's series of murders. It tried to describe all the ways in which the murders were similar.

The last inclusion in Ingmarsson's report was an attempt to explain something about Rosse's mentality. He started it, and destroyed what he wrote several times. He finally had to admit to himself he was out of his element. The FBI never trained him for any of this sort of crime investigation. Perhaps some time in the future, the Bureau would have an applicable science to address and unravel these mysteries.

As Ingmarsson wrapped up his report, he flagged the file for the attention of an agent in Washington that he heard about. He was working as something called a "psychological profiler." The agent's name was Robert Ressler. *

The whole business of criminal psychology was new to the Bureau. There were not many Bureau people involved directly in it. Like many large organizations, it had its supporters and detractors. There was actual resistance to it. The detractors considered it a way of coddling criminals, and confusing already complex investigations with psychiatric gobbledygook.

In unraveling the many complexities of the case, Ingmarsson came across Cary's admission that he had viewed the auras of the two agents with whom he worked.

Cary revealed how confused he was to find that both men were in extremely agitated, and in hostile states of mind.

When debriefing Agent Denny about Cary's report, the man admitted that he was in fact being driven nearly insane at the time of the investigation. The problem was his wife. She was divorcing him.

Mrs. Denny's lawyer was a real go-getter, and out to prove himself by ruining Roger Denny's life. The little twerp already admitted that winning a case against an FBI agent would be the thing he needed to establish himself as the "go-to" divorce lawyer in St. Louis.

None of this divorce business sat well with Agent Denny. He felt victimized by the legal profession. He also had undeniable hostile intentions toward his wife. Their investigations all centered around women. He couldn't help but be reminded of how much he hated his wife. He kept it all to himself, or at least he thought he did. Unaware that Cary Lang would "view his aura," he just suffered his emotions silently.

Ingmarsson took all of Agent Denny's debrief to heart. He knew the man's divorce decree was only recently finalized. He chalked it up to the fact that everybody had trials and tribulations of their own, even FBI agents.

***

Sitting in the Captain's office made Detective First Grade Beckestone uncomfortable. He just finished his explanation of how he came to be at the scene of an FBI agent's killing – at the hands of another FBI man, yet. The Captain sat through every word of it with the same unwavering scowl on his face.

366

Benji Beckestone was fairly sure it would all wash – just fairly sure. The business of how Cary Lang aided the Department in several investigations had all gone across the Captain's desk. He knew as much about aural viewing as anybody.

Aural viewing was a strange, new – if somewhat quirky – tool for crime investigators to use. Beckestone hoped that the possibility of using it again meant more to the Captain than any of his out-of-jurisdiction shenanigans.

While he waited for the Captain to say something, Benji Beckestone reassured himself that something very positive had come out of the investigation for him. Marie Rader and he exchanged telephone numbers when they last saw each other. That was the afternoon of the killing in the park. Exactly why he asked her for hers, he didn't know.

More importantly, Marie called him a couple of nights ago. As far as he was concerned, it was of no consequence that she called him, instead of the other way around. They talked for quite a while. They set a date to meet for drinks and possibly dinner. Whatever the outcome here, he had that to look forward to. Beckestone was roused from his momentary reverie by the Captain starting to speak.

"Well, Detective Beckestone, it seems your activities have become famous, at least to some important people." He paused to let the impact of his words settle in.

"I have a letter here, from Fort Meade, Maryland. Apparently, the FBI shared your participation in their investigation with people fairly high up in the government. It seems another federal agency wants you, and your friend Mr. Lang, to help them out."

367

Silent Sight

EPILOGUE

The small church in Red Bud, Illinois was full. Cary stood across the alter from his beloved Lennie. They both looked at each other, each as starry-eyed as the other. The weekend they selected was going to turn out to be spectacularly beautiful. Their plans for an outdoor reception were likely to come off without a hitch.

The calm intonations of the minister belied his dislike of having an animal on the altar. The young couple had insisted on it. In the end, the minister acquiesced to the request because he knew the Baerd family so well.

The wedding processional, with the dog walking so calmly, behind his master, caused quite a stir in the congregation. The dog walked calmly, almost serenely down the aisle. It had a small basket handle in its mouth.

The basket held a small pillow upon which rested the wedding rings.

There, between him and the groom, is where the golden retriever sat. The dog sat quietly looking at his master. The minister didn't know that dogs could be so well-behaved. Nonplussed, he carried on.

The bride's side of the knave of the church was filled with many people that the minister recognized. Relatives and friends, from all over southern Illinois, came to the Baerd's daughter's wedding. Many of the attendees were people he had baptized, married, and conducted funerals for family members.

Lenora's parents were there, seated in the front row. The minister could only wonder at the look on their faces. It seemed to be as much a look of satisfaction as it was the look of two people who just shared a joke. The tiny smirks gave that away. He wondered what the joke could be.

The truth about the Baerd's was simple. They made a promise to themselves when they were married to enjoy life. In that vein, they both kept a sense of humor about everything in general. The tiny bit of chicanery with Cary, the first time they met, was typical of them.

Today was a special, happy day. The crowd seated across from them was so colorful that they took turns citing little oddities they observed, under their breath to each other. Smirking went right along with the fun.

The groom's side of the seated assembly was another matter entirely. The minister didn't recognize a single face. He did know that the church parking lot was filled with government cars. There was also a police car from St.

Louis, a Missouri Department of Conservation truck, and a very unusual old Dodge Polara sedan, with over-sized tires on the back. He could only think that the mixture of people would lead to a very memorable wedding reception.

Glancing down one last time at the dog, the minister continued, "Repeat after me: I, Cary Lang, take thee…"

***

June 16th, 1994. The intervening years were hard on Hamor Drubedta. His hollow eyes stared blankly ahead. Twenty years of appeals had come to nothing. Every wheedling explanation and excuse had been consumed, spent, exhausted. The stony countenances of the judges belied their intent even before the arguments were presented. The juries were no better.

Hamor Drubedta sat, strapped to the metal "throne." The gas chamber in the Missouri State Penitentiary reeked of dried sweat. Drubedta realized it was the leather belts that bound him. The number of people who must have poured their last ounce of perspiration into the effort of struggling against the straps was, no doubt, large.

The steel chair was welded to the raised screen floor. The box on which the chair rested elevated the person sitting in it to almost normal standing height. The steel doors clanged shut. The airtight latches turned into place. The poison gas would soon be rising. He was waiting.

He looked at the window. The gas chamber itself was a room within a room. The viewing gallery was another room outside the double room. The faces that he could see there meant nothing to him. Even his newest appeal lawyer was a very recent appointment by the state.

He vainly contemplated the outcome of his trial. He received life-without-parole sentences for the killing of the three men. Arranged as successive sentences, they ensured that he would never leave prison. It was nothing more than he expected, once he was arrested.

What he couldn't believe was that the prosecutors asked for the death penalty for the killing of the women. It turned out to be a sure bet. The juries couldn't resist the descriptions of the two women's children, who would be orphaned forever, by Hamor Drubedta's foul acts.

The truth was that neither woman had been in any contact with their children for years. Their involvement as prostitutes and drug "mules" was glossed over in the cases that were presented in the sentencing trials. The truth was...

He heard the sound of several clicks and clacks, followed by the sound of balls rolling down a track, or trough. A brief silence – too brief – was followed by the multiple splashes of the poison balls falling into the mild acid solution that would dissolve them. A faint hissing sound began.

Hamor Drubedta looked own. His arms, forearms, wrists, legs, knees, and ankles were all bound to the steel seat. He tested every leather strap. The strap across his abdomen completed the bindings that prevented any purposeful movement. Sweat was pouring out of him. His heart pounded in his chest.

The first whiff of bitter almonds assailed his nostrils. He held his breath...

***

In his penitentiary cell, Victor Forsyth thought to himself, At least Drubedta is outta here. The shits on the parole board basically told me that another sixteen years in this shit-hole were ahead of me.

The End

Notes

- *FBI agent Robert Ressler coined (began using it in forensic psychology) the term "Serial Killer" in 1974, the year after the year in which this story is set.

- An article entitled: Origin of the Term "Serial Killer", Serial killers have operated for centuries but the terminology is new. Written by Scott A. Bonn Ph.D., in his column "Wicked Deeds," for Psychology Today can be found at the following web address:

https://www.psychologytoday.com/us/blog/wicked-deeds/201406/origin-the-term-serial-killer

- An article entitled: Who Coined "Serial Killer"? Despite FBI profiler's claim, he wasn't the first. Written by Katherine Ramsland Ph.D. in her column "Shadow Boxing" for Psychology Today can be found at the following web address:

https://www.psychologytoday.com/us/blog/shadow-boxing/201410/who-coined-serial-killer

Acknowledgements

Thanks to Marilyn Nardin for her editorial support. Thanks also to Linda Sieve, whose artwork adorns this book's cover.

Thanks, also, to my wife, Christine, who listened to all my complaints with sympathy, lamented my setbacks and problems right along with me, and enjoyed all the small and great victories that accompanied the creation of this work.

A good deal of gratitude is due The St. Louis Writers Guild (Missouri Writers Guild), and the St. Louis Publishers Association. Their members, staff, presenters and lecturers have given me not only the skills used in writing, but valuable insight into the processes of writing and publishing.